Praise for Andrew Kane's Previous Novels

JOSHUA: A BROOKLYN TALE

"Gripping, multi-layered [illegible] drawing readers in... Using lively dialogue and vivid d[illegible] of three specific characters and tran[illegible] ar time and place in contempora[illegible] themes explored are universal and w[illegible] relatable to many."

– *ForeWord Reviews*

"In revealing the very human side of racial tension, Kane offers up an engaging and heartfelt tale."

– *Kirkus Reviews*

"We read about deep familial love and hopeless romantic love, about desperation and acceptance... the author interweaves vivid details of real-life tragic events with fiction... this is a fine novel about a piece of New York history that is still unfolding."

– *Jewish Book World*

"This is a completely engrossing story with well defined characters that the reader can't help but care about... a fast paced story as well."

– *Stacy Alesi (bookbitch.com)*

"This summary doesn't do justice to the wide-ranging plot and numerous other characters, many of whom are also richly described. Kane made me care about these people as individuals. He manages not only to offer excellent psychological portraits, but shows how the communities in which they live affect their lives and the way cultural attitudes constrict their behavior…showing how their desires, hopes, strengths and weaknesses make them all equally human. This richness and depth makes *Joshua: a Brooklyn Tale* one of the best novels I've read about race relations in America."

– Rachel Esserman (*The Reporter Group*)

"This book is incredible. A Shakespearean tragedy wrapped in the thorny issues of race, religion, politics and class, this book grabs the reader and does not let go until the last page. This book is a must read."

– Adina Bernstein (*WriterGurlNY)*

RABBI, RABBI

"An enjoyably lightweight page-turner… exotic fun."

– *The Jerusalem Report*

"Kane delivers some stunning portraits…this first novel is a warm, richly colored story that will move readers of any faith."

– *Booklist*

"In true potboiler fashion… walks us through his characters' journeys with insight, sensitivity, and fine attention to detail that are rare."

– *Hadassah Magazine*

"Andrew Kane writes with keen wit and well crafted insight… a must read, literary and spiritual journey."

– *Faye Kellerman, Novelist*

"Kane has a penchant for scandal...he has written a first novel that is likely to be enjoyed by religious enthusiasts, heretics, and most people who are undoubtedly somewhere in between."

– *Long Island Jewish World*

"Beautifully constructed...hard to put down...fast paced story that sustains suspense and holds the interest."

– *Catskill-Hudson Jewish Star*

"A moving story of the power of love and faith...a richly textured tapestry."

– *Bayside Tribune*

"An unusual and original novel...absorbing tale... filled with impressive learning...wrapped around by a touching romance."

– *South Shore Record*

"A worthy edition...provides us with an understanding that profundity and complexity are not the same thing."

– *Great Neck Record*

"Kane brings in numerous characters who are well drawn...insightful commentary on the contemporary Jewish scene which is well worthy of note."

– *Dade Jewish Journal*

THE NIGHT, THE DAY

"From the exciting prologue on, the reader intensely follows the suspenseful action and psychological warfare...Kane brings his own psychology background, expertise, and input to the narrative ...

This immensely readable book presents the themes of forgiveness, guilt, love, and justice."

– *Jewish Book World*

"Kane weaves a complex and interesting tale with a rather shocking ending."

– *Stacy Alesi (bookbitch.com)*

"A fast-paced, psychological game of chess."

– *Ronald Balson, Novelist*

The Other Hand

by

Andrew Kane

BERWICK COURT PUBLISHING CO.
Chicago, Il

This is a work of fiction. Any resemblance to specific persons, living or dead, is purely coincidental.

Berwick Court Publishing Company
Chicago, Illinois
http://www.berwickcourt.com

Names: Kane, Andrew (Andrew L.), 1958- author.
Title: The other hand / by Andrew Kane.
Description: Chicago, IL : Berwick Court Publishing Co., [2019]
Identifiers: ISBN 9781944376086 | ISBN 9781944376093 (ebook)
Subjects: LCSH: Jewish families--New York (State)--Lawrence--Fiction. | Rabbis--New York (State)--Lawrence--Fiction. | Gay youth--Family relationships--Fiction. | Interfaith dating--Fiction. | Interracial dating--Religious aspects--Judaism--Fiction. | Jewish ethics--Fiction. | Jewish fiction. | LCGFT: Domestic fiction.
Classification: LCC PS3561.A465 O84 2019 (print) | LCC PS3561.A465 (ebook) | DDC 813/.54--dc23

Library of Congress Control Number: 2019933953

For Max

Our Hero

How can I turn my back on my faith, my people?
If I try and bend that far, I'll break. On the other hand ... NO!
There is no other hand!

– Tevye

1

THIS WAS IT: THE moment of truth, the moment he had been dreading.

"Noah, are you listening?" she asked.

He nodded, pretending to be present, his thoughts elsewhere. He knew everything was about to change.

She'd been stuck on the subject of marriage for weeks now. They had been dating just over four months, a lifetime in their circles. Most of their close friends were either engaged or already married. He, unfortunately, had been through this a few times before, with three other women, each more suitable than the last. And now it was her, Ilana Lustig, with looks, charm, and sensibility far eclipsing any of her predecessors. Many had placed their bets on this match—his family, her family, the rabbi who matched them up. Possibly even God Himself.

Ilana's pedigree was impressive. Her father was a renowned oncologist at Sloan-Kettering, and her mother was the principal of an Orthodox Jewish high school for girls. Noah, for his part, had descended from many generations of rabbis and women determined to keep them grounded in this world, with his parents as the latest incarnation of this paradigm. His mother was a pediatrician and his father led an Orthodox congregation in Lawrence, Long Island, filled with wealthy, politically conservative, religiously observant families. The rabbi was also a non-practicing attorney and enjoyed international acclaim for his scholarship in both Talmudic and American law.

The restaurant Noah had chosen for this date, Roma 86, was a small, quaint place on the upper east side of Manhattan, Glatt Kosher, Northern Italian, and quite pricey. On a prior visit some time ago with another young lady, Noah had noticed a private table for two tucked in a corner behind a partial wall—an ideal spot. Secluded enough to say what he had to without worrying about eavesdroppers, and public enough to avert an embarrassing emotional reaction from Ilana. A bit calculating, perhaps, even callous. But what choice did he have? There wasn't a good place or a good way to do this.

His right hand rested on the base of his wine glass, while his left propped up his chin. He was attempting to appear relaxed. He had replayed this scene many times in his head, had rehearsed his words *ad nauseam*, and had imagined the countless scenarios that might ensue. But at the end of the day, he knew there was only one thing to say, and it had to be said.

"I really think we should do it before *Pesach*," she continued, referring to the Passover holiday just two months away.

"That seems awfully soon, don't you think?" Peering into those sapphire eyes reminded him of his first impression: *Definitely could be a supermodel, if only she weren't Orthodox.* Statuesque,

Jennifer Lopez nose and lips, wavy dark hair, and olive skin betraying the Sephardic heritage on her mother's side.

"It feels that way only if you're not ready." She waited a beat. "Aren't you ready?" she asked innocently, as if she couldn't imagine otherwise.

To him it sounded more as a statement than a question. He couldn't blame her, nor did he see her as presumptuous, for he had clearly led her to believe that he was in this for the long haul. And in his heart of hearts, he knew he hadn't been deceptive, at least not intentionally. He had truly wanted this to be it, had once even believed it *could* be. But sitting here now, across from her, he knew he had been unrealistic. What's more, he knew he had to come clean.

"There's something I need to tell you," he said.

She could see in his eyes that it wasn't good news. She focused on him, waiting for more.

Silence.

"Look, Noah," her tone turning impatient, "if you have something to say, I just wish you'd say it."

"It isn't that easy."

"I'm sure it isn't." Her discomfort was palpable. Just a few minutes ago, things had been going wonderfully. They had been talking marriage! And now he has *something* that he's finding hard to say.

"Well, the first thing is that I... I want you to know that I do love you, that you're the only one with whom I can see myself sharing the type of life I want, the type of life I should have." He felt himself trembling as he watched her eyes well up.

"What are you trying to say, Noah?" she asked, bewildered, finding it hard to get her words out. She loved him, and he loved her. They were great together. *What could possibly be wrong?*

"Ilana." He stared at her as if no one else in the room existed. "I think..." Wavering. "No, I know that..."

"Just tell me already," she interjected.

He thought for a second. It was time. No need to dance around it any longer. "I'm gay."

"Gay?" Dismay. Disbelief.

He waited a moment for her to process. "I think I've always sort of known," he said.

"Always? *What does that mean*?"

He contemplated her question, wondering if she really wanted an answer or if she simply didn't know what else to say. "Pretty much as far back as I can remember thinking about such things," he said as he reached for her hand.

Touching wasn't something they typically did, for they observed the traditional Orthodox Jewish norms of dating, which prohibited physical contact. But this was a unique circumstance, and it just seemed to him the right thing to do at the moment.

Though tempted to, she didn't pull away.

"What sort of things?" she asked.

"You're not making this easy."

"Am I supposed to? We've been together almost five months. I thought we'd fallen in love. I thought we were going to get married, have kids, a home, share a life. And now I learn my boyfriend's gay, that he's kept this from me all this time, and I'm supposed to make it easy?"

"I'm sorry, you're right."

"I really don't understand any of this. How can this be happening? And if you knew, how could you let this happen? What were you expecting?"

"I know you're angry, and I'm not sure how to explain any of this. It's just that I've always had feelings for men. I've spent years not wanting to feel that way, denying that I felt that way, hating myself for feeling that way. I even believed that if I truly fell in love with a woman, then all that would go away. And I do love you! But those other feelings are still there, and I can't shake them. God knows I've tried, but now I see that I can't."

She was silent.

"It's ironic," he added.

"Ironic?"

"That through loving you I came to realize who I truly am."

More tears. "What are you going to do?" she asked.

He was struck by her ability to express concern at a time like this, though not surprised. This was the Ilana he loved. And it was just like her to hit on the very question that plagued him. For years, his inner world had been in upheaval, and now his outer world was about to follow suit. His family, friends, and teachers were all steeped in a culture that couldn't possibly accept him as he is. His only plan right now was to tell her. Beyond that, he had no clue. "I don't know."

"Have you ever actually..."

"No," he interrupted. It was a lie, but at this juncture he saw no point in sharing his adolescent escapades with her. And that's all it had been to him anyway—some experimenting with a high school friend and nothing else—or so he had thought.

"Then how do you know for sure?"

"I just know."

She considered his response, then asked, "Have you told anyone else about this?"

"Absolutely not!" he said, thinking she was referring to his family or friends.

"I mean, have you spoken with someone?"

"Like a shrink or something?"

"A shrink. Or a rabbi."

He nodded. "Both."

"And?"

"I actually saw two shrinks. The first was about a year ago. He was Orthodox, and I went to him because I heard he specialized in this sort of thing."

She waited for more.

"He was okay, but after about six months it felt like he didn't know what to do with me. He encouraged me to keep dating women, which I did, and he also tried a few other things which you don't want to know about. He called them 'conversion' or 'reparative' techniques."

"I've heard of that," she said. "It's pretty controversial."

He looked at her perplexed, wondering how someone from her background and with her interests would even know about this. They both attended Yeshiva University—she, a junior majoring in Early Childhood Education, and he a senior headed for Harvard Law school next year—and awareness of such matters was somewhat uncommon in their cloistered circles. But then again, he reminded himself, she was often full of surprises.

"What about the second one?" she asked.

"He's actually a really good guy, and I still see him."

"So, what does he say?

"That it's really unhealthy and miserable to live a life in which I'm dishonest with myself and others."

She looked down for a second, trying to absorb what she was hearing. "And the rabbi?" she asked.

"He sent me to the psychologist who did the reparative therapy."

She waited for more.

"He said pretty much what I'd thought he'd say: It doesn't matter what I feel. I'm being tested and all I need to do is pray harder, study more Torah, find a good woman, get married, have children and, above all, *never* sleep with a man."

"I'm sure he didn't say it quite that way."

"He didn't, but that was the bottom line."

She realized that she didn't know what else to say or do. Trying to contain an emotional outpouring, she once again lowered her head. Eye contact was getting hard. Sitting there was becoming impossible. And while parting seemed unbearable, it was all she could think of. "I really want to go," she said in an almost childlike manner.

"I understand. Let's get the check."

"No, you get the check. I just want to go."

"You just want to leave alone?"

She nodded.

He stared at her for an instant, trying to take a picture in his mind. This was it, he told himself, realizing she was about to exit from his life. He had hoped they would continue to talk, perhaps remain friends, but the look on her face told him otherwise. He reached into his pocket for her coat check, handed it to her and said, "I'm so sorry."

"I know," she said, her voice trembling. "Me too."

2

RABBI JONATHAN BAUMAN LOOKED out at his congregation. It was a dreary, blustery late January day, yet many of his congregants managed to trek their way to the synagogue this Sabbath morning. The sanctuary was at its 600-person capacity, as usual.

It was 11:05 a.m. and the Torah had been placed back into the ark—time for his weekly sermon, or *drasha*, as it was called in Hebrew. He scanned the faces of his audience. Aside from a cough here and there, and the faint sounds of children playing in other parts of the building, silence permeated the room.

In an Orthodox synagogue, the noise of children was acceptable, even welcome. They were the future and any expectation of silence from them was viewed as somehow sacrilege. It was difficult enough to command decorum from the adults, many of whom came primarily to socialize. *Davening*, or prayer, certainly rated, but for most it was the draw of reconnecting with friends and neighbors that brought them in on a day like this.

And the rabbi understood this, as he understood most of what drove his flock. After twenty-eight years in this very pulpit, there was almost nothing about these people that escaped him. He had officiated at bar and bat mitzvahs, weddings and funerals, and had been with them through illnesses, religious crises, bankruptcies, and divorces. He had played the role of confidant, spiritual advisor, couples counselor, referee, and teacher. And at this same time every Saturday morning, he was expected to capture their unbridled attention for fifteen or so minutes and inspire them to greater religious heights and devotion.

He looked down at his notes, some scribblings on an index card, then back to the pews. He wondered when it was that he started seeing this occasion as more of a chore than a challenge. What had become of his enthusiasm and passion? Was he the only one in the room who was finding his sermons dull? Had he really lost his touch? The only thing he knew for sure was that he was growing tired.

He was 23 years old and fresh from rabbinical school. His plan was to study a few more years and eventually become a *Rosh Yeshiva*, a Talmud teacher, as his father had been. But everything changed the moment he met Sarah Kaplowitz.

His reputation as a brilliant student coupled with his ancestry of famed rabbinic scholars made him a most desirable commodity on the *shidduch*, or matchmaking, market. His appearance—tall, slender, handsome face, hazel eyes, sandy hair—didn't hurt much either. But his parents were getting worried. In their world, he should have been married with at least one child by now, and he hadn't even managed to get to a third date. "She's very nice and pretty," he would tell his mother, "but a little boring." Or, "She's quite interesting, but I'm not so attracted."

And that's how it usually went, until his childhood friend, Shimmy Katz, introduced him to Sarah. Shimmy had veered a bit off the *derech*, or path. He had always been a restless soul in high school, misplacing his black hat, showing up late to prayers, missing Talmud classes, and had even confided in Jonathan about some dabbling with pot now and then.

But Shimmy was the single smartest person Jonathan knew, with a huge heart to boot. The two had been close friends since the second grade, a bond that proved immune to the differences that would eventually develop between them. After high school, Shimmy left their Flatbush *shtetl* for Morningside Heights and Columbia University, and Jonathan stayed put.

"I'm really not going far, Yoni," Shimmy said. Yoni was Jonathan's nickname, what his friends called him, while Yonasan, his formal Jewish name, was what he was called by his teachers, parents, and family. "And I do expect you to visit me, even for Shabbos."

"You know I wouldn't exactly fit in up there. And how would I ever explain where I was going?"

"Oh, you'll figure it out. You always figure things out," Shimmy responded, cleverly mimicking their Talmud teacher, Rabbi Saperstein, who often complimented Jonathan in front of the class with those very same words: *you always figure things out.*

Once Shimmy moved and started college, their relationship evolved into phone calls and occasional get-togethers when Shimmy visited his family for holidays. Whenever they spoke,

Shimmy reiterated his invitation and, after four years of badgering, Jonathan finally gave in. His discontent with the Brooklyn social scene was becoming unbearable.

"It's the best Purim party in the city, across the street at Barnard," Shimmy said. "A costume party. It's perfect, you can dress up as a normal person," he added, teasing Jonathan's usual uniform—black hat, black jacket, black pants and white button-down shirt. "Everyone in Brooklyn will be drunk, so it should be easy for you to sneak away."

It was only one night, Jonathan reasoned. Most of the yeshiva would indeed be inebriated, as was customary on Purim. He could get away for a few hours and be back in the dorm by *shacharis*, the morning prayers. He actually owned a pair of jeans and borrowed a shirt from Shimmy, making him look like just another college kid. He convinced himself that what he was doing was harmless; after all, it was Purim.

Jonathan was amazed as he entered a large hall on the Barnard campus. He had never even imagined such an event: hundreds of young men and women fraternizing with one another, most holding a beer bottle, wine cooler, or red Solo cup. More than a fish out of water, he felt like he was from another planet.

Shimmy introduced Jonathan to many of his friends, including the alluring Sarah Kaplowitz, a senior pre-med major at Barnard. Jonathan was taken the instant they met. Fetching smile, long, wavy ginger hair, freckly complexion, green eyes, tall and curvy figure, and an energy about her that enchanted him. Somehow, from that very moment, he knew she was the woman he was going to marry. And the fact that they clearly came from different places didn't deter those thoughts.

Sarah was from an Orthodox family, but had grown up in Riverdale, a religiously diverse community, far more secular and modern than the ultra-Orthodox Brooklyn enclave of Jonathan's youth. She was definitely curious about this new young man from Brooklyn, who made no bones about his background and the fact that he was studying to be a rabbi, but didn't for the life of her ever imagine actually dating him. Yet she found him quite intriguing. She had spent the past three-plus years dating Columbia, NYU, and occasionally Yeshiva University guys, most of them impressive by anyone's standards, but she simply couldn't deny that Jonathan piqued her interest. So they spent most of that evening by each other's side, until about 2:00 a.m. when he walked her to the building of the off-campus apartment she shared with three other seniors.

It seemed a quite natural thing that went on between them, neither nervous, each eager to continue the conversation. But it was late, and Jonathan felt he had to get back to Brooklyn. His absence from the yeshiva's party might be noticed, but his early appearance for morning prayers would hopefully obviate any inquiries.

"I'd really like to see you again," he said as they stood at the entrance to her building.

She wasn't surprised. Despite her misgivings, there was definitely some chemistry. "I don't know," she responded. Vacillating.

His face fell.

"I mean, I know the world you live in, and it's not the same as mine. We're very different."

"I know," he said, matter-of-factly.

"It'll never go anywhere," she said in as delicate a manner as such words could possibly be uttered.

"I would take that bet," he said, surprised at his own confidence.

"Oh, so now it's a wager?"

"I think 'gamble' is a better word."

"Touché."

"So, next Thursday night?" Thursday, rather than Saturday, was the most common night for dating in yeshiva circles. This was because Friday, the eve of Shabbos, was a day off for preparation and taking care of the mundane chores that got neglected during the busy week, while Sunday was just another day for Torah study.

"You assume I don't have class on Friday."

"I assume nothing. Shimmy's told me many times almost nobody has class on Friday. He says it's kind of a thing that professors don't want to teach Fridays."

"Most don't. There are a few that do."

"Well, do you have classes Friday?"

"No, I'm off."

"Do we have a date?"

"I suppose."

"I'll take it. You don't sound too excited, but I'll take it."

She smiled at this young man who was neither easily offended nor discouraged.

And that was how it started.

Their first date was that next Thursday. He showed up in his hat and suit, as he would for a date in his usual circles. He had thought long and hard about donning something that she would be more accustomed to, but he was who he was and chose not to pretend otherwise. Purim had come and gone.

He entered the front door to her building, pushed the buzzer for her apartment as instructed, and was buzzed in. Once in the elevator, he started to feel a bit jittery. He had never been to a woman's apartment. Typically, he picked up his dates at their family homes and met their parents first. He stepped off the elevator, found her door and rang the bell.

She opened the door with a smile and immediately said, “Hi.” He watched her eyes peruse his getup. “Are we going to a wedding?”

“Ha ha,” He looked himself over, then asked, “You still want to go out?”

“Sure.” Pause. “Why not?”

“There’s that enthusiasm again. It’s killing me.”

“Killing you, really? Well I hope you stay alive at least through dinner.”

He smiled and said, “I’ll do my best.”

They went downtown to Moshe Peking on West 37th Street, one of the city’s most famed kosher establishments and a popular place for *shidduch* dates. He wasn’t sure that the two of them would easily blend into that scene, but he really didn’t know of much else beyond his usual venues, and he thought that this was among the nicest.

After being seated, she looked around. “Seems like a lot of *shidduch* dates,” she said.

“And others.” Slightly defensive.

“I know. I’ve actually been here a few times before.”

“On dates?”

“With my family. Most of my dates are kind of... movies, pizza. And I really like those burgers that are wrapped in foil.”

“Like the ones at Kosher Delight?” he asked, referring to a popular fast food place.

“Love those.”

“I guess this is a little over the top for a first date,” he admitted.

“Or a second or a third,” she said with a smile.

“Sorry.” Also smiling.

No reply. She just gazed at him.

"Seems our differences are quite..." He searched for the word.

"Obvious."

"That's probably the right word." He considered the point, then said, "So, why'd you agree to see me?"

"Because you're interesting. And because you *are* different. At least, for me you're different. I don't mean that you're different..."

"I get it," he interrupted.

Her gaze intensified. "And why did you ask me?"

"Because you're different."

The waiter arrived for their drink orders. She chose a glass of Chardonnay, taking it up a notch from her usual preference for Corona, while he went with Glenlivet 12 on the rocks. Scotch was fairly commonplace in yeshiva circles, especially on Shabbos, but most of his peers were still stuck on the likes of Chivas Regal or Johnny Walker Black. He had discovered the single malt a few months back at the recommendation of his father, a Torah scholar who knew how to enjoy a good drink from time to time.

Their conversation segued into the dissimilarities among the various types of Orthodox Jews, especially between the modern and the ultra-Orthodox, and how these were sometimes more pronounced than the distinctions between Orthodoxy and the other Jewish denominations.

"Maybe I'm not quite as *Charedi* as you think," he said, using the Hebrew term for ultra-Orthodox.

"I agree. My guess is that you're a little confused. You've got the penguin outfit thing going, but you're also here with me." She held her arms up to emphasize that her sleeves were the shortest in the room, then looked down to make the same point about her skirt.

"I suppose you could put it that way, but I don't feel confused."

She looked at him curiously.

He shrugged his shoulders.

"Well, it is a bit inconsistent," she said.

"A bit. But I don't have a problem with it. Wasn't it Emerson who said, 'A foolish consistency is the hobgoblin of little minds'?"

"You're quoting Emerson!"

"So surprised! Seems you have a stereotype of us *Charedi* folks."

"I'm sorry. I probably do. I shouldn't have said that." Embarrassed.

His smile told her it was fine. "What about you?" he asked. "Being here with me isn't exactly typical for you? Is that a problem?"

"Honestly, I'm still not sure." She took a breath. "But there is something I have to tell you."

He raised his eyebrows.

"Well, I don't think you know this, but..." Another breath. "We were supposed to meet."

"We were?" He thought a moment. "Oh yes, of course we were! It was ordained in heaven."

"Cute, but that's not what I'm talking about."

That smile of his was really getting to her. He just seemed so comfortable, so much at peace with who he was and what he was doing, she had a hard time making sense of it. And she was a little jealous.

"It was Shimmy," she said. "He's been talking about you for years. Yoni this, and Yoni that, and Yoni the other thing. It's always Yoni."

Now *he* was embarrassed. "We're good friends."

"He adores you. Thinks you're the smartest and best person he knows."

"Trust me, he knows many who are smarter and better. And *he* is truly the smartest person I know."

"Ah, but you didn't say he was the best person you know."

"Good catch. To tell you the truth, he is a great person, and probably the finest of all my friends when I think about it, but..."

"Not the best you know."

"Correct."

"Then who is?"

He hesitated. "It's going to sound trite."

"Try me."

"Okay. My parents."

She thought about that for a second. "Actually, it doesn't sound trite at all, at least not from you."

"Thanks."

"Anytime."

"And who's the best person you know?"

"Well now that I can't say my parents, I need to think about it. But I want to get back to the other story."

"Right, the one about how we were supposed to meet."

"Yes. Like I said, Shimmy's been talking you up for some time, not in relation to me, but just in general. And I recently broke up with someone I was seeing for a while, so he's been laying it on quite thick. 'You gotta meet Yoni, he's perfect for you.' Like that."

"You must have thought he was crazy."

"I didn't get it. He really is a perceptive guy, and with everything he knows about the two of us, I just didn't know what to think."

"So, what did you tell him?"

"That it's a ridiculous idea." Realizing she may have offended him, she added, "That was before I met you."

"I understand. You don't have to explain."

"No," she said, contemplating. "I do."

"You mean you feel differently now?"

"Well, I guess it's not ridiculous."

"There's that enthusiasm again."

"All kidding aside, why don't we just call it uncertainty?"

"Beats ridiculous. Works for me."

The waiter arrived with their drinks and took their order. Sarah selected wonton soup, an egg roll, and chicken with broccoli. Jonathan went for hot and sour soup, veal spare ribs, beef lo mein, and another egg roll. The soup came within minutes. The egg rolls and spare ribs followed shortly.

As she eyed the ribs on the table, she said, "Clearly not the best first-date food."

"Yeah. I wasn't thinking about that when I ordered them."

"But they look really good."

"They do." He reached for a rib with his hand to break the ice. "Feel free to use a fork and knife if you like."

"I'll be brave," she said as she also reached for one.

Through their entrées and desserts of orange and lemon sorbet, their conversation turned to talk of their families, backgrounds, and aspirations. He had much to say: about descending from many generations of prominent rabbis; about his older brother who had just gotten ordained and was teaching in a yeshiva high school; about his younger sister who was recently married to one of his classmates in the rabbinical seminary. And she was just as talkative about her parents' nursing home business and how her older brother, who had become more religious than the rest of the family after studying for a year in a yeshiva in Israel, had recently started working with them. Jonathan talked about his eventual plans to teach alongside his father in the rabbinic seminary, and she talked of her passion to become a pediatrician. And when the manager approached to tell them it was past closing time, they both seemed surprised. They looked around to see that the restaurant had emptied.

They arrived back uptown at her building shortly before midnight and decided to walk and talk for another hour or so. As she showed him around her campus, she tried to conceal her apprehension. Seeing faces she recognized, she couldn't help wonder what they might be thinking about her and this guy. But this was the easy part, she supposed, admitting a gnawing sense that she was eventually going to have to introduce him to her parents. That would be the hard part.

"This was great," he said as they were standing outside her building, about to part ways. "I'd really like to do it again soon."

"Okay, but I have another thing to say."

He waited for more.

"This was nice. Nicer than I thought. Nicer than I wanted it to be. And I guess Shimmy is as smart as we think he is, because I do want to see you again. But there's something I need to say first."

"Say anything you want, it's fine."

"I don't mean to be presumptuous, but, given our differences, I'm having a hard time seeing how we fit into each other's dreams."

"I understand."

"Don't get me wrong. Judaism is important to me. I want to raise my children in a religious community, but not in some secluded ghetto split off from the world. I like television, I like movies, I like concerts, and I'm a really big fan of coed schools and camps."

He gazed at her impassively.

"And I'm not even saying that we're headed in that direction or anything like that—I mean, we barely even know each other—

but I just want to put it out there. Sort of how you needed to wear your hat and suit. You needed to be who you are. I need you to know from the get-go who I am."

Still wordless.

"I'd love to know what you're thinking. Please, say something."

"I'm honestly not sure what to say. All I know is that I want to see you again. I get what you're saying, but I still think we have potential." He paused, realizing that he wasn't very convincing, then said, "Why don't we each make a promise that we won't try to force anything on the other, and let's just see where this takes us?"

"I can do that," she said. "As long as we both know it's going to be a bumpy road."

"I see it more as an adventure."

"Okay. A bumpy adventure."

And that was the beginning. They dated for six months—a drop in the bucket in her circles and an inordinate amount of time in his—and were engaged by the end of summer. While it was his idea to observe the laws of having no physical contact before marriage, she came to appreciate it, and him for his self-discipline. But they could stand it for only so long. The wedding was scheduled for mid-December of her first year in medical school.

Both sets of parents were more supportive than anticipated. His were simply happy he had finally found someone. Hers were familiar with, and surprisingly impressed by, his family background.

The first concession he made was abandoning his plans to teach in the rabbinical seminary, instead landing a position as assistant rabbi of the prestigious Modern Orthodox Beth Israel Synagogue of Lawrence, in the famed Five Towns of Long Island. The money was decent and the senior rabbi's age rendered it an excellent opportunity.

The neighborhood was classic suburbia, home to one of the country's most robust Orthodox Jewish communities, and had a plethora of Orthodox day schools. Though most of these schools were single-sex, courtesy of a large influx of ultra-Orthodox in recent years, there was one that remained coed and thus acceptable to Sarah.

In the end, the only drawback seemed to be Sarah's commute to medical school, which consisted of the Long Island Railroad and a couple of subways. It was definitely tough in the beginning, but she eventually came to appreciate it as an opportunity to study or, when she was really lucky, to nap.

Another development was Jonathan's application to law school. Although she had never pushed for anything of this sort, he somehow felt a need to do more academically. Law school was a natural choice for someone with such vast Talmudic training and a fairly common path for yeshiva students. He knew his rabbinic responsibilities would allow him to do it only part time, so he applied and was admitted to Fordham, reputedly the best night program in the city and only about an hour commute that time of day. Further breaking with family custom, he started keeping his beard closely trimmed, and added light gray and blue suits to his wardrobe. His hat, however, remained the traditional black Borsalino fedora. Sarah had a few thoughts about that but kept them to herself. Everything in its time.

She, too, had made some compromises in accepting the demands of her position as a *rebbetzin*, a rabbi's wife. Her dresses and sleeves grew longer, and her hair was covered with either a hat or a *sheitel*, a wig. It was hard at first, but she truly loved Jonathan and wanted to make a life with him. There were certain things they each agreed to before they got married. He was upholding his end of the bargain, and she would uphold hers. And with it all, she still remained steadfast in her views, committed to becoming a physician and raising her children to appreciate both their religion and the secular world in which they lived. And he, in a way he hadn't necessarily expected, grew to appreciate these things as well.

It was just short of the completion of his first year as assistant rabbi, six weeks after the birth of his first child, Aaron, when the senior rabbi, Mordecai Friedman, informed Jonathan that he would be retiring. "It's been thirty years, and I've had enough," Friedman said to him in a candid discussion one night in the rabbi's study.

Friedman had three daughters and a son, all of whom were married with children and lived in Israel. "It's time for me to go join my family."

Jonathan was disheartened by the news. He was fond of Friedman, both as a person and a mentor. And he felt unprepared at that point to assume the mantle of leadership, if the congregation would even want him to do so.

"Oh, they're going to want you!" Friedman said. "They love you, probably a lot more than they love me. Me, they're sick of. But you? You're young, fresh and brilliant. I hear them talking about you all the time."

"They're not sick of you at all," Jonathan demurred.

"Ah, but they are. Anyway, I'm exhausted. Thirty years is too long to be doing this job."

Jonathan understood. The demands of the job were daunting. Even as assistant rabbi, his phone never stopped ringing.

"I, for one, think you're prepared for the position, and I'm going to recommend it. Law school may become a problem for you, but I'm sure you'll figure it out."

Why do people always think that? Jonathan wondered.

"Just a warning..."

Jonathan raised his eyebrows.

"These people will come to you for everything under the sun—family problems, marriage problems, neighbor problems, financial problems, legal problems, medical problems. And at the end of the day, you're going to have to burp them."

"Burp them?" Jonathan said.

"Yes, burp them. Just like you burp a baby. You have to pick them up, rub their bellies, pat their backs, all until they let out a big burp, and only then do they stop crying."

Jonathan was taken aback by the cynicism. Friedman had always been supportive and encouraging. But then again, Friedman had never even hinted about retiring till that moment, so there were clearly things he had been holding back.

"And one more piece of advice," Friedman said. "The minute you stop indulging them, they're going to want to replace you with another model."

"But the whole purpose of being a rabbi is to teach and guide."

"That's true only so long as you teach the things they want to learn, say the things they want to hear, and guide them along the path they prefer. If you forget that, you're finished."

Jonathan couldn't hide his astonishment.

Seeing his apprentice disillusioned, Friedman dialed it back a bit. "Don't worry, you're going to be great. You've got the entire package and they know it. You can pretty much write your own ticket. Just remember, play by the rules. Set an example, a very strong example, but don't expect them to follow. And *never* show your disappointment when they don't."

3

NO ONE EVER NOTICED Jonathan's furtive glance toward the women's balcony at the conclusion of every sermon. No one except Sarah, for whom it was intended. A single nod from her meant *nice job;* a shoulder shrug, *I'm not sure what they think;* and a blank stare with open palms, *better luck next week.*

This time it was the nod, which pleased the rabbi as he stepped away from the podium and returned to his seat. He'd recently been growing unsure of his influence. For twenty-eight years he'd preached about every topic under the sun regarding one's relationship with God, one's self, and others. His sermons had gained an international reputation, and he was often invited to other communities to speak. Lately, though, he felt as if he was running out of things to say and wondered if his congregation felt likewise.

Sarah's approval meant more to him than any accolades from congregants, and there were always plenty of the latter. She was the perennial truth teller—honest, perhaps to a fault. She also had an excellent feel for the pulse of the congregation. If she said the speech was good, then it was. His initial doubts, he now realized, had been but a projection of his own tedium onto his listeners.

It was at moments like this when he wondered how life would have turned out if he'd heeded the advice of Professor Carmichael, his favorite teacher and law school dean.

"You're a brilliant student," Carmichael had said. "A natural! Come on board, teach for us. Before you know it, you'll be tenured. You can write, publish, earn recognition. Eventually, you'll be able to consult to firms. *That's* where the money is."

Sarah had found the idea tempting at the time. "Professor Jonathan Bauman. It has a ring to it," she had said.

But Jonathan's heart had been elsewhere. He wanted to be a teacher of Torah, to spread the gospel—so to speak—of Jewish scholarship and lore, to inspire others to greater religious heights and observance. He hadn't known at the time that most of his audience would be less interested in learning than being entertained, a reality he had eventually come to accept.

The image of Professor Carmichael entered his mind. The two of them still caught up over lunch at least once a year, where Carmichael continued to press him to return to Fordham. The professor's physical appearance hadn't changed much over time. A few added wrinkles and white hair, but otherwise the same—tall, stocky, bespectacled, goateed, and impeccably attired. Carmichael had retired as dean a few years earlier but was still teaching, and still *quite* influential, to hear him tell it. "Just say the word and you're in," was always the last thing he mentioned before they parted.

It was funny, Jonathan thought, how Carmichael refused to give up on him. Was the professor that stubborn, or did he simply sense a restlessness in his former student? In either case, such was not to be. And as the years wore on, Jonathan wondered from time to time if he had really made the right choice.

At the conclusion of *davening,* the congregation gathered in an adjacent hall for food and mingling. The *Kiddush,* named after the benediction made on the wine or liquor immediately prior to eating on the Sabbath, was a vast improvement from the cookies, cakes and soda of Jonathan's childhood. This was a smorgasbord of various hot dishes, herrings, salads, spreads, desserts, and of course an array of top-shelf single-malt scotches, bourbons, and an occasional rye.

While Jonathan enjoyed a libation now and then, he had been growing disdainful of the custom of drinking after *davening* over the past few years. It had become a problem in his eyes, week after week, watching many of the men imbibe to various states of intoxication, ranging from tipsy to outright drunkenness. The term "Shabbos alcoholic" had been bantered about at recent rabbinic meetings, but Jonathan knew that for some of his congregants such a designation was misleading. Shabbos only scratched the surface.

He had grown jealous of one of his colleagues, who insisted on having a "dry" synagogue—absolutely no alcohol under any circumstances. He had considered the idea, had floated it to his board, and was told emphatically that it would jeopardize his position. The other synagogue had already lost a large portion of its membership, which was now gathering as a "breakaway *minyan*" in the basement of a Conservative synagogue, boasting the most elaborate *Kiddush* in all the Five Towns.

Jonathan rarely ate or drank anything at the *Kiddush*. A sumptuous lunch awaited him at home, and this was a time when he had to be available to the myriads of congregants jockeying for a moment with him and Sarah, who always spent this time by his side. Often it was a comment on the speech, a compliment, criticism, or question. And occasionally it was about politics or other recent newsworthy events. Jonathan always shied away from expressing his political opinions, but it was basically known that he, as most Orthodox rabbis, harbored fairly conservative views. Sarah, on the other hand, was somewhat more liberal leaning, and this was known only among her most intimate friends, all of whom pretty much shared her perspectives.

"A homerun!" said Benjamin Marcus, the president of the congregation, as he approached Jonathan. Marcus was a hearty sort, tall and imposing. Not much hair atop his head, but a nicely trimmed beard to compensate. An immensely successful real estate mogul, he was one of the more strictly observant members, and deeply appreciative of Jonathan's ultra-Orthodox background and lineage. He was also a genuine devotee, highly respectful of the rabbi's intellect, and almost always present for the daily 6 a.m. Talmud class. "Brilliant and well said," he added.

"Thank you, Benjy," Jonathan responded as the two men shook hands.

The wives embraced, kissed, and exchanged inquiries about their kids. And then it was onto the next in line, one after another until everyone had gotten a chance.

By the time they arrived home for lunch, Jonathan was ravenous. It was 12:30 and he hadn't eaten anything all day. In his view, it was against *halakha*, Jewish law, to eat before *davening*. Sarah had often encouraged him to take something at the *Kiddush*, but he just never felt comfortable having a fork and plate in hand or a mouthful of food while talking to a congregant.

As usual, the lunch table was crowded. His eldest son, Aaron, his daughter-in-law and three young children were in from Los Angeles where Aaron was following in his father's footsteps as a congregational rabbi. Aaron had always been the dutiful, studious son who watched and mimicked every step his father took, excepting his short-lived career as a basketball star in the yeshiva high school circuit. Jonathan never had much of an interest in sports but was an avid runner who still managed five miles most days.

Also visiting that week was Miriam, their middle child and only daughter. In her second year of a Clinical Psychology doctoral program at New York University she, like her younger brother, Noah, was still single with seemingly no prospects on the horizon. Jonathan's anxiety over this far exceeded Sarah's, and in conversations with her, he often referred to them as "unmarried" rather than "single." She wasn't enamored with his terminology but understood that this was all rather difficult for him.

As far as Jonathan was concerned, Miriam was the sharpest intellect of the Bauman clan and, courtesy of her mother, quite independent minded. This, of course, engendered more than a few father-daughter clashes over the years. Diffidence wasn't his long suit, especially on those occasions when she challenged the very foundations of his thoughts and beliefs. But he never broached the subject of her dating woes. There had been several impressive suitors, none of whom had quite made the cut with her, and he was always careful to hide his disappointment, always mindful that she was a sensitive soul and his little girl. And never ignoring the irony of how he had put his own parents through similar travails.

As for Noah, whose absence this Shabbos was felt by all, the situation was altogether different. While Jonathan saw Aaron as the perfect child and Miriam as a rebellious one, Noah was always somewhat of a mystery. For the most part, he did what was expected when it came to school and religion, but his actual feelings, thoughts and beliefs were undiscernible, hidden beneath a veneer of compliance and equanimity.

Jonathan worried about Noah more than Miriam, because with Miriam he was confident he always knew what was going on. And despite Sarah's frequent reminders that every child was different, some more in need of privacy than others, he just couldn't shake the gnawing sense that, with Noah, it was about more than just privacy.

4

NOAH BAUMAN SAT ON the couch in his living room, staring out the window of the fourth floor Washington Heights apartment he shared with three other students. His roommates were away this Shabbos, as he was supposed to have been. A last-minute change of plans prompted by a state of utter despondency left him alone inside these walls. Alone with ruminations of the other night with Ilana. And of the family he would eventually have to face.

He was close with his sister, Miriam. They spoke several times a week, and it was easy for them to get together for dinner now and then because she lived in a shared apartment just a few subway stops south on the Upper West Side. Being only a year apart, they also had a few mutual friends.

But things were different with Aaron, his older brother, who he hadn't seen in over six months. They spoke once every month or so, generally about sports, which was pretty much the only thing they had in common. They were both huge Knicks, Mets, Jets, and Rangers fans, basically covering them for conversation the entire year. Noah had also played basketball in high school but had fallen short of his big brother's skills and reputation, an inequity that bothered him some, but had never detracted from their relationship.

His mind returned to Ilana, their last moments together, the understanding that he might never see her or speak with her again. He just couldn't fathom that, but knew it was beyond his control.

Just like everything else.

He was roused from a deep sleep by the ring of his cell phone. Hesitant to answer, he glanced at the clock and saw that Shabbos had ended an hour ago. He had slept most of the day away.

"Hello," he said, his voice groggy.

"Sounds like you just woke up," his sister said.

"Yeah." Hesitation. "Sort of."

"Are you okay?"

"Yes, sorry, I'm fine. Where are you?"

"I'm on the train. Rushed out of the house after *Shabbos* to get back to the city. I have a party tonight. Why don't you and Ilana come?"

"I don't think so." Subdued.

"You know, little brother, we missed you this *Shabbos.*"

"I know."

"You want to tell me why you didn't show?"

"Just wasn't feeling it."

"Like you aren't feeling the party I'm going to."

"Sort of."

"I may not be a psychologist yet, but it doesn't sound like you're doing very well."

There wasn't much he could hide from her. She was ever the intuitive one, and he had even occasionally wondered if she had guessed his big secret. "You're right, I'm not," he admitted.

"What? What's going on?"

Realizing that evasiveness was stupid at this point, he answered, "Ilana and I broke up."

Momentary silence. "I'm so sorry," she said softly.

Her conspicuous omission of asking what happened, coupled with her total lack of surprise, reinforced his belief that she knew the truth. "I am too," he said.

"Any chance of reconciliation?"

She definitely knows, he told himself. "I don't think so."

"I'm going to skip the party and come up to see you," she said.

"That's really unnecessary."

"I want to."

"I'm too tired."

"Tired? I'll bet you've been sleeping all day. I'll come by, we'll go out for pizza or something and we'll talk."

"I don't feel like talking."

"Okay," she said hesitantly. "I won't push. I'll call you tomorrow."

"Sounds good," he said.

"But if you change your mind about tonight just call me. The party isn't that important."

"If I do, I will."

As soon as they hung up, he shut off the phone. He didn't want to deal with anyone else that evening. He recited the prayers for ending Shabbos, fixed himself something to eat, and tried to study. Unable to focus, he got into bed and turned on the TV. Surfing the channels proved useless. Nothing held his attention. He attempted sleep, but, after a seeming eternity of tossing, turning and looking at the ceiling, he got out of bed.

What now? he mused, feeling an acute need for distraction. He turned his phone back on and saw a missed call from his mother. He would talk to her tomorrow, he told himself, dreading the inevitable barrage of questions about the breakup. He was hoping she wouldn't hear about it before speaking with him. He knew for certain that Miriam wouldn't say anything but was worried about whom Ilana may have told and the breakneck speed of gossip in the incestuous Orthodox world. As for the other thing, his secret, he wasn't really concerned. He just didn't imagine Ilana ever betraying him that way.

He dialed his sister's number.

"Change your mind?" she answered.

He heard in the background that she was already at the party. "I guess so."

"You want to come here, or would you like me to come to you?"

"I'll come down there," he said, thinking it was better she not ride the subways alone so late at night through some of Manhattan's seedier neighborhoods. He knew better than to actually voice this concern to her, lest she take it as a challenge and insist. "It's probably better for me to get away from here," he said.

She gave him the exact location of the party and they both figured it would take him a little over an hour to shower, primp, and travel down there. He hung up the phone, ambled his way to the bathroom, and examined his reflection in the mirror. *Dreary eyes,* he told himself, mindful that he needed to perk up a bit. *Maybe a shave?* He wasn't sure. He usually shaved once a week, just before Shabbos. But yesterday, things being what they were, he hadn't been very motivated and skipped it. To be honest, he kind of liked the scruffy look. He wasn't sure why. Perhaps because it made him feel more rugged or manly, he reflected, admitting that he probably needed that—a byproduct of years of self-doubt and self-loathing. But more than a week's worth might be pushing it. Or was it? He decided to leave it be.

He took a quick shower and got dressed. Skinny blue jeans, Ugg moccasins and a checkered Polo button-down beneath a burgundy shawl-collar pullover sweater. He glanced at himself once more in the mirror. He had never quite taken much stock in the accolades he'd gotten about his appearance over the years—handsome, striking, gorgeous—always thinking people were simply trying to curry favor with his parents.

At a little over 6 feet with jet-black hair, baby blue eyes and eye-catching facial features, he still wasn't convinced. In fact, there was a time when he thought he was too tall, another time when he thought he was too thin, and yet another time when he thought his hair was too thick and wavy. It wasn't surprising, all things considered, that he wasn't able to put the whole picture together and appreciate what he had going on. Though he was getting better as of late, and at this moment he had to admit, *not bad.*

He wondered what kind of crowd he would encounter at the party. Miriam had an eclectic circle. There were her religious friends from childhood, most of whom were married; her slightly less religious friends from the Upper West Side, none of whom were married; and her friends from graduate school, many of whom weren't Jewish.

He assumed from her initially including Ilana in the invite that it wasn't going to be very rowdy, and that suited him just fine.

He didn't love crowded gatherings to begin with, but his choice was simple: Miriam's party or the pity party he'd been stuck in over the past two days. He glanced at himself in the mirror yet again. A sad, confused, and fearful face peered back at him as somewhere in his distant mind he heard a small voice saying, *You really need to get out!*

5

SARAH BAUMAN CURLED UP on the den couch with her latest novel. Between her pediatric practice and duties as the rabbi's wife, she had little time for herself—maybe an hour or two on a Shabbos afternoon and an occasional Saturday night. Fiction was her favorite pastime, and her present project, Ronald Balson's *Karolina's Twins*, was moving along at a good pace. She needed to finish the book before its scheduled discussion at the upcoming sisterhood book club meeting next Thursday evening. Leading that monthly gathering was one of her favorite activities.

While the story was compelling and well written, she couldn't keep her mind from drifting. She had been worrying about Noah for quite some time, and his unexplained absence this past Shabbos wasn't helping. She couldn't put her finger on it, but she knew that something was amiss. Her recent attempts to probe him proved fruitless, usually provoking something like: "everything's good," followed by a swift change of subject. And whenever she brought up Ilana, who she thought was perfect, she sensed emptiness in his eyes and dispassion in his voice. She had perceived such things in his previous relationships and had always been right. And was always bewildered.

She put the book down on the table and got up to find Jonathan. It was an unusual Saturday night. Not a single phone call since the end of Shabbos. It was nice, she thought, that people in the community knew better than to bother the rabbi while his oldest son's family was visiting from across the country. What they didn't know, however, was that Aaron and family were actually out for the evening seeing old friends in Brooklyn. Undoubtedly, there were some pastoral tasks requiring Jonathan's attention and, undoubtedly, he would pay for this peaceful night during the next few days. But for now, he was tucked away in his study laboring over a challenging page of Talmud—*his* favorite pastime.

She gently opened the door to his study so as not to startle him. "Hi," she said as he lifted his eyes from his book and smiled.

"Everything okay?" he asked, surprised that she was taking a break from her reading.

"I called Noah. No answer." She planted herself in a chair in front of his desk, a spot usually reserved for a congregant needing the rabbi's time outside of normal synagogue hours. His job always involved late-night phone calls and meetings, so they had set up a study in a room that had originally been intended for a live-in housekeeper. The décor was simple: walls covered from floor to ceiling with jam-packed book shelves, an artisanal maple desk Sarah had picked up years earlier from an estate sale, and two matching brown leather guest chairs in front of the desk. The room's sole indulgence was a Herman Miller graphite executive chair she had given Jonathan for his forty-fifth birthday, dreamily ergonomic for his chronically sore back.

"He's probably out with Ilana. I'm sure we'll hear from him tomorrow."

"I'm sure we will." Sarcasm.

"What? What's the matter?"

"Doesn't it bother you that he just didn't show this *Shabbos*, not even to see his brother and the children?"

"He didn't just not show. He called," Jonathan said.

"At the last minute. And with some cockamamie excuse of needing to study. He can't study here?"

"So, what are you saying?"

"Something's wrong. I just know it."

So much for trying to assuage her. He got up from his seat, came around the desk and planted himself in the other guest chair to be closer to her. "And what do you think is wrong?" he asked, figuring she had an idea. It was unlike her to worry for no reason.

"I honestly don't know. I've just been sensing that he hasn't really been happy for a long time."

"Like, forever," he muttered.

"So, you see it too."

"Sort of, but I think that's just him—he's not exactly the poster boy for bubbliness."

"I know," she said. "But this seems different."

"Different?" he said, reminding himself that she was generally more in tune with the kids. It wasn't that he was unaware or aloof, only that she had a real gift when it came to reading minds, his included. "How so?"

She was wordless, seemingly lost in thought.

"Do you think he's unhappy with Ilana?" he asked.

A tear fell from her eye as she nodded. "He's never happy with anyone. And this time he seems to be forcing himself, I can tell."

"Forcing himself?"

"Because he feels pressured. He's the rabbi's son, all his friends are married, the list goes on..."

"I know." Regretful. "You think he didn't show because he's uncomfortable seeing Aaron with Sheindy and the kids?"

"No, that's not it. I think he's way past competing with Aaron."

"Oh, I don't agree. From a man's perspective, and one with an older brother no less, there are some forms of competition you *never* get past." He paused for her to digest his point, then continued, "And what about Miriam? You're not worried about *her*?"

"You know I am, but it's different. She may be *unmarried*, as you like to refer to her, but she's not unhappy." Sarah frequently called him out on his double standard when it came to Miriam and Noah, though, truth be told, she understood it.

Having married late himself, he had to give Noah a pass. But with Miriam, he just couldn't get his head around her still being single. And then there was the fact that she was at NYU studying for a PhD in clinical psychology while being single, a potentially risky situation for an Orthodox Jewish woman. He'd expressed this opinion to Sarah many times. But Sarah had always had an abundance of patience for Miriam's free spirit, even years back when Miriam's favorite hobby was picking fights with her father about religion, politics, or just about anything under the sun.

"Well, maybe she should be a little unhappy? It might motivate her," he said.

"Are we going to rehash all that again?"

He thought for a moment. "No, let's not," he said. He had stopped arguing with or about Miriam long ago, mostly because it had become unproductive. For some reason beyond his comprehension his daughter had always seemed heavily invested in viewing the world differently than he did. For years this had caused a great deal of conflict between them. But lately, owing to their vastly improved relationship, he had become more acquiescent, while quietly hoping she would one day grasp the wisdom of his ways.

Sarah looked at him relieved.

"So, back to Noah," he said.

"I don't know."

6

STEPPING OFF THE ELEVATOR, Noah Bauman heard the party down the hall. He arrived at the door and pressed the buzzer, convinced no one would hear it above the music and voices. To his surprise, the door opened almost immediately. It was his sister.

"You heard the bell?" he said.

"I was waiting for you, so I stayed near the door."

"Good thinking."

"Yeah, I'm just a genius."

He smiled. She was always able to get him to do that.

She pulled him into the apartment. "Looks like you found the place okay," she said.

"It's an address. It's New York City. Not so complicated."

"Fair enough," she said.

He smelled the alcohol on her breath. "You've been drinking, Sis?"

"It's Saturday night. It's a party." Almost defensive. "You could probably use a few beers yourself." She helped him out of his coat. "I'll take care of this. Why don't you circulate?"

"Okay," he said tentatively.

"Actually, wait here," she said, backpedaling her suggestion, realizing he might need some hand-holding.

She disappeared with his coat and left him standing alone in the foyer. He could see people in the living room and kitchen, both of which were crowded and noisy. Out of habit, he searched for another head with a yarmulke, but there were none to be found. Beyond feeling self-conscious, he wondered about his sister's social circles. They were certainly different than his. And different from the way hers used to be.

The apartment was typical Upper West Side tiny, and also sweltering, not the best combination for someone who had a touch of social anxiety to begin with. He took a deep breath. *I'll manage.*

Miriam returned within a minute. "So?" she said. "Are you ready for me to introduce you to a few folks?"

He offered a reticent shrug.

She led him into the living room. "Oh, there's Raj," she said with a smile, pointing to an Indian-looking fellow involved in a group conversation on the other side of the room. They eased through the crowd toward Raj, Noah wondering what Raj and the smile were all about.

She came up behind Raj and put her hand on his shoulder to get his attention. He grabbed her hand, turned around delighted and eyed Noah.

"Raj, this is Noah," she said.

"Ah, the mysterious little brother."

The two men shook hands.

"Good to meet you," Noah said.

"You too," Raj said.

Noah watched Miriam slowly pull her hand from Raj's as the two of them shared an awkward glance. He had a suspicion that he wasn't the only one with a secret.

"Raj is in my doctoral program," Miriam said.

"Oh," Noah responded. "Same year?"

"Same year, same class, same everything," Raj said.

Noah didn't know what else to do besides nod and smile. His wonderment about his sister and Raj was actually helping to distract him from the anxiety he normally felt in parties and crowds, at least as much as possible. It was also easing any worries he may have had of her knowing the truth about him.

Miriam introduced him to a few more friends as he responded with more graciousness, smiles, and nods. Realizing that he was doing the best he could, she offered him a reprieve. "Let's get out of here."

"You sure?"

"Absolutely. I've had enough of this myself. Let's go somewhere we can talk."

He suspected she was being kind but opted to go with it. The talking idea didn't thrill him—he wasn't really up for it after his last encounter with Ilana—but it was better than the alternative. He watched as she made her way back to Raj to tell him they were leaving, his eyes widening as Raj embraced her and kissed her on the lips. Clearly, there was a lot to talk about.

It was too frigid for a long walk, so they quickly found a place around the corner on Broadway. An open café on a Saturday night in this neighborhood wasn't unheard of. And the fact that it was relatively uncrowded enabled them to find a table in the back with plenty of privacy.

The walk from the apartment building had been quiet and brisk—minimal chit-chat about the arctic weather and the need to find a warm spot quickly. Now they sat looking at each other, wondering who would start.

"So, who's Raj?"

She glanced into space, immediately realizing she had been foolish not to have jumped in with the first question. Now she was on the spot while his issues would enjoy a momentary reprieve.

"A friend." Tentative.

"Who you hold hands with and kiss on the lips?"

"Oh, that's nothing."

"Really?"

"Sort of," she said.

"Look, I'm not judging. Just asking."

"I know."

He considered how swiftly she responded. "You say that with such certainty. How do you know I wouldn't judge?"

"Because that's not you, little brother. And..." Hesitation. "You have your own stuff, so you wouldn't..."

"Judge?"

"Yeah, judge."

"Because I have my own stuff?"

She nodded.

He realized that she'd skillfully turned the conversation his way. "Okay, what are we talking about? My stuff or yours?" he asked.

"Which do you want to talk about?"

He contemplated her question. "You first."

"Then you?"

He nodded.

"Tonight?"

"Tonight."

"Okay, Raj is a guy from school." Faltering. "And we're friendly."

"Friendly, as in friends?"

"Sort of."

"Well, that certainly clears it up."

"Okay, okay, so we're a little more than friends."

"And how long has it been going on?"

"The friends? Or the more than friends?"

He gave her a look that said, *cut the crap already*!

"Not long. About a month," she said.

Noah considered asking about Raj's ethnicity, wondering if it was Indian, Pakistani, or some other possibility that would share similar features. He decided not to, as it really didn't matter. The main issue was that Raj wasn't Jewish, plain and simple. If he had been, which was remotely possible though unlikely, then Miriam would have led with that. "How come you never told me about him?" Noah asked.

"Never told you!" She chuckled. "You're kidding, aren't you?"

"Why would I be kidding?"

"Because *that* question, coming from *you*, is funny. You're the king of hiding things!"

Touché. She had him, he presumed. But before revealing anything, he had to be sure she really knew. "And what am I hiding?" he asked, trying to sound as innocent as possible.

"Are we now switching to you?"

"I guess." Vacillating.

"There's more about me and Raj."

"It can wait." A tinge of resolve. It was time.

"Can I ask you a question?" Delicate.

"Anything," he said.

"Why did you break up with Ilana?"

"It's complicated."

"Do you not want to get married?"

"Also complicated."

She felt bad, as he was obviously uneasy. The last thing she wanted was to embarrass him but, in her heart, she was certain that he wanted to tell her. "Are you sexually attracted to women?" she asked, purposely wording her question as unambiguously as possible.

He stared at her, then said, "How long have you suspected?"

"A little while. Maybe a year or so."

"What gave it away?"

"You've dated some really good women—beautiful, smart, funny, caring, and you just never seemed..."

"Happy," he interjected.

"Happy's part of it, but it isn't exactly what I was thinking of."

"Okay, what were you thinking?"

"That you never seemed excited or enthusiastic. Even with Ilana, I kept watching the two of you together, and it just didn't look to me like you were in love with her. Then I started thinking about the others. Then I started wondering."

They were both silent for a moment, just gazing at each other.

"I don't know what to do," he said, as if speaking to himself and letting her listen.

"I know," she said empathically. Then she added, "I don't either."

"You don't know what I should do? Or you don't know what you should do?"

"I was talking about you, but now that you mention it..."

"Ironic that we're each in a similar conundrum," he observed. Both of their situations were completely unimaginable in the world from which they came.

"Different conundrums," she said. Pensive.

"Different, I suppose." Contemplating. "And similar."

"I hear you. But let's face it, your problem is definitely worse than mine."

"Because?" He happened to agree but was curious about her reasoning.

"Because mine is temporary. It's just a thing, not a real or lasting thing. More like a distraction—for now. And even if it weren't, it's fixable, at least in Dad's eyes. He'd probably be upset, and maybe even rant a little bit, but in the end there's always the option for Raj to convert. I'm not saying that any of this is going to happen, because it isn't. I'm just pointing out the difference."

"Dad doesn't rant."

"I know, but he can get really upset."

"He's entitled. None of this fits into his worldview."

"And what about Mom?" she asked. "I don't exactly see her jumping for joy over this. And let's not forget Aaron, he's probably going to have a really hard time with it."

"Aaron? I don't think so," he said with an uncharacteristic certainty. To the world, Aaron Bauman was the poster boy for an ultra-Orthodox rabbi, but to Noah, he was big brother first and foremost. It was inconceivable to him that Aaron would be anything less than supportive and protective.

"I don't mean that he would be angry," she said defensively. "I just think he would be...more like sad."

"Like Mom," he muttered.

"Yeah, like Mom. I think she'll be sad too." She looked like she was holding back tears.

"I can't blame her," he said, acknowledging that his situation was going to create immense problems for him in his community, problems that no parent would want a child to have to encounter.

"She'll come around," she said, trying to sound reassuring.

"So will Aaron."

"I agree." Hesitation. "It's Dad I'm worried about."

"What? You think he's going to disown me or something?"

"No, of course not." She paused. "I just don't see him ever being at peace with it."

Silence.

"So when are you planning to tell them?" she asked.

"I don't know." He considered the fact that he really had no idea what his next move was. "And what about you?"

"What about me?" Feigned innocence.

"Are you going to tell them about Raj?"

"Like I said, there's nothing to tell."

"And what happens if there is something to tell?"

"Let's worry about that when it happens, which, by the way, it isn't going to."

"Uh huh."

She managed a faint smile. "Look at us. Not exactly what Mom and Dad expected."

He raised his eyebrows. "No shit!"

7

MIRIAM'S BAUMAN'S FIRST MEMORY, which wasn't really her memory at all, was her father's oft-repeated recollection of the time she peed on him. Told with humor and irony against the backdrop of Jonathan's never having experienced this from either of his sons, it was always intended as an expression of Jonathan's deep affection for, and acknowledgement of, his daughter's feistiness.

"I was changing her, and she started to cry," he would usually begin. "Probably because it was me and not her mother." At this point, some of the people around the table—usually a Shabbos table—would smile. "She's getting all upset and squirming around, I can't even get the diaper on her, so I just pick her up and try to console her, and then it happened, a warm liquid is all over me."

Laughter typically filled the room at this point, and later Sarah and the kids would remind Jonathan that his story wasn't really that funny. They frequently relished in reminding him that he wasn't as funny as he thought.

"But they laughed," he would protest.

"Only because you're the rabbi," Sarah would answer, usually followed by something like, "You could have told them why the fireman wears red suspenders and they'd still be hysterical. They respect and revere you, it's that simple."

Eventually Jonathan ceased using his audience's laughter as proof of anything, and at some point—though Miriam could never quite pin down exactly when—he had stopped recounting this particular story altogether. It was probably, she guessed, when she had reached the age at which such a thing would sound more embarrassing than cute. But she was actually somewhat saddened when he stopped. She liked being reminded that the two of them shared something that he hadn't had with her brothers, and that it became, over time, an increasingly delicate subject, had made it even more special.

The tension, if one can call it that, between Miriam and her father started shortly before high school. While Jonathan had conceded to sending the children to a coed and thus more modern Jewish day school, Aaron Bauman had raised the bar in his father's eyes by actually requesting to attend a same sex yeshiva once he reached high school. He had grown to be a serious religious scholar and felt strongly that his proclivities would fare better in such an atmosphere.

Sarah had never insisted on her preference, nor had she actually stated it as a condition for marriage. Jonathan appreciated this, and he knew that his choices also mattered, especially once their relationship had been well underway. He also knew what was important to her, and he felt confident enough that their children's ultimate influences would come more from the home than anywhere else. When Aaron came around on his own, Jonathan was pleased and relieved, so when it became Miriam's turn to apply to high school, he was disappointed that she didn't want to follow in her brother's footsteps.

His reaction was quickly quelled by Sarah's gentle reminder that a child's happiness was one of the strongest predictors for remaining in the fold. After watching many families suffer from their children veering from the Orthodox path, Jonathan's single greatest anxiety was of such a thing happening to him. He was humble enough to know that there was no absolute way to ensure the outcome he so desired, no guarantees whatsoever. He accepted his wife's sage advice. And he also prayed.

It was about three months into high school when Miriam's behavior really began to concern him. First, it was her newfound wardrobe: shorter sleeves, low cut necklines, pants now and then. Never during school, of course, for even the Hebrew Academy of South Nassau, one of the more liberal Orthodox institutions, had a strict dress code. But on some evenings, especially Saturday nights when she went out with friends, Miriam Bauman was looking less and less like a yeshiva girl, and nothing like an Orthodox rabbi's daughter. Her strong resemblance to her mother—wavy red hair, shapely figure, and light, freckly skin—didn't help matters either. And while this bothered Jonathan and Sarah alike, their respective approaches were poles apart.

"Where did she get that outfit?" he asked immediately after the first time he saw her leave the house that way.

"That's how the girls dress," Sarah responded, a bit defensively.

"What girls?"

"Her friends."

"Any other rabbi's daughters in this clique of hers?"

"Probably not..."

"You didn't answer my question," he snapped, not allowing her to finish her response. This was most unusual. "Where did she get those clothes?"

"I bought them for her," she said in a subtly defiant way.

"You bought them for her?" Dismay.

"Yes." Steadfast.

"You think it's okay for her to dress that way?"

"It doesn't matter what I think."

"How can you say that?"

"Because it's true... Look, she knows I don't exactly approve, and that you definitely don't either. I just decided that this isn't a battle I wish to fight."

He considered her words. She had a point. Parenting an adolescent was endlessly tricky. Battles were to be chosen wisely. But he simply couldn't help but worry about what this portended, what was next. He knew something was next. Something was always next. "I'm certain that if you didn't buy her those clothes, she wouldn't wear them. It's that simple."

"Come on, Yoni! You know it's never that simple. Do you want her to be one of those girls who leaves her house with long sleeves and a skirt and then changes in some restroom?"

He had to admit, she had a point. As the community rabbi, he was well aware of such cagey practices. He also understood that denying his daughter something like this could engender even worse consequences. There was no way to win. He simply had to hold his breath and wait till these years passed.

And then came other things, like Miriam's mind drifting when she should have been reciting the grace after meals, or her interest in trendy teen novels rather than religious texts. Jonathan always preferred to discuss Torah matters with the family, especially at the Shabbos table, and it was at these moments that Miriam's disinterest was palpable.

She also had a beautiful singing voice, even took lessons for a while, and for many years was the loudest voice of the Bauman clan when the family sang *Zemiros,* the traditional songs during the Shabbos meal. But at some point toward the end of high school, she became stingy about lending her voice to the family singing, seemingly bored with the Jewish tunes she had once loved so much. Yet throughout the house, on a constant basis, she would carol the latest that pop music had to offer, almost as if she were doing it deliberately.

"What's wrong with regular music?" she had once asked him, purposely choosing the word "regular" instead of his preferred term, "secular."

"Actually, I think it's terrible. The lyrics, they're always about sex, and often filthy."

"Not always." She sounded almost exactly like her mother might have under similar circumstances. "You should listen some time instead of judging. You know, Dad, you can be very judgmental," she said, trying to soften her criticism with as gentle a tone as possible.

So, listen he did when she presented him with some of her favorites. "Yeah, but you're not going to share the bad ones with me," he reacted.

"Is that what you think, Dad? I'm trying to fool you?"

"You're telling me that none of the music you listen to is explicit or has obscenities?"

"Curses sometimes, but if I hear something explicit or really inappropriate I don't listen to it again, and I certainly don't walk around singing it."

"I don't think that 'sometimes' is okay, and I'm sure we have a different definition of what's appropriate."

"I'm sure we do. That's because you're you and I'm me. I love you, Dad, but I'm not you, and I'm not Aaron, and I'm not Noah."

You're most certainly not, he didn't say. "It's not about being anyone else. It's about what's right and what's wrong."

"According to you, Dad."

"According to the Torah."

"Well, that depends on your interpretation," she asserted.

And so it went. Whether it was wardrobe, music, ritual observance, or even questioning some of the basic tenets of the Judaism she was taught, Miriam Bauman clearly had her own ideas.

"It's really not a bad thing," Sarah had once explained to Jonathan. "This way, if she ever does come around, it will be on her own, and not because we forced her to."

"If she ever comes around," he had responded.

"Why don't you try being less cynical?"

Maybe you should try being less naïve was what he had initially thought but had chosen not to say. Instead, he moved toward her, took hold of her hands and uttered, "OK, I'll try."

8

NOAH BAUMAN STEPPED OFF the train at the Long Island Railroad's Great Neck Station. It was a long trek from Washington Heights, but well worth it. After it hadn't worked out with his first psychotherapist, he did a lot of research before finding Dr. Martin Rosen. During their first meeting, he realized he had made the right choice. The weekly commute—initially a considerable inconvenience—had become an opportunity to catch up on studying.

As a clinical psychology grad student, Noah's sister could have helped find him a suitable referral, but he hadn't been ready to come out to her at the time. He could have invented another reason why he wanted to see someone but knew better than to try that with her.

He first heard Dr. Rosen's name being bandied about at a support group for gay Orthodox Jews, which he had been attending on and off for a couple of months. He researched Rosen on the internet and found that the doctor had authored five best sellers, the most recent of which dealt with how families reconcile conflict. Noah ordered the book with overnight shipping and started on it as soon as it arrived.

Although it was nonfiction, it read like a novel, and he finished it in one weekend. In it, Rosen discussed how he had come from an ultra-Orthodox background himself, how he had married out of the faith, how his wife and young son had died tragically in a car accident, and how it had taken years for a rapprochement with his parents. As he closed the book, Noah felt confident that Rosen was someone who could understand and help him.

Noah came out of the train station and started walking north on Middle Neck Road toward Rosen's office. Middle Neck was the main commercial thoroughfare through Great Neck, an affluent area with many high-end boutiques and eateries. Rosen's office was quite a stretch north in what was called the "old village," where the elegant shops made way for fast food stops, grocery stores, apartment buildings, several synagogues, a Catholic church, and a park.

Noah could easily have justified a cab, considering the cold and the distance, but he preferred the walk to gather his thoughts prior to the session. He was also conscientious of the money he was already spending to see Rosen. He had built a nice reserve for himself from years of being a highly sought-after Bar Mitzvah teacher. He was the first choice of all the families in his father's community and, notwithstanding the demands of his school schedule, was able to manage three students at a time. He commanded top dollar, a great gig for a college student, but the visits with the shrink were adding up, and he was starting to feel the crunch.

He walked briskly and made it to Rosen's office in just over twenty minutes. He entered the waiting room with five minutes to spare before his appointment. This was going to be a big one. Much had happened since they'd last seen each other, and much would happen in the next week or so, at least that was his plan. There was a lot to discuss.

Rosen didn't have a receptionist or secretary. It was a single-office suite with a waiting room and a consultation room, both of which had been tastefully decorated. Noah had sensed a woman's touch the first time he'd seen the surroundings, and had once offered a compliment. Rosen had simply smiled and said, "Thanks, I had some help with it."

The door to the consultation room opened, and Rosen came out to greet him. He was distinguished looking, about 6 feet tall, trim, short gray hair, closely cut beard, Tom Ford framed glasses, and casually attired in brown cords, a periwinkle half-zip sweater, and cordovan penny loafers. "Hi, Noah," the psychologist said, holding the door open for Noah to enter.

"Hi," Noah responded as he walked through and took his usual spot on the comfortable black leather couch.

Rosen planted himself in his black leather recliner on which he only reclined now and then during breaks between patients. He crossed his legs, revealing bright red Happy Socks patterned with dogs sporting neckties, a glaring contrast to his otherwise conventional appearance. It had taken a few sessions before Noah became comfortable to actually ask about the socks.

"They make me happy," Rosen had said. "I recommend them to all my patients."

Noah appreciated the humor, but also saw in Rosen's choice of footwear a semblance of underlying yet controlled iconoclasm. From the very start, Rosen had impressed him as a complicated man in his own right.

They looked at each other. Rosen noted the tension in Noah's expression. "What's going on?" he asked. He didn't always start the conversation, but this time felt it was appropriate.

"I guess you can tell I'm a little..."

"A little...something," Rosen said.

"Stressed," Noah offered.

"Yes, you look stressed," Rosen confirmed. "What's it about?"

Noah took a breath. "I broke up with Ilana."

Rosen nodded. He had been expecting this sooner or later.

"And I told Miriam," Noah added.

"Told Miriam what?"

"I came out to her."

Rosen contemplated what he'd just heard. "Did you also come out to Ilana?"

Noah nodded. "Yeah, I told her."

Rosen looked pleased. They'd had many discussions about Noah's conflict over how to handle things with Ilana, whether to tell her the truth or make up something else. Rosen had been pushing for the truth, he believed it to be the healthiest way, which also meant that it would be difficult and painful.

"Pretty courageous," Rosen said.

"Or stupid."

"Stupid?"

"What if she says something? That's all it takes. She would only have to tell one person. News travels very fast in the Orthodox world."

Rosen nodded. He understood. "Do you think she'd do that?"

"Not really. I don't. She's a good person, and as upset as she is, I just don't believe she'd do anything to hurt me."

"But you're still worried?"

"A little, I suppose." Wavering. "It kind of forces my hand, makes me think that I have to tell my parents sooner than later, before they find out from someone else."

"Do you have a plan for telling them?"

"Not really. I figure it'll just be a game-time decision, and it will come out the way it comes out."

"No pun intended, of course."

"Of course." Noah smiled.

"So, back to Ilana. How did she take it?"

"As expected. No, take that back, better than expected."

Rosen looked curious.

"She was surprised, and very upset. But she really tried not to make me feel awful. She understood how hard it was for me. She even seemed..."

"Concerned for you," Rosen interjected.

Noah nodded.

"Not surprising," Rosen added, "from what you've told me about her."

"Not surprising at all," Noah said pensively.

"Are the two of you talking?"

"Not now. Maybe at some point... I don't know." Sadness.

Rosen was silent.

Noah wiped a tear. "I didn't think it was going to be this tough."

"How did you think it was going to be?"

"I don't know. I guess I just didn't think about it."

"It would seem so," Rosen said, contemplating. "You avoided. You hid. And now that you're not hiding anymore, you realize how hard it's going to be. But the truth is, you really knew how it was going to play out, you just didn't want to see it."

"I still don't."

"I can't blame you."

"But I have to do it. I just can't live like this anymore."

Rosen was impressed with Noah's resolve. They'd come a long way. "How'd it go with Miriam?" he asked.

"That part was actually easy. As we guessed, she kind of knew all along."

"Did the two of you talk about how you were going to approach your parents?"

"We sure did."

Rosen waited for more, but Noah seemed lost in thought. "And?" Rosen said.

"And, nothing. We both agreed that it's going to be..."

"Quite challenging," Rosen interjected.

"To say the least."

The two men looked at each other.

"Oh, by the way," Noah said, "I almost forgot to tell you the most important part."

Rosen raised his eyebrows, as if saying, *What could possibly be more important than what we're already talking about?*

"My sister is seeing a gentile."

"Seeing? As in dating?"

"As in dating, sleeping with, and whatever else goes with that." Noah considered what he had just said, then added, "Okay, I don't know for sure if they're sleeping together, but that would be my guess."

Rosen wore his *I'm processing* face.

"He's Indian."

Rosen nodded impassively.

"Think my parents can survive all this?"

The irony of everything wasn't lost on either of them. Rosen knew that Noah had read his recent book and was well aware of his own personal history. "Is she planning on telling them about this?" he asked.

"She says no. Claims she doesn't have to because it isn't anything serious, and if it gets serious it can be remedied."

"Remedied?"

"She's thinking that he could convert, but insists it'll never even come to that."

"And what if it does come to that and he doesn't want to convert?"

"I agree, but that hasn't seemed to cross her mind."

"Oh, so she also plays the avoidance game. The two of you have something in common."

Noah nodded. "It appears we have *much* in common."

"Yes, it does," Rosen remarked.

Noah contemplated a moment. "As if my situation wasn't bad enough, and now this."

"And does this change things for you? Are you having second thoughts?"

"I think it's obvious," Noah said.

"Why don't you spell it out."

Noah knew Rosen well enough to realize that there was some purpose to this beyond simply wanting to hear him state the problem. He was accustomed to Rosen's style and assumed that Rosen was entertaining the possibility that they each might be thinking different things.

"Well, you know I've been worried all this time—no, I've been afraid all this time of how my parents would react if I came out to them. Now, between Miriam's situation and mine, I'm really scared what all this will do, more to my father than my mother."

Rosen understood. They'd had much discussion on the differences between Jonathan and Sarah.

"My father's such a good man, the best I've ever known, and I just can't help thinking that this is going to break him. I know he's strong. I know he's capable of seeing things differently than he does, especially when my mother gets involved. But all this—it's going to be too much." Noah began to cry.

Rosen remained silent. Noah had gotten past much of his self-loathing, which had been a recurring theme throughout his treatment, and now it was sounding like some of it was once again resurfacing. He wanted to hear more before responding.

"And then there's his position," Noah continued. "He's truly beloved by his congregants, but I can't imagine that continuing—at least not the way it's been—once they learn about all this. Jews are very fickle when it comes to their rabbis."

"I think all people are fickle when it comes to those they put on pedestals."

"I guess you're right. I'm just echoing things I've heard him say over the years. He lives his life almost in anticipation of the day that some of them turn on him. And this would be just the thing to bring that about."

"So, he's cynical?"

"Only about this. He has many friends in the rabbinate who have had issues with their congregations over things far less problematic than this. As for everything else, he's quite optimistic and positive."

"You really believe that this could jeopardize his position?"

"I wouldn't exactly say jeopardize. But I've grown up in that synagogue, and I know the people well, and I can assure you that something like this can cause him serious difficulties."

"And would you see that as your fault?"

Noah thought a moment. "Yes, I would see it as my fault."

"Ah, so it's your fault that you're gay, as if you had a choice. And it's your fault that your father is going to have a rough time with that. And it's your fault that some people in his congregation are going to be intolerant of it. And while I'm at it, is it also your fault that your sister's dating a gentile?"

Noah considered Rosen's point. "I hear you," he responded.

"Okay, now that we're done attributing fault, maybe we can find a way out of this mess."

"I'd love to," Noah said.

Noah took his vibrating cell out of his pocket and saw it was his mother calling. He didn't bother to answer because he was on the subway where it was too noisy to have a conversation. And he was pretty sure he knew why she was calling.

News traveled quickly in the Orthodox circles, and he figured his parents must have already heard about his breakup. He would have preferred to go home this coming Shabbos and tell them himself. Doing so over the phone just didn't seem appropriate, not for news such as this. But the community gossipers got in the way. He couldn't help but wonder whether he had unconsciously hoped for this. It just made things easier.

As soon as he ascended from the station, he listened to her voicemail: *Hi honey, it's Mom, give us a call. Love you.*

He called her back as he walked.

9

JONATHAN BAUMAN HAD BARELY REMOVED his hat and scarf when he heard Sarah calling him from the kitchen, a startling departure from their usual routine. Normally, he would have to distract her from her laptop or cellphone to let her know he was home. The urgency in her tone worried him.

"What? What's going on?" he said as he undid his coat.

"I just heard from Noah," she said, approaching him. "I didn't want to tell you till I spoke to him."

"Tell me what?"

"I had heard through the grapevine that he broke up with Ilana, but I didn't want to say anything to upset you until I knew for sure." She took a breath. "Now I know for sure."

The grapevine was code for her weekly Shabbos walk with her girlfriends. They were a group of five who had been walking every Shabbos afternoon for years, regardless of the weather. He had frequently referred to them in jest as the *lashon hara* club, using the Hebrew term for gossip. In truth, however, there wasn't much gossip at all. They were a group of women who had grown close over the years, catching up on their own family stuff while trying to avoid discussions about people who weren't present. Jonathan knew that Sarah was careful when it came to the laws of "guarding one's tongue," especially with members of the congregation, and he assumed that the news about Noah was probably delivered by one of her friends, likely during a private moment when the others were out of earshot. "You could have told me," he said softly, reflecting his disappointment.

She shrugged her shoulders.

He understood. She was always cautious about such matters. He knew that, between her medical practice and her relationships, there were often things that came her way that she chose either not to share with him at all or to share only at appropriate times. For the most part, he appreciated that she shielded and protected him. But when it came to issues concerning their own kids, he occasionally felt that she was actually protecting them from him. That, he didn't appreciate so much. Of course, he could see how from her perspective, his expectations could be unreasonable, or "a bit much," as she would put it. And on those rare occasions when he was disappointed, she tried to help him see things differently. "Sometimes you can be a little too hard on them," she had once explained. "I know you don't intend to be, but I think it's because you worry a lot about the perceptions of others."

He recalled his exact response at the time: "I'm the rabbi. We live in a glass house." It was the only response he ever had to such matters. And he believed it.

He sighed as his thoughts returned to the present. "What's with that boy?"

"That's a good question," she said, taking his hand and leading him to the kitchen. "Sit, I'll get your dinner."

It was past 9 p.m. and she had eaten hours earlier. With the exception of Shabbos, which was pretty much the only night they ate together, he was always home late and never sure whether he would find her on the couch busy with work stuff or already in bed. Since his dinner often consisted of Shabbos leftovers—the product of their mutually busy professional lives and the general overabundance of Shabbos food in the house—getting it together didn't really take much, and he usually fended for himself.

"No, no, no. You sit, I'll do it," he insisted.

"It's fine. I'll get it," she said.

He sat down at the table while she pulled a few trays from the fridge. "Did he tell you anything about why they broke up?" he asked.

"He was on his cell walking to his apartment from the subway, and he didn't want to get into details. You know that kid, you can't push him."

"That's for sure."

"He said he'll be home this Shabbos, and we'll talk then."

"Wow, I can't wait." Sarcasm.

"Yeah, neither can I." Hesitation. "So, how was your day?"

Jonathan attempted to lose himself in the Talmudic text on his desk but wasn't making any headway. What could possibly have gone wrong between Noah and Ilana, he wondered. She had been perfect—at least in his eyes—lovely, smart, funny, from a good family, and a genuine *menschette*, a word Jonathan liked to think he had coined, feminizing the Yiddish term *mensch*, meaning an exceptionally fine individual.

It was Monday night and Shabbos seemed far away, a long time to wait to hear what really happened. He was tempted to pick up the phone but knew better. If Noah's preference was to speak in person, it would have to wait.

Jonathan considered the possibility that it might be his fault that Noah had such a hard time finding someone. After all, he'd had the very same problem back when he dated women. He knew this line of thinking was irrational, that there really was no connection between these two things. But blaming himself somehow seemed fitting at the moment.

The Bauman family saga was an open book, and the children were well acquainted with every detail of the Story of Mom and Dad. Perhaps Noah, in his determination to find a woman like his mother, unconsciously drove himself through the very same steps his father had taken, or perhaps it was something hereditary, a genetic mutation causing one to date umpteen women before actually finding one to marry.

Jonathan's foolishness—he understood it to be foolishness—was interrupted by his cell phone. It was Benjamin Marcus, the president of the congregation.

"Benjy," Jonathan said.

"*Rav* Yoni," Benjamin said. Most congregants called him "rabbi," but those closest to him called him "*Rav* Yoni," reflecting an odd blend of reverence and intimacy. "Do you have a few minutes?"

"For you? Of course!"

"But I need to talk to you in person, not over the phone."

You too? Jonathan thought. "No problem. I'm home now. Can you come over?"

"I'll be right there." Urgency.

Jonathan was concerned. A pressing late-night meeting with the rabbi at home portended something unpleasant. That it wasn't five minutes before he heard the front doorbell worried him even more.

He opened the door and saw on Benjy's face a tense expression. This was quite out of character for a man whom Jonathan regarded as calm, and always confident. Benjamin Marcus had been a leader in the community for years prior to assuming the presidency of the congregation. He was known to be a tremendous philanthropist and the go-to guy for anyone who had hit on hard times. Among the top tier of earners in what was considered one of the wealthiest Jewish communities anywhere, his empire included commercial and residential properties in every borough. More recently, he was rumored to be venturing in some of the untapped outer reaches of NYC.

"Is everything okay?" Jonathan asked as Benjy entered the house.

"No. Not really."

"Come, let's go to my study," Jonathan suggested, realizing that this conversation would require more privacy than the living room.

They each took one of the guest chairs. Jonathan offered an expression encouraging Benjy to start.

"I have some bad news," Benjy said.

Jonathan stayed silent, waiting for more.

"I'm going to be arrested."

"Arrested?"

"Yes. Avi Gerstein called me about a half hour ago to tell me."

Abraham "Avi" Gerstein, was another member of the synagogue and a prominent criminal attorney who was often in the news representing crooked politicians and troubled celebrities. Jonathan, himself a member of the bar, enjoyed a special relationship with Avi, occasionally teasing the lawyer about some of the outrageous accusations against many of his clients. And Avi gave as good as he got, using the utmost of his lawyerly skills in frequently challenging Jonathan during his daily 6 a.m. Talmud class, as the other attendees simply enjoyed watching the two of them go at it.

"He's representing you?" Jonathan said.

Benjy nodded, anticipating the rabbi's next question.

"What's this about?"

"It's financial. The state attorney general's been investigating me for over a year. You know how it is—if they look, they find."

Jonathan nodded. It wasn't the first time one of his congregants was in trouble with the law, albeit the first for a sitting president of the synagogue. He also understood that if the AG was investigating for more than a year, Avi Gerstein was involved, and an arrest was imminent, it had to be something serious. And most of all, he understood that Benjy was being deliberately vague. Whatever the allegations, he would learn the details soon enough, as would everyone else. He didn't need to probe right now and cause his friend any additional embarrassment.

"How can I help?"

"Esther. The kids. It's going to be really hard for them," Benjy said. He and Esther were actually empty nesters in a large waterfront mansion in the back of Lawrence. They had four children, two daughters, two sons, all married with their own children, and all in one way or another part of his business.

"Is anyone else in trouble?" Jonathan asked.

"That's just it. My sons are also under investigation but, so far, they're not being charged with anything. Avi thinks he can work out a deal—I may have to do some time, but they'll be left alone."

It didn't escape Jonathan that Benjy wasn't claiming innocence. It also struck him how matter-of-factly Benjy was discussing all this. The nervousness he had seen on the man's face at the door seemed to disappear as soon as Benjy unburdened himself with the news. Now it was only a matter of figuring things out, staying cool, making the right moves and choices, and getting the best deal. It was odd to Jonathan how a man could seem almost unflappable as his entire life was about to unravel. But then again, he reminded himself, it was Benjamin Marcus. "That's Avi's advice?" Jonathan asked.

"He thinks that's the best-case scenario, if he can convince them. It's a big 'if,' but Avi's the best there is."

Jonathan nodded. There were many things he wanted to ask but chose not to.

"There's one more thing," Benjy said, a trace of consternation reappearing.

Jonathan nodded, again waiting for more, and assuming it wasn't going to be any better than what he'd already heard.

"Avi's arranged for me to surrender myself tomorrow morning at 8. Once that happens, there's probably going to be some press, and more things are going to come out."

"More things?" Jonathan asked.

"Well," Benjy responded, obviously discomfited. "One thing."

Jonathan stared in silence.

"It's..." He faltered. "It's a woman."

"A woman?" Jonathan was unable to hide his astonishment. Benjamin Marcus had always seemed the consummate family man.

"My assistant," Benjy said, dropping his head. "It's been going on for years."

"Years?" Stupefied.

Benjy nodded. "Yeah, I've been an idiot. I've really messed things up."

Jonathan looked at his friend, realizing that this was no time for chastising. It was clear that Benjy was doing a good enough job of that on his own. "How does this relate to the case against you?"

"She was involved. She knew about everything, and she's made a deal for herself: she's become a witness for the state."

Jonathan stroked his beard and adjusted his glasses, which he often did when lost in thought. Aside from Benjy being among the most prestigious members of the synagogue, the Baumans and Marcuses were friends. Esther was close with Sarah, and the children had all grown up together. Beyond Jonathan's rabbinic role at bar and bat mitzvahs, weddings and funerals, there had also been carpools, birthday parties, sporting events, and so much more.

Benjy clammed up and stared at Jonathan, seemingly searching for a reaction.

"I don't know what to say," Jonathan offered.

"Neither do I," Benjy said, his eyes tearing up. "It's bad. I'm going to prison, I don't even know for how long. Esther's probably going to divorce me. And the kids...they're going to be humiliated and ostracized, and they're definitely going to hate me for what I did to their mother."

Jonathan listened, then said, "I know your children pretty well, and I know that they love you unconditionally. They're going to be hurt and angry, but everyone's going to get through this. Together."

Benjy noticed that Jonathan's assurances excluded Esther. "I hope you're right, but you know the community we live in. Once this gets out, I'll be the topic of gossip, the butt of bad jokes, and it won't be long before I'm a pariah... That's how it's going to be."

"I don't think so," Jonathan said.

"Of course you don't, you're the rabbi. You're going to tell me how much support and sympathy we're going to get, how kind and compassionate everyone is, how my family isn't going to be alienated."

"I'm not saying there won't be problems, or challenges. But you're painting the absolute worst-case scenario."

Benjy thought for a moment, then said, "I think I'm being realistic."

Jonathan considered Benjy's perspective. There was no denying it, this was going to be quite a storm. Benjamin Marcus was a major benefactor for countless institutions in both America and Israel, some of which depended on him for their very existence. Jonathan's own synagogue's mortgage had been paid off two years earlier single-handedly by Benjy, and in the Five Towns alone, there were two yeshiva high schools and a rabbinic seminary that were named after the family. Then there were the homeless shelters in Jerusalem and Tiberius, rabbinic seminaries in Brooklyn and Baltimore, and the various hospitals, poverty organizations, and medical research programs. It was going to be a mess. "We'll get through it, Benjy," he said.

"We?"

Jonathan nodded.

"You're going to stick with me, after all I've done?"

"I'm your friend."

"I don't want to lose Esther."

"Hopefully, you won't. I assume she knows that you're being arrested?"

"Yeah. She's supposed to come with me in the morning when I turn myself in. Avi says it's important that I project the image of a family man." He paused, absorbing his own words. "Oh my God, what have I done!" He covered his face with his hands, trying to compose himself, then lifted his head, looked at Jonathan, and asked, "What should I do?"

Jonathan weighed his response. "It might be a good idea for you to tell her about the affair before it becomes public knowledge." He had been hesitant to use the word "affair" earlier. It was a pejorative label, no doubt, but it was also what happened, and he simply saw no need to dance around it at this point. "If I were you, I would say all I can to convince her of my love. And my remorse."

The two men looked at each other, then Jonathan continued, "You also need to accept whatever her reaction is. Your world is falling apart and so is hers. She's going to be shocked and angry. Whatever she says, whatever she wants, I would just do it, even if she asks you to leave."

Benjy nodded. He knew he was getting the honest advice he needed.

"She's going to need a lot of time to figure all this out. With *Hashem's* help," Jonathan said, using the traditional Hebrew expression for God, "she'll hopefully find a way in her heart to forgive you." He considered his words, then added, "It's a deep wound. It will take a while to heal."

"If it ever does heal," Benjy said.

Jonathan nodded.

Jonathan switched off his laptop and released a deep yawn. It had been an hour since Benjy had left and he was still feeling quite restless. Unable to focus on studying Talmud and too wired for sleep, he had turned his attention to some unanswered emails, of which there were always plenty. He'd spent about an hour at this until he couldn't look at the screen anymore. Still convinced that sleep wasn't in the cards, he decided nevertheless to go upstairs.

He entered the bedroom, his mind still racing with thoughts of Noah, Benjy, and the incredibly long day he was eager to dispose of. Sarah, already in bed half asleep, offered a slight wave to greet him as she turned over to evade the light from the hallway. He removed his clothing down to his boxers and T-shirt and slipped in beside her.

"Hi," she whispered.

"Hi back," he said as he inched closer and put his hand on her waist.

"Everything okay?"

"Yeah," he said. "Why do you ask?"

"It's just very late."

He looked at the clock. It was 1:20 a.m., definitely later than usual. "I know. Just had a lot of stuff going on and Benjy came by."

"I heard the doorbell ring, figured it was someone for you. Anything special?"

"Just stuff," he said, feeling it wasn't the right time to get into it. "I'll tell you all about it in the morning," he added as he caressed her. Usually at such an hour, he'd be way too spent for anything, but tonight he was strangely awake and in need of her to help him find some repose.

She moved herself against him, took his face in her hands and brought their lips together. It seemed she needed the very same thing.

10

NOAH BAUMAN HAD BEEN DRAWN to his own sex from as far back as he could remember. His first reminiscence was a prepubescent fixation on one of his peers, Josh Friedman, whose family belonged to the congregation. It wasn't a sexual attraction per se, at least not to Noah's awareness at the time. All he knew was that he couldn't get Josh out of his head.

The irony was that they weren't even friends. Josh went to a different school, and in those days the cliques among the kids were very much stratified by the schools they attended. He mostly only saw Josh on Shabbos at junior congregation. He would try to sit as close to Josh as possible and occasionally initiate some conversation, despite feeling jittery when doing so. He wanted to be around Josh so much that, on weekdays, he frequently rode his bike past Josh's house in the hope of spying a mere glance of the boy.

Everything about Josh somehow seemed magnetic. He was blessed with the looks of a young movie star, was medium height, thin with soft facial features, short blond hair, and always well put together—to an extent that was unusual for a kid his age. Noah found this all quite appealing and, at the time, didn't even question himself about what he was thinking or doing. It took years and some time with Dr. Rosen before he realized that his fascination with Josh had actually been a crush.

Once he entered high school, Noah's sights fell upon another young man, Jacob Stein, but this time it became more complicated. Jacob and Noah instantly struck up a friendship, and it wasn't long before they were the best of friends. They hadn't previously known each other because they came from different neighborhoods, and each attended a different elementary and middle school prior to entering the Hebrew Academy of South Nassau. They wound up in the same Talmud class, which took up most of the morning, and were also on the basketball team together. Jacob was quite different from Josh—tall, robust stature, longish dark hair, and a somewhat rugged face. For Noah it was undoubtedly genuine love. Still not sexual, at least not at the beginning, but true depth and admiration. And it was mutual.

Noah and Jacob began each school day as study partners in the *beis midrash*, the study hall where students prepared for the Talmud class. They always ate lunch together, and in the afternoons during math and science, the only other classes they shared, they sat together. Their opinions of teachers were identical, as were their opinions of their peers, favorite sports teams, movies—just about everything and anything. They were seen as inseparable, so much so that some of the other kids occasionally teased them, though all in good fun. And while in another milieu there may have been some suspicion about this "couple," in the Orthodox yeshiva world, such a thought would have been blasphemous.

It wasn't till their junior year when their relationship took a turn. They both enjoyed much popularity, courtesy of being jocks, and a plethora of interested girls. Jacob seemed more into the girls, as well as drinking and smoking pot. Noah's enthusiasm for girls was somewhat blunted compared to Jacob's, and the booze and weed didn't quite appeal to him either. He saw little value in losing control of his feelings that way. And being the son of a rabbi also played a role. That "glass house" thing had been drilled into him his entire life, and he was always cognizant of how his actions reflected on his family and, more specifically, on his father. This wasn't easy, considering that there was plenty of partying going on, even in the Modern Orthodox high school scene.

Jacob often regaled Noah with tales of his hookups with girls. He was also open about his fascination with pornography. Noah didn't seem to care much for that either. While he wasn't immune to pleasuring himself now and then, porn just wasn't his thing. He was discomfited enough by the imagery flashing through his mind, which always left him with a deep sense of guilt and dejection. Still desperately avoiding the acknowledgement of his true inner conflict, he convinced himself that his guilt was solely due to the expressly forbidden nature of masturbation according to Jewish law. Though eventually it became clear to him that his denial would no longer work.

"Have you ever thought about doing it together?" Jacob said.

It was a late Friday night and Noah was sleeping over at Jacob's house. Jacob lived in West Hempstead, another Orthodox Jewish enclave not too far from the Five Towns, but far enough that if the boys wanted to spend Shabbos together they would have to sleep at each other's homes. Jacob had a sizeable family, four siblings, and lived in a large colonial. His bedroom was in the renovated basement, removed from the rest of the family on the second floor. He was lying in his bed and Noah, nearby on a blowup mattress, was half asleep.

Noah was taken aback. He had an idea of what Jacob was asking, yet still looked at him incredulously. "Doing what?"

"You know, like... jerking off together."

"Why would I want to do that?" Defensive.

"Might be fun. Don't knock it till you've tried it."

Noah stared into space, admitting to himself that the idea stirred something within him. He eyes turned to Jacob. "Have you tried it?" he asked.

"No, but I've thought about it."

"You never talked about it before."

"I'm talking about it now."

And so it began. Tentatively at first, each taking care of himself, until eventually they graduated to taking care of each other. And that was as far as it ever went. Neither was interested in exploring other avenues, or so they claimed.

Noah would later discover that Jacob must have sensed something in him that made him amenable to such an arrangement. For now, all he knew was that he really enjoyed these encounters with Jacob, and it wasn't long before this became the sum and substance of their relationship. It lasted for about nine months when, somewhere in the middle of their senior year, Jacob started withdrawing, choosing instead to spend most of his time with a young lady, Shira Friedman. Shira had been friendly with both Jacob and Noah before she and Jacob discovered something starry-eyed between them. For Noah, this was a sad and confusing time; he was, in a way, losing both of them. Shira was still a friend, of sorts. But with Jacob, things dwindled to the point that even others around them noticed. While their peers saw this as a typical relationship shift now that Jacob had a girlfriend, Noah knew better. Jacob now needed to pretend that his bond with Noah had never really existed.

Noah, unfortunately, couldn't do the same. He spent the rest of his senior year hanging out with other friends, going through the motions, though deep down he found himself in turmoil, unable to forget and discard the lingering feelings and fantasies that haunted him.

The following year, during his so called "gap year" studying in Israel he was still distracted, at least at the beginning. He found new friends among his fellow yeshiva students, but no one with whom he connected in quite the same way he had with Jacob. So, he set his sights on women, thinking and hoping that if Jacob could do it, so could he.

Her name was Ruthie Klein, and she was on her gap year at a women's seminary in Jerusalem. She was from a fine Orthodox family in Montreal, and they were introduced by one of Noah's new classmates, also from Montreal. By all objective standards, she was attractive—brunette, emerald eyes, petite with nice curves—but what really caught Noah was her wit, intellect, and the tenderness of her smile. She was also quite religious and observant of the prohibition of physical contact between men and women before marriage. This, no doubt, suited Noah just fine.

They met at the beginning of November and started seeing each other as frequently as their schedules allowed. As was the case in the yeshiva circles of America, Thursday was the popular night out for yeshiva and seminary students in Israel. They usually rendezvoused on Ben Yehuda Street in the center of Jerusalem, grabbed a bite, walked around, and then met up with other friends or sometimes found a quiet spot in one of the hotels just to talk.

And talk they did, for hours and hours, about anything and everything—politics, religion, philosophy, their dreams and aspirations. She was headed for McGill University the following year with hopes of pursuing dentistry, and for him it was Yeshiva University with eventual plans for law.

Yeshiva University was a choice he had made toward the end of his senior year in high school, and it hadn't been an easy one. He knew that his father's hope was for him to follow the Bauman family legacy, as his brother had: *Yeshiva Sha'arei T'shuvah* and college at night. Jonathan Bauman had yielded to his wife's preferences as the children grew up, but after years of serving in a Modern Orthodox congregation, witnessing the primacy of "modern" over "Orthodox," and the growing assimilation to contemporary culture of many of the young people, he'd become increasingly skeptical of the Modern Orthodox way. Over time, it became his not-so-secret desire that his children eventually choose a more traditionalist path. And while he wasn't extremely outspoken about it, once Aaron had made the shift, the pressure grew ever more palpable for Noah.

Having become more aware of his proclivities, Noah figured that Yeshiva University might be a better fit for him. At the time, he wasn't yet convinced that he was "totally gay," as he conceived of it, and he still harbored hopes of managing in the heterosexual world as Jacob seemed to be doing. But something within told him that he needed a less restrictive environment than he would find in the hallowed halls of his father's alma mater. He knew that the ideal choice would have been a purely secular institution but realized that this would have been out of the question for a son of Rabbi Jonathan Bauman.

He recalled how, just a few years earlier, the entire Orthodox community had been in an uproar over Yeshiva University hosting a conference entitled "Being Gay in the Modern Orthodox World."

It had been a historic gathering, the first of its kind, and had been discussed all over the internet. It became *the* topic at a few Shabbos meals in the Bauman home. And Jonathan, not normally one to opine on such matters publicly, felt compelled to do so from the pulpit. None of this left Noah feeling very good. The anti-gay jokes among the boys in high school had never bothered him much, nor the homophobic diatribes he'd heard throughout his life from some of the more right-wing rabbis, but his father's reproach most certainly distressed him, leading him to wonder what might become of their relationship should he be fated to the life of a gay man. But of course, that wasn't going to happen. Or so he told himself.

So, Yeshiva University became his best option. In his research, he had learned about a "tolerance club" on campus, not only for gays, but also for those simply opposed to intolerance. He had also found that a national organization for Orthodox gays, Eshel, taking its name from the Tamarisk tree under which the biblical Abraham sat as he welcomed wandering travelers, had members on campus, and that there was an LGBTQ and Allies student group chapter on Facebook. He hadn't fully understood why he was so compelled to look into all of this—probably just curiosity, he had told himself. But in truth, he knew the answer. He just hadn't been ready to accept it. And wouldn't be for quite some time.

It was the second Thursday in December when Noah and Ruthie were sitting in the lobby of the David Citadel Hotel when they ran into Jacob and Shira. Noah had actually seen Jacob on two other occasions in the *shuk*, a popular outdoor market, and both times the two had shared brief, perfunctory greetings. In their first encounter, Jacob looked just as he had back in high school. In the second, Noah noted how Jacob was wearing a white button-down shirt, dark pants, and sporting more than a couple of weeks' worth of stubble on his face. It caused him to wonder at the time if Jacob was "flipping," a term used for individuals who become very religious. Flipping was not an uncommon occurrence among the men and women who spent their gap year studying in yeshivas or seminaries in Israel, and the first indication was usually a change in wardrobe such as Jacob's. Had they been as close as they once were, Noah would have said something, or perhaps may even have teased Jacob. Instead, he had simply made a mental note and went on his way.

Jacob had now progressed to a complete beard, at least as complete as his 19 years could muster, and *peyes*, ear locks, awkwardly tucked behind his ears, suggesting a rather severe flip. Shira, too, was dressing the part, having gone from tight jeans and lowcut tops whenever she wasn't in school or synagogue to an ankle-length wavy skirt and modest long sleeve blouse.

Noah and Ruthie were sitting on a couch in a back corner of the lobby, engrossed in conversation, when Noah looked up and happened to see them on another couch just a few yards away. His eyes met Jacob's as an awkwardness swept over each of them. There was no escaping the encounter, no turning away. It was just a question of who would take the initiative. Surprising himself, Noah instantly offered a pleasant "hi" to both of them, as he turned to Ruthie and said, "This is Jacob and Shira. They're friends from high school."

The two couples were situated close enough for conversation, yet all stood at the same moment to relocate a little closer.

"No, sit. We'll come to you," Noah said, projecting more boldness than he actually felt. The next thing he knew, they were sitting and talking.

He learned that evening that Jacob and Shira's relationship had become very serious. They were planning on staying in Israel for another year of study and were also talking about getting engaged. They had both become quite religious and, like Ruthie, were observing the laws forbidding physical contact before marriage. For the three of them, it was about subjugating their desires and inclinations to the will of God. For Noah, who had simply fallen into this by circumstance, it was altogether something else. He wasn't physically drawn to Ruthie, no matter how hard he tried, so abstinence was easy, a perfect opportunity for avoidance. He didn't even pretend to himself that it had anything to do with religion.

Noah surmised that Jacob must have given up partying. That's how it went during the Israel gap year: some flipped, some stayed the same, and some went over to "the dark side," falling prey to the drinking and drugs that so often accompanies leaving home at 18. Usually one could predict who would end up in which group by the degree of rebelliousness and defiance exhibited in high school, but it wasn't an exact science. Every now and then there was a big surprise and, for Noah, Jacob was just that.

Noah and Ruthie's story was definitely lackluster in comparison. They had nothing to say regarding plans for a future together. They got along delightfully and were very much enjoying the here and now. It was assumed, in the absence of any explicit understanding, that this would continue until they hit a snag. Noah hoped that the snag wasn't inevitable, though part of him sensed it might be. He tried not to think about that, holding fast to the possibility that maybe he could choose just as Jacob had. So he clung to Ruthie as if she were his last chance for what he believed was normalcy, though, in his heart of hearts, he knew that he and Jacob weren't the same.

The small talk went on for about a half hour before they parted ways, and it struck Ruthie as odd that such "good friends" would so naturally say goodbye without any mention of another get-together. "It felt like you guys were pretty close in high school," she said to Noah.

"We were."

"But you never even mentioned either of them."

"I suppose I didn't."

She was tempted to probe further but stopped herself. It was obvious that he didn't really want to talk about it. Something had happened here, some type of falling out or growing apart. Maybe it had to do with Shira, she wondered, which would explain why Noah was being so cryptic. Either way, it seemed to have worked out for the best. Jacob and Shira looked great together, and she and Noah felt right as well.

Their relationship lasted through their gap year and their first year of college. Then she started talking about marriage. In her worldview, getting married at 20 or 21 was perfectly reasonable, and Noah had to admit that along with Jacob he had other high school friends who were doing just that. But he knew he couldn't be one of them. Firstly, he couldn't see himself marrying anyone at this point. Secondly, and more painfully, he was still finding himself unable to love Ruthie in that way.

She saw that he wasn't on the same page, and they started fighting. She wanted more of his time and attention, for their parents to meet, and for them to spend Shabbos with each other's families more often. He managed to dodge pretty much all of it and was unable to bring himself to tell her the truth, for he hadn't even told himself the truth yet. It ended poorly.

He spent the next few months recuperating. There were many offers to fix him up, coming from family and friends and even a couple of rabbis at school, all thinking it a great *mitzvah* to find a mate for the son of such a prestigious rabbinical family. He wasn't interested. It was starting to creep in that all this may not be for him.

Toward the end of his freshman year, he decided to give it another try. Another perfectly well-suited young lady. Another six months. Same result.

After three letdowns, Rabbi Jonathan Bauman seriously started to worry about his younger son. Sarah advocated for patience. "Not everyone is like Aaron," she repeatedly reminded him. "Not even you."

Then came Ilana Lustig. Everyone was convinced this would be it. Everyone except Noah, that is. At the start of their courtship, he began seeing Dr. Rosen and, in doing so, came to realize that he could no longer deny who and what he was.

He secretly started attending a support group for Orthodox gays and struck up a friendship with another male attendee, Zach Abramson. Zach was from a typical Modern Orthodox family in Riverdale, a senior majoring in pre-law at City College, and a nice-looking fellow—6 feet, beefy physique, curly brown hair and chestnut eyes. It began as a friendship, but both knew there was more to it. Zach, having been out since his first year of college, was ready for a full relationship from the start, but he understood the special circumstances of Noah's situation. Noah just wasn't there yet, and Zach didn't push. They shared an unspoken agreement that any intimacy would have to wait until both of them were fully invested.

They talked often, but the growing sexual tension was making it difficult for them to see each other in person. Noah had finally reached a turning point. He could no longer hide. He had to out himself. Ilana would be the first to learn, then his family—Miriam, Aaron, Mom and Dad, in order from easiest to hardest. Or, more accurately, from easiest to most daunting.

11

AARON BAUMAN WAS BORN with perfect genes, especially according to his father. Being the first born and a son, he held the prominent status of the *bekhor*, who in Biblical times had been marked for death by Pharaoh in his efforts to destroy the Jewish people. The Torah later decreed that they inherit a double portion from their fathers, and serve as the priests of Israel, though that was annulled after the worship of the golden calf when the priestly responsibilities were reassigned to the descendants of Moses' brother, the original Aaron.

From his first days, little Aaron was a crier, almost impossible to console. At his *bris* ceremony, the screams were so earsplitting that people cringed. Jonathan had initially regarded this as a sign that his firstborn somehow possessed a unique understanding of the pain and turmoil inherent in being a Jew. But after weeks of endlessly walking him around the house, hoping to elicit a burp and some repose, the pediatrician decided that the baby was having difficulty digesting his mother's milk and suggested switching to formula.

Sarah, surprised that she—a pediatrician herself—didn't figure this out on her own, realized that she had been in denial of the possibility her provisions might be insufficient. Such was her first lesson in parenting. And a good dose of reality for Jonathan as well.

The years that followed revealed perhaps another dimension to Aaron's early wailing: intense passion. Whatever his interests, at whatever age, his devotion was total. At 5, a fascination with firefighters made him a leading expert in the equipment, various types of trucks, drills, and lingo of the trade. At 8, he knew the stats of every New York Met, and many other major league players, and was glued to the TV screen for every game that wasn't on Shabbos. It was hard, but Jonathan, a quasi-Mets fan himself, frequently managed to arrange his schedule to be able to take Aaron to games. And Mom also stepped in now and then when Dad had a last-minute crisis on his hands.

Aaron became one of the top pitchers in the Yeshiva Little League, but gradually baseball gave way to basketball. Baseball would always remain an interest, but his tall and lanky stature all but assured that his truest talents would be found on the court. Another young man might have continued with both sports, but not Aaron Bauman. His fixation on excellence, rare for his age, engendered total devotion to his studies and time for only one extracurricular interest. Even socializing fell by the wayside.

It wasn't that Aaron was in any way reclusive. On the contrary, he had many friends and was invited to just about everything. But by the end of middle school, he had evolved into someone with an austere sense of obligation and regarded all distractions as somehow mundane. Yes, there were secular studies and basketball, but that was as much as he would allow himself. His job, he believed, was to become a Torah scholar, as his father and grandfathers before him. Hence, his choice to go to an all-boys yeshiva high school, then two years studying at one of the more prestigious Talmudic academies in Jerusalem, then four years in his father's alma mater in Brooklyn while attending Brooklyn College at night. Lacking any detours or doubts, his was a relentless pursuit, a perfect trajectory towards sustaining the Bauman family rabbinic heritage.

Growing up in the shadow of his older brother, Noah Bauman often felt lacking. He was interested enough in religious studies, though never terribly enthusiastic, and did well in secular studies, though not to the exclusion of healthy social and recreational pastimes. While Aaron was spending his evenings studying Talmud, Noah was in front of the TV, on Facebook, or texting with friends—sometimes all three at once. He was also a fairly decent basketball player, making both junior varsity and varsity in high school, but he always wondered about that: The son of a prominent rabbi and brother of a famed player, had he made the teams on his own merit?

His relationship with Aaron was neither overtly competitive nor covertly hostile. They were brothers and friends who shared a mutual understanding that they were different. It was only in relation to their parents' expectations that Noah felt that he somehow always came up short. And all things considered, those very feelings were now quite pronounced.

Noah's plan was to come out to Aaron before he did so with his parents. Aaron's family was still visiting but was heading back to LA on Thursday afternoon. The brothers hadn't yet seen each other on this visit, which was quite unusual, and Noah felt strongly that such a conversation should be had in person.

Fortunately, Noah happened to have access to a pair of Knicks tickets for Tuesday night, a perfect excuse for the brothers to get together without Sheindy and the kids. Noah was still close with his high school basketball coach who had season tickets and, due to the Knicks poor showing this season, was rarely using them. The coach, Rabbi Daniel Bernstein, was also the youth director of Jonathan's synagogue. Noah enjoyed a special relationship with Rabbi Dan, as did Aaron. He had secured the tickets two weeks earlier, knowing that Aaron was coming in and that it would be a fun thing for them to do together. He hadn't planned it to be a "coming-out party," but what the hell.

The brothers met at the Long Island Railroad concourse in Penn Station just below the Knicks home venue, Madison Square Garden. It had been over six months since Aaron's last visit. Occasional Skyping, and even more occasional FaceTiming and texting had left them both eager for some in-person contact.

Despite their dissimilarities, they were strongly bonded through love, familiarity, respect, and the few interests they shared. Political discussions were always feisty, Aaron being staunchly conservative and Noah being just as staunchly non-committal. Religious discussions found a bit more commonality, though Noah was far less dogmatic. Sports discussions were always a fight, mostly purposeful, just for the fun of it.

Their eyes made contact the instant Aaron emerged from the gate. Mutual smiles. Each sporting earbuds. For Noah it was Springsteen; for Aaron it was a lecture on some esoteric matter of Jewish law. Each had some idea of what the other was listening to. They shared an enthusiastic embrace, then stepped back to observe each other.

Noah was in skinny jeans, Nike shoes, an untucked sky-blue button-down shirt under a V-neck brown sweater with sleeves folded out over the sweater. Knicks cap, black leather jacket in hand, and claret wool scarf.

"You look the same," Aaron said.

"You don't. Your beard seems a little longer." Aaron also wore his Knicks cap, as if they'd planned it, though they hadn't. Otherwise, it was black Rockport lace ups, black slacks, gray sweater over a white button-down, black scarf and an olive parka. An Orthodox rabbi going to a basketball game in the dead of winter.

"A little longer?" Aaron said, fully aware of what Noah was implying. "I'm the *rav* of a *shul* now. Have to look the part."

"I suppose so," Noah said, a tad derisively, reflecting his discomfort with the community's emphasis on appearance. He knew that his brother was a genuinely pious person—long beard, short beard or no beard—and assumed that Aaron must have his own conflicts over having to accede to such superficialities. He chose not to pursue it. They'd had plenty of discussions on such topics in the past, and now wasn't the time for yet another. Aaron had made a personal choice, and Noah didn't want to put him on the defensive.

Aaron glanced at his watch. "Half hour till the game."

"Let's go find our seats."

"Rabbi Dan's seats, you mean."

"Yup."

"Then we know where they are," Aaron said. "Center court, 15th row."

The two started making their way from Penn Station to the Garden. Almost as soon as they began walking Aaron came out with the question Noah had been anticipating. "So, what happened with Ilana?"

Noah knew that this evening wasn't going to afford them even a minute of privacy and it was just as well. Coming out to Miriam had required more of a sit-down, face-to-face setting, more because of Miriam's persona than his own. She was always the serious, thoughtful, sensitive one—useful traits for her chosen profession. With Aaron, however, it was different. Theirs was a more blunt and unceremonious connection, requiring nothing from Noah on this matter beyond his own vocal cords and a touch of audacity. Walking through this crowd was as good a time and place as any. "I've been meaning to tell you about it," he said.

"So here I am."

Noah took a deep breath and said, "I'm gay."

Aaron stopped dead in his tracks and looked at his brother. "Did I hear you right? Did you just say..."

"I'm gay. Yes, now I've said it twice."

The two brothers stared each other down for a moment. Aaron saw Noah's eyes welling up. He reached out, grabbed his brother's shoulders and drew him into a hug. They stood there for a few minutes holding each other in silence, oblivious to the passersby, until Aaron asked, "Are you sure you want to go to the game?"

Noah nodded, took another deep breath, and said, "Yeah, I'm sure."

Aaron put his arm around Noah's shoulder. "It's going to be okay," he said, almost instinctively, not really understanding why those words came out. Then an image entered his mind of another time he uttered the same exact phrase.

He winds up for a fastball and releases it just as a loud noise comes from the street. It sounds like a car crash, startling, distracting. Suddenly, Noah falls over and is screaming.

He runs across the yard. Noah lies in a fetal position, his hands covering his face. More screaming.

"What? What's going on?" he says, frightened, not knowing what to do.

"My eye," Noah screams. "My eye."

He realizes his fastball found his brother's eye. He bends over to take a look. "Let me see."

Noah removes his hands, revealing a swollen left eye socket. The eye is bright red, and the swelling is increasing by the second. "Here," he says as he grabs hold of Noah's torso, "let me help you up."

"I can't get up," Noah says.

"What do you mean you can't get up? Your eye's injured, your legs are fine. Let me help you."

"Okay." Tentative.

They stand together. He looks at his 11-year-old brother's eye and feels awful.

"How did you miss it?" he asks.

"I heard a crash. It startled me."

He's tempted to lecture Noah: "always keep your eye on the ball, no matter what, especially when catching my pitches." But this isn't the time. He puts his arm around Noah, who is still obviously traumatized. "Come, let's go inside." As they walk to the back door, he tries to comfort his little brother.

"It's going to be okay."

Aaron recalled how they later learned that there had indeed been a car crash, not on their quiet cul-de-sac but on the busy cross street. Noah's eye had been fine in the end, and it hadn't been long before he was helping Aaron practice pitching again. Aaron had been correct; everything had turned out okay. This time, however, he wasn't so sure.

"I suppose," Noah said, also unconvinced.

Not knowing what to say next, Aaron looked at his watch again. "We should get going."

Noah nodded, and they resumed walking up to the Garden.

Noah could tell Aaron was lost in thought and had a good idea of what he was thinking. He appreciated Aaron's initial reaction, though had expected nothing less. As fervent as Aaron was in his religiosity, he was never one to pass judgement on others, and was also very much about family. More than anything, Aaron loved him, and he knew it. He also knew that Aaron would be troubled by this news and would worry about him, their family, and the impact it would have on everyone.

The silence lasted a few minutes before Aaron broke it, asking, "So, when did you come to this conclusion?"

It sounded like an odd and somewhat clinical way to phrase the question, but Noah understood that Aaron was doing his best in what was a difficult situation for both of them. "There wasn't a specific point in time or moment when I had an epiphany. It's something that evolved," he said.

Aaron looked at him inquisitively.

"I mean I always sort of knew," Noah explained. "Or suspected, but I also had a lot of denial, even hopes that maybe it wasn't so. I've struggled with it for a long time."

"It must have been very hard for you," Aaron said, his voice trembling slightly with sadness.

Noah nodded.

"And you're sure?" Aaron asked.

Noah had anticipated that question as well. It was probably the most natural thing for someone in Aaron's position to ask.

"Yeah." He waited a beat. "I'm sure."

"And what's your plan in terms of telling Mom. And Dad?"

"I'm going home this Shabbos and I'm going to tell them then," Noah said, realizing that he had just committed to what had only been an idea. Now it was, as Aaron had put it, a "plan." Now it was no longer daunting. Now it was terrifying.

Aaron had a fleeting inclination to say *good luck with that* but held his tongue. It wasn't the time for sarcasm. "It isn't going to be easy," he said instead.

"I know."

The Knicks were having a bad season, and their 97-89 loss to the Celtics only added insult to injury. Aside from a few glimmers of hope, Noah and Aaron spent most of the game critiquing their own team. It was almost as if their prior conversation hadn't even occurred. Almost, but not quite.

Aaron seemed slightly adrift. Noah understood that his brother would need time to digest this revelation but was undoubting of Aaron's fealty in the end. He assumed Aaron was contemplating how to break the news to Sheindy, and at some point—most likely in the distant future—the ever-so-challenging task of explaining this to his children. Noah desperately loved his nieces and nephew and relished every minute he got to spend and play with them. But they were being raised in an ultra-Orthodox culture that regarded him as a deviant sinner. Putting Aaron in the position of somehow teaching them to defy any aspect of their tradition felt like quite an imposition.

Noah's guilt over disrupting the lives of everyone important to him was inescapable. Until just days ago that very same guilt had condemned him to fear and inaction. Now, no longer paralyzing yet still palpable, it had him wondering if he would ever get beyond it.

In addition to the back and forth about the game, they shared some small talk about Aaron and family in LA and Noah's plans for Harvard Law next year.

"That's so awesome," Aaron said, praising his brother's accomplishments. "I keep forgetting, what was your score on the LSAT?

"178," Noah responded, seemingly uncomfortable with the question, almost embarrassed.

"That's like perfect."

"Perfect is 180," Noah whispered as if talking to himself.

"Whatever. And your GPA was like..."

Noah was hesitant.

"C'mon!"

"It was 3.8"

"Wow! I worked hard and did well, but you were always such a slack off when it came to school. And now look at you, the brainy one."

"If you say so," Noah responded, reluctant in that moment to accept anything positive about himself whatsoever.

12

MIRIAM BAUMAN STARED INTO Rajesh Bhatt's eyes as she strategized how to let him down easy. Their "friendship" had been blossoming into so much more and was intensifying with each passing day. *I've got to put the kibosh on this. I can't let it go any further! Noah's going to drop the bomb on my parents this weekend, my family's going to be in crisis, and I just can't be doing this. I can't!*

They sat across from each other at Mike's Sports Bar, a popular spot just a few blocks from the university, and were surrounded by friends, many of whom were somber from the basketball game that had ended just minutes earlier. Miriam would normally have been upset over the Knicks loss to the Celtics—she shared her brothers' allegiance to the struggling New York team—but tonight, her thoughts were elsewhere.

She also knew that Noah and Aaron were together tonight, and how Noah was planning to use the opportunity. Everything was getting way too complicated. She needed some simplicity in her life and figured that putting the brakes on this thing with Raj would be a good start. *Or would it? Why am I the one who has to make the sacrifice?*

She was caught between rational and irrational inclinations. Part of her believed the "right" thing to do was to find a nice Orthodox guy, marry quickly, and have lots of babies. That would certainly soften the blow that her parents would suffer from Noah. But was that really right for her? And would it truly soften anything in the end? It was all quite confusing, and it was at moments like this when she admired her father for his keen, unflinching sense of right and wrong, good and bad, proper and improper. She was jealous of his clarity, as annoying as it sometimes was.

And Raj. What an appealing man, she reflected. Thick black hair, South Asian complexion, inviting face, tall, slim—an Adonis with smarts, wit, depth and charm—a package she hadn't found among the Jewish men she'd dated. Or maybe she hadn't really looked hard enough. Perhaps she hadn't wanted to. After all, she'd always had a penchant for something different, something atypical or unexpected in the sheltered world from which she came.

On the other hand, she could never imagine actually marrying a man who wasn't Jewish. As rebellious as she was, she'd always thought she would eventually settle into a traditional religious life in an Orthodox community with a family much like her own. Daydreaming as a young girl, she had pictured her husband dressed in his finest suit, wearing the yarmulke she had knitted for him when they dated, blessing their children at the start of Shabbos dinner—just as her father had blessed her and her brothers. He would be a man of the world, at ease in both Talmudic texts and the latest social media craze, reciting the benediction over the wine with fervor, and telling their children stories from the Torah portion of the week as they sat around the table, hanging on his every word. And when the festive meal drew to a close, he would sway back and forth with their youngest on his lap, her family singing the traditional Shabbos songs she loved so very much.

In reality, Adonis or no Adonis, she knew a life with Raj would mean rejecting the heritage she cherished, a part of her she could never truly abandon. The very thought was absurd, impossible. They were just having fun together, enjoying themselves, that's all. It could never turn into anything serious. She wouldn't let it.

The night was late, the game was over, and her beer was warm. Time to go. Her group simultaneously arose from the table and said their goodnights. Once out on the street, everyone split up to go their separate ways, leaving her and Raj alone. They started walking as if it were expected that he would see her home.

"You seem pensive tonight," Raj observed.

"Oh, I'm sorry," she reacted. "Just a lot on my mind."

"That family stuff you alluded to?"

She had told him there was something going on but was still withholding the details. In truth, she wanted to tell him the whole story. He would never say anything, and even if it were to somehow slip out, the only friends they shared were her fellow graduate students. None of them would think twice about her brother being gay, and none had any connections to her community at home. Nevertheless, she felt it would be wrong. It wasn't her place to be outing her brother, even to Raj. "Yeah," she said.

"Want to talk about it?" he asked.

"Not especially." She clarified, "Not right now."

"Okay. Whenever you want, whatever you need, you know I'm here."

"I know." And she did know. That was the problem. He was just so... wonderful.

"Some game," he said, changing the subject to the Knicks' loss.

"The Knicks suck."

"Maybe I should try out."

"Maybe you should. They need all the help they can get."

"I agree. I'll look into it tomorrow."

She smiled, her first of the evening, realizing that her plan to tell him they needed to cool things down wasn't happening. She wasn't sure what to say or do, only that she couldn't say it was over. She didn't want to. They went on chatting until they found themselves in front of her building.

"Well, here we are," she said, feeling awkward. They had kissed goodnight before, but somehow she knew the next kiss was going to be different. As if possessed by a force beyond her control or reason, she said, "It's freezing. Would you like to come up?"

It was late and they both had class the following morning, but he, too, was driven by instinct. "Sure, that'd be great."

Miriam awoke abruptly, as if jolted from a loud noise. Despite the darkness, she gazed at the ceiling for a few seconds and regained her bearings. Realizing she was naked, she glanced to her right to confirm her thoughts. *Oh my God!*

She felt a wave of panic as she saw Raj, fast asleep, facing her. She eased herself from the bed, slipped on her panties and tee-shirt, and quietly tiptoed to the bathroom. She looked at herself in the mirror, aghast—*What have I done!*

Miriam Bauman had never gone any further than "making out" with a guy, and even that was of recent vintage and meant that her clothes always stayed on. Despite years of rebelliousness, she had pretty much managed to confine her defiance to the realm of intellect, and continued to see herself as a rabbi's daughter, especially when it came to men. Sure, there had been a few missteps along the way, coupled with confusion and conflict. And the past year had been particularly challenging. But *this* was beyond the pale, beyond anything she ever saw herself doing before marriage. And the worst part of it was her undeniable awareness that she had really enjoyed it.

She tried mollifying herself with the fact that they hadn't actually had intercourse, but the distinction seemed trivial in light of everything else they did do. *He must think I'm so weird.*

She searched her face for signs of shame but found none. Guilt, yes. But no sense that she was somehow bad or reprehensible. Hers was a feeling that she'd done something she simply wasn't supposed to be doing. A subtle distinction, perhaps, and one which Raj might label a "distinction without a difference," but meaningful to her nonetheless.

What am I going to do now?

She thought about Noah, how her parents were going to react to the news they were soon to learn about him, and how her own situation would only add fuel to the flame.

Nobody can know.

But how can I possibly keep this a secret? Can I sneak around with Raj? Is that fair to him? Someone's bound to see us, sooner or later. Then what? Oh my God!

Maybe I should just tell him we made a mistake? But did we? I really love being with him, the way he treats me, the way he talks to me. The way he touches me.

Realizing her conundrum had no easy solutions, she made her way back to the bed, slipped under the covers and closed her eyes. Sleep was out of the question, but she hoped the darkness might offer some peace. Yet she knew it wouldn't.

13

THE ARREST OF BENJAMIN Marcus shook the Orthodox Jewish community, both in Lawrence and throughout the world. The papers reported it with fervor, all eagerly highlighting that the philanthropist charged with multiple counts of fraud was an Orthodox Jew, president of his congregation, and had allegedly been having an extramarital affair with his assistant who recently turned state's evidence against him. The synagogue's phone rang incessantly throughout the day, reporter after reporter seeking comment from the rabbi, only to be stonewalled by his secretary, who stated simply that he was unavailable. The Bauman's home voicemail was also filled with similar entreaties.

A local TV news station was camped outside the synagogue for hours trying to grab a statement from whomever came and went, hoping ultimately for an audience with the rabbi. It was 9 p.m. and Jonathan had just finished his last meeting of the evening with a lovely young couple he was soon to marry. He walked out to the parking lot knowing the press would be waiting. He no longer cared. He hadn't eaten dinner yet and was hungry and tired.

It wasn't a second before he heard a female voice shout, "That's him, that's the rabbi!"

A barrage of bright lights, a camera, and the female reporter were instantaneously in his face. He figured she'd identified him from his picture on the synagogue's website.

"Rabbi, Sharon O'Neil with Channel 11. Would you care to comment on the arrest of Benjamin Marcus today?"

Boxed in, Jonathan squinted from the lights but managed to focus on the reporter. "Excuse me, Sharon, but would you mind asking your people to allow me to go to my car." He was tempted to point out that she was on private property, and the lawyer within him might even have mentioned something about her restricting his movement or harassment. But confrontation wasn't his style and, again, he simply wanted to get home.

"Sorry about that, Rabbi," she said. Feigned sincerity. "Guys, let the rabbi through!"

Jonathan made his way to his car, the reporter and crew following in tow.

"Rabbi, would you care to comment?" She said it as if he owed her something for letting him pass.

"Not really." Impassive. He slid into the driver's seat and shut the door.

Sarah heard the front door open while tied up in a phone conversation with a nervous mother whose 6-year-old daughter was sick with the flu. She emerged from the den with the phone to her ear and a hand gesture indicating she would be off soon. Jonathan, in turn, gestured *don't worry, I'm fine* as he hung his charcoal Biltmore Homburg on the second rung of the hat rack, just below the black one he wore on Shabbos and holidays, and above the wide-brimmed black Borsalino fedora he had given up a few years ago.

The black fedora was the classic hat of both yeshiva students and most of Jonathan's rabbinic colleagues. The Homburg, however, with its narrow, perched up brims had been Sarah's preference, born of her penchant for nonconformity and a keen sense of style. For Jonathan, who had conceded on this issue relatively recently compared to how long Sarah had been pushing, the new hat ironically represented just the opposite of Sarah's intentions.

To wit: it was an even stronger tie to tradition. A relic of yesteryear, it had been the chosen headware of many great rabbinic luminaries of past generations, including his grandfather. His only discomfort with it was the seeming pretentiousness of placing himself in such company. But the fact that his weekday hat was gray ameliorated that somewhat, for anything other than black would never have been worn by his predecessors. And while he still went with black on Shabbos and holidays, his inevitable tinges of unworthiness were not sufficient for him to return to the fedora and disappoint his wife.

He walked into the kitchen and found some food in the fridge. As usual, Shabbos leftovers. This week: sliced London broil, roasted chicken, a faux potato kugel actually made of cauliflower and stewed zucchini. He grunted, longing for the days of french fries, pasta, and some sort of bread. This carb-counting business was the last thing he needed on a night like this. The stress was definitely getting to him.

He placed the plate in the microwave as Sarah appeared, minus phone. "Everything okay?" he asked.

"Another kid with the flu." Edginess.

"Seems to be going around."

"Indeed. It's keeping me quite busy."

"So I see."

She observed him a bit more carefully. "Hard day, huh?"

"I suppose that's one way of putting it." He grabbed a bottle of red Cabernet sitting on the counter and examined it to see how much was left. "Half a bottle. That should do."

Sarah chuckled. "Sure that's enough? Maybe you should go for something stronger." She turned and eyed the small antique bar in the dining room, upon which sat several fine single malts and bourbons.

"No, this'll do."

"Maybe I'll join you," she said.

He looked at her astonished. She detested dry reds, tolerated sweet whites, and only drank when out to dinner or at social gatherings. "Sure," he said as he pulled two glasses from the cabinet. "I can open a different bottle."

"No, that's fine."

Ignoring the ring from the microwave, he poured the wine and handed her a glass. "To good things," he said, extending his glass for a toast.

"To good things," she responded as their glasses clinked.

He whispered the blessing for wine, she responded with *amen* and they sipped. He smiled and said, "We may wind up opening another bottle after all."

"Maybe we will."

He moved toward the microwave to get his plate. "So, what's going on with Esther?" he asked. During their brief phone and text conversations throughout the day, she'd informed him that she had spoken with Esther Marcus. "There's a lot. I'll tell you tonight," had been her last communication. As usual, they'd each had an overloaded day.

They both sat down. "She's falling apart," Sarah said.

"I can just imagine," he said under his breath.

"She called me three times. She doesn't know what to do. She was packing a suitcase for Benjy and was going to hand it to him at the court after he posted bail. Instead she brought him home."

"Maybe she did the right thing."

"Maybe she didn't."

"They have a lot to work through."

Silence.

"Benjy's a good man who made some bad mistakes," he said, almost as if trying to convince her.

"Do you really know Benjy?"

He considered her question. "As much as I know anyone."

"Yeah...it's kind of scary..."

"That it is." He started at his dinner.

"By the way," she said, "I do have some good news."

"Good news would be...good," he muttered through a mouth filled with food. It was too late, and he was simply way too hungry and exhausted to worry about his manners.

"Noah's coming home for Shabbos."

He sipped his wine. "How kind of him to make an appearance." Snide.

She threw him a frown.

"Yes," he said, losing the sarcasm, "that is good news."

She took her own sip, winced from the taste, faked a cough, then smiled. "Indeed. Very good news."

14

THE BAUMAN FAMILY HADN'T planned to have guests at the table this particular Friday night. With the community in a state of shock and dismay, it was an all-around bad time for entertaining, but a good opportunity for Sarah and Jonathan to spend some eagerly awaited quality time with Noah. A welcome respite from an otherwise traumatic few days.

Sarah had given Jonathan the obligatory lecture on not asking Noah what happened with Ilana. They had long accepted Noah's unusual attachment to his privacy. Each child had his or her quirks, as Sarah often put it, and this was Noah's. It had been hard for Jonathan—pretty much an open book most of his life—to get his head around this. But, as always, he eventually hearkened to his wife's sensibilities.

He agreed to her "request," but warned that they both ran the risk of being disappointed. "It would be just like him to go through an entire Shabbos, say nothing about it and then just leave."

"It's possible," she responded. "It's just not easy for him to talk about these things. But I think he wants to. It's important we let him do it in his own way."

"It's not easy for him to talk to us about *anything.*"

"I agree. That's exactly why we shouldn't force it. We should sit back and let him take the lead."

"Could be a quiet meal."

"I think it will be fine."

"I hope you're right."

"Me too."

Jonathan's concern with getting to *shul* early, coupled with Noah's tendency to arrive at the house at the very last minute, typically resulted in their having to wait till after the service to greet each other. It made Jonathan yearn for the years when little Noah always accompanied him to *shul* on Shabbos and sat by his side, enthusiastically playing the role of the rabbi's son. Fighting back the urge to turn around to see if Noah had arrived, a move that might embarrass Noah, Jonathan faced the ark and focused on his prayers.

In many Modern Orthodox synagogues, the rabbi sits in a special chair on the bimah beside the ark, facing the congregation. When Jonathan became senior rabbi, the first thing he did was move his seat. Notwithstanding objections—and there were plenty—he simply stated his position.

"I am part of the congregation and should *daven* with them, not on a stage in front of them," had been his exact words. His compromise was taking a seat in the far corner of the front row of the pews, distinguishing himself ever so slightly.

At the conclusion of the service, Jonathan stood at the front of the sanctuary as congregants passed by to exchange wishes for a peaceful, good Shabbos. This usually took about five minutes or so. But tonight, things were different. Many felt the need to express something to Jonathan about Benjy Marcus. Some were supportive, others simply observed how sad it was. Nobody actually dared being openly critical to Jonathan about one of his closest friends and the president of the congregation. Though there were likely more than a few, Jonathan surmised, who held such feelings, and it wasn't hard for him to guess who they were.

In all, the procession took about fifteen minutes. Noah waited at the end of the line, talking with a couple of friends who also happened to be around that weekend. Finally, he stood face to face with the father he hadn't seen in weeks. The two men beheld each other for a moment before Jonathan reached out, grabbed his son in a vigorous hug, and planted a kiss on his cheek. Sarah was very much into lips when kissing her children, and Jonathan was a cheek guy. Each of their styles mirrored exactly how it had been with their own parents. Noah was used to this, and he always felt a depth of affection from both parents in whatever form it came.

"I've missed you," Jonathan said.

"I've missed you, too."

They released each other, and Jonathan reached out to touch Noah's face. "I'm glad you're here," his tone unusually emotive.

"You say it like I've been away for a lifetime."

"When it comes to you, Noey, even a few weeks feels like a lifetime."

Noah smiled when his father used the childhood nickname everyone else had stopped using years ago. He had begun insisting people call him by his proper name when he was 14. Jonathan, having himself been called Yoni his entire life, didn't quite get it at first but eventually came to realize that Noah, the youngest in a family of strong personalities, was struggling to take some control over how he was defined. So, Jonathan complied for many years, until that time when Noah was 20 and he slipped. He swiftly caught himself and immediately apologized, to which Noah had just as quickly responded, "For what?" Since then, Jonathan often called him by his nickname, but only between the two of them, as if it were a special secret. With anyone else present, including Sarah, it was always "Noah."

They gathered their coats and left for home. Another blustery evening dictated a hurried pace and minimal dialogue—just enough for Noah to report about his evening with Aaron at the Knicks game. Jonathan was pleased that the boys had gotten together and couldn't have cared less about the Knicks. The walk was only four blocks and there would be plenty of time for more meaningful conversation at dinner—or so Jonathan hoped.

The warmth of the house was most welcoming after their walk through the cold. The aromas of Shabbos food permeated the air as Jonathan, Sarah, and Noah took their places at the dining room table. Off to the side on the antique bar stood five flickering candles in Sarah's grandmother's silver candlesticks, one for each member of the family. On the table sat two home baked *challahs* covered by a cloth with a pastel drawing of the city of Jerusalem.

Jonathan chose a bottle of red from the rack and handed it to Noah for approval. He took pleasure in having passed on his beverage appreciation to all the children, occasionally jesting how this was one of the few contributions he made compared to Sarah. Noah perused the label—*Galil Mountain - Yiron 2013*—a Northern Israeli blend of Cabernet, Merlot, and Syrah that his father knew to be his favorite. He handed back the bottle, along with his endorsement in the form of a smile and a nod.

"Good, then it's decided," Jonathan said.

"Yay!" Sarah roared teasingly, once again displaying her lack of enthusiasm for reds. She was also, admittedly, a little jealous that her children's pallets, in this regard, followed their father's.

Jonathan popped the bottle with a two-step Rabbit lever corkscrew Sarah had gotten him for Father's Day a few years back. He was enamored with its propensity for a seamless, perfect uncorking since the first time he'd seen it in an upscale restaurant. He had been thrilled when Sarah presented it, and it became one of his favorite toys, both for its utility and sentimental value.

He poured the wine into an oversized silver goblet they'd received as a wedding gift from a generous friend of Sarah's parents. He then commenced with the pre-benediction rituals: *Shalom Alechem*, a song for the Shabbos angels, and another song, *Eishes Chayil*, taken from the poetic verses in Proverbs 31, describing a "Woman of Valor." It was widely believed that the latter was a dedication to the "woman of the house," recited at this time in acknowledgement of her meticulous preparation for Shabbos. But for Jonathan, based on the interpretations of his teachers, it was really a statement about God in the feminine, honoring the Friday night presence of the "Shabbos Queen." It was a teaching he had passed on to his children, hoping they too would always recite the poem, regardless of the presence of a "woman of the house."

Noah and Sarah joined along in the singing as Jonathan closed his eyes and lost himself in the melody. After a week such as this, he relished the escape, however fleeting. When the songs concluded, Noah stepped to Jonathan for the Blessing of the Children, a ritual in which the father places his hands on his child's head and beseeches God that the child become as the patriarchs or matriarchs of Israel, followed by the Biblical priestly benediction. The two men faced each other as Jonathan whispered the blessing and planted three loving kisses on Noah's forehead. They hugged briefly before Noah returned to his spot at the table and Jonathan recited the special *Kiddush* for Friday night, a prayer bearing testimony to God's creation of the world and sanctifying the Sabbath as a day to refrain from creating, a day that gives man an opportunity to imitate God—a concept flowing through many Jewish dictates.

Following the *Kiddush*, they all washed their hands with a special cup before reciting the blessing of *Hamotzi,* the benediction for breaking bread and beginning the meal. Then, Sarah's famed chicken matzah ball soup, prepared in a rich short rib base, always beloved but especially craved on freezing nights such as this. She smiled as she observed both men devour the soup while she worked on hers more slowly, careful not to burn her tongue, a concern her men seemingly didn't have.

"How was *shul*?" Sarah asked. A conversation starter. She already knew the answer to her question.

"Somber," Jonathan replied.

Noah nodded.

"I assume Benjy wasn't there." Sarah said.

"No, he wasn't. I doubt he'll show up tomorrow, either," Jonathan said.

"Probably not," Sarah said. "Esther's devastated and he's... He's embarrassed."

"It's probably best if he lays low for a while," Jonathan said under his breath, as if thinking aloud.

"Best for him or for the community?" Noah asked, a bit more acerbically than he'd intended.

"Probably both," Jonathan responded, ignoring Noah's tone.

Sarah looked on, particularly at Noah, wondering what was really on his mind.

Noah's plan was to have *the* conversation at some point during the evening, intending to give Sarah and Jonathan time to digest and react before he returned to the city Saturday night. He hadn't figured exactly how he was going to do this, and he certainly hadn't imagined that an opportunity would present itself. Yet, willy-nilly, one just had.

"I'm just saying that I don't get why you both think it's a good idea for him to hide," Noah said. "Whatever happened, he's a member of the community and has done many incredibly good things. If the charges are true, then he made a mistake, or even a few mistakes, and he's going to be punished big time for that. He shouldn't be afraid to be among his friends and all the people he's helped over the years. He has a lot to be proud about, and he should always feel comfortable in the *shul*."

"You've been spending a lot of time with your sister," Jonathan said, cracking a smile and melting tensions momentarily.

"If she were here, I'm sure she would have said the same thing," Noah said.

"No doubt," Jonathan uttered.

"And she would have a point," Noah said.

Jonathan nodded.

"But it isn't an easy thing to do," Sarah said. "In a perfect world, he should just go about his business and not care what others think or say, but we don't live in a perfect world. Benjy's human. He has fears and insecurities just like the rest of us. So, I understand why he's hiding. I understand why he's embarrassed."

"Another good point," Jonathan said.

Noah was quiet as they all brought the soup bowls into the kitchen and gathered the trays of food for the table. There was the usual sliced London broil—always a favorite of the Bauman men—roasted chicken, potato kugel, sautéed spinach and a recent ratatouille concoction Sarah had found on a kosher foodies website. Enough for the three of them and about ten others. Sarah suggested that Jonathan go easy on the kugel and smiled as her men filled their plates.

Noah took a deep breath, so to speak, between bites. "Since we're talking about people hiding," he said hesitantly, "and being scared about what others will say and think, I have something to tell you."

Sarah and Jonathan stopped eating, glanced at each other briefly and turned their sights on Noah.

"That's some introduction," Jonathan commented, feeling a twinge of anxiety about what was to follow.

"Yoni," Sarah interjected, "let's just hear what he has to say." Also anxious.

Noah lowered his head for a moment, then raised it and looked back and forth at each of them. "I know you're both wondering about what happened with Ilana. I also imagine you're wondering what happened with all the others. I want you to know that I've been seeing a therapist."

Sarah reached out and put her hand on his. "There's nothing wrong with that."

"I know." He took another breath. "I'm not finished."

Silence.

Noah's body began to quiver, and his eyes started to water. "I'm not attracted to women," he said as clearly and succinctly as he could muster.

Sarah and Jonathan looked at each other, her expression begging for him to be careful with what he said next, his indicating that he didn't know what to say at all. Sarah squeezed Noah's hand. Jonathan sat frozen, a pit in his stomach, his appetite completely vanished, his mind muddled as Noah began to cry.

Sarah moved over beside Noah and wrapped her arms around him. Tears began to flow from her eyes as she held him tight, saying, "Don't worry, honey. Everything's going to be okay."

Thinking he should participate somehow in comforting his son, Jonathan found that he simply couldn't. *Is everything going to be okay? Really?* He stared into space, his mind blank, his ears filled with the sounds of sobbing. Sarah's eyes caught him, hoping to elicit a response, but none was to be had. He was lost, some place she knew she couldn't reach.

Unable to bare his inertia any longer, Jonathan said, "I love you, Noey."

Noah raised his head. For an instant, father and son faced each other as if Sarah wasn't in the room. "I want you to know that I love you," Jonathan repeated as he stood up. Then he declared, "I need to get some air."

Sarah looked at him inquisitively. "Yoni?"

"I need to take a walk," he repeated.

What she wanted to say was: *You need to stay right here with us and tell your son that everything's going to be okay, that we're going to work all this out, and that we're going to stick together no matter what. That he is a wonderful, wonderful man, and that none of this changes anything!* Instead, she said, "A walk? It's freezing outside!"

Noah was silent. He understood that each of them would have to process this differently and that in some ways it would be easier for Sarah than Jonathan. "It's okay," he said, hoping to mollify his mother.

Sarah was speechless as Jonathan nodded to her and Noah before stepping away to get his coat. Jonathan didn't know how long he'd be, so he didn't say. He didn't know where exactly he was heading, so he didn't say. He didn't know anything. So he said nothing.

Sarah sat beside Noah, her arms still around him, her face resting on his head as they heard the front door close. She rubbed his back while saying all the encouraging things she'd hoped his father would have said.

All she had was hope. And an unbridled devotion to those she loved. And a lingering fear that even these things might not be enough.

It was freezing, as Sarah had warned, but Jonathan didn't mind. He needed to be alone, to walk, to think, and the wintry night pretty much guaranteed there would be no one about to disrupt his solitude. He felt a tear escape his left eye and wiped it with his glove. *Hold it together! You have to figure this out. After all, you're the one who always figures things out, at least that's what everybody thinks. Little do they know.*

He thought about Noah, the suffering his son must have endured all these years. He couldn't imagine the turmoil, fear, and self-loathing of growing up in the Orthodox Jewish community while feeling fundamentally aberrant. And what of the future? he wondered. Could Noah ever really find fulfillment and happiness in their world? Was marrying and raising children in the Orthodox tradition no longer within Noah's reach? And did Noah even want those things?

Jonathan realized he was more worried about Noah's future as an Orthodox Jew than as a homosexual, and he understood why. For him, it was quite simple: If Noah was gay—he still felt the need to pose it as a hypothetical though he knew the truth—then his only option was to accept it. *I'm not God. I didn't write the Torah, and I can't judge my son for something beyond his control. I can't and I won't!*

But Noah's staying within the Orthodox fold was another matter altogether, and a most uncertain one at that. Or was it? Was it even fair to expect Noah to continue in a lifestyle that condemned his very essence?

Amid all the uncertainty, two things seemed clear to him: First, the only way for a gay person to really observe the Torah's commandments would be to commit himself to a life of celibacy. Second, he could never expect such a thing from his son.

His thoughts then turned to analyzing how his life had brought him to this place. Images flashed through his mind—his parents, the home in which he grew up, himself at Noah's age before he met Sarah. He had been at a crossroads then, facing the decision of whether to remain within the confines of ultra-Orthodoxy, marry someone from that background, and raise his children to follow that path. But a single night, a party he probably shouldn't have been at, and the most alluring green eyes he'd ever seen all conspired to compel him in a different direction. And although his parents had seemed pleased with his choice of Sarah, he had always known that this had been more about his finally having settled down than anything else. Pondering this, he reminded himself how his parents did indeed grow to love and respect his wife in time. But he also reminded himself of how he had never quite been able to shake the feeling that they still would have preferred someone less "modern."

His parents had both been gone a few years now, but that didn't stop him from wondering how they would have reacted to such tidings about their grandson. Imagining their profound dismay and disapproval, he immediately dismissed the thought. *That's really not what I need to worry about right now!*

The real question burning inside him was whether things would have turned out differently had he chosen the world from which he came. Could he have exerted a stronger influence living in the Brooklyn ghetto, teaching in the rabbinic seminary, sending his children to the same schools in which he had been reared, depriving them of smartphones, television, and carte blanche internet? Was it simply Noah's biological destiny to be gay, or had environmental influences played a role as well? *And could those influences have been thwarted had I been more protective?*

Come on Yoni, who are you kidding? You made your choices not because you were forced, but because you wanted to. As for all this self-blaming, how about some reality? Noah is a wonderful, smart, stable, happy young man. Okay, maybe not that last part so much, but that might be starting to change. And as for these so-called outside influences of modern culture and their effect on Noah's sexuality, how does that explain the presence of so many closeted homosexuals in the protected enclaves of the ultra-Orthodox world?

This conclusion seemed sound to him, though only briefly, until other questions invaded his mind. *Could this be a form of punishment? Is this God's way of imposing consequences for my actions and decisions? Had I been stauncher, less compromising, might this not have happened?*

It occurred to him how ironic it was to be torturing himself with the same sort of thinking for which many of his congregants often sought his help. He could even hear himself advising them how no one can truly understand why God does what He does, and then reminding them how God, Himself, stated this very same idea to Job in the Bible. Now the only trick was to convince himself, a hard thing to do when you feel that things are somehow your fault.

He knew it was only a matter of time until Noah's secret became common knowledge throughout the community. That was just the way things worked. Between the Benjy Marcus crisis and this, his congregation was in for quite a jolt, to say nothing of what was in store for him and Sarah. Rough days were ahead, his leadership was certainly going to be tested. And he was tired. Tired of living in a glass house, the politics, and the incessant demand of always having to be the perfect and wise one in the room. At this moment, he was feeling far from either.

He continued walking as his thoughts seemed to only deepen his frenzy. He regretted having left Sarah and Noah the way he had, and the cold was getting to him. It was time to return home, so he started on his way, still stunned and helpless, bereft of even a clue of what to do about any of this.

15

JONATHAN BAUMAN ENTERED THE house still expecting to find Noah and Sarah in the dining room. Not realizing how long he'd been out, he was a bit surprised to find Sarah sitting on the den couch with a pediatric medical journal. He appreciated that reading her journals was actually a respite for her, similar to a page of Talmud for him. She looked up as he entered the room.

"Noah?" he asked.

"Upstairs. Probably asleep."

This was one of those moments when two people talk to each other calmly, yet feel anything but. He wasn't sure if she was angry at him for disappearing, and she had no idea what was going on with him. He planted himself in his usual spot: a soft, brown leather La-Z-Boy rocker, and stared at her blankly.

"Maybe you should go upstairs and talk to him," she suggested.

"You said he was sleeping."

"I said he was *probably* sleeping, and I'm sure he wouldn't mind if you woke him up."

He nodded. "Okay, I think I'll do that," he said as he got up. "Not sure what to say to him," he added under his breath.

"You'll figure it out."

Oh, how he hated those words.

Jonathan found Noah lying in his bed, awake. He sat down on the edge of the bed as Noah shifted to make room for him. "How you doing, Noey?" he asked.

"I'm okay." Tentative. "You?"

"I'm all right."

"Good walk?"

"Cold."

They looked at each other, neither knowing what to say next.

Jonathan reached out and ran his hand through Noah's hair. "I love you," he said softly.

"I know." He took a deep breath. "I love you too."

"I'm sorry I walked out."

"You don't have to be sorry. I understand."

Jonathan appreciated the reprieve but still felt a need to explain. "It's just that...it was quite a surprise."

"That's putting mildly. More like an earthquake."

The two men smiled. It was so typical of Noah to jest at a time like this.

"Yeah, it does shake things up some," Jonathan admitted, managing a faint smile. He caught a glimpse of the bookcase across the room. The hallway light was just enough for him to make out the title of one of the books, *The Little Midrash Says*, triggering a fleeting reverie of sitting in this very same spot so many years ago, reading those ancient stories to a 5-year-old boy who was begging for just one more tale before Daddy kissed him goodnight. Jonathan thought it curious how that book remained on the shelf, its fate distinguished from the multitudes of other children's books that had found their way to the trash. He wondered if Noah had intentionally kept it, cherishing those memories as he had.

"It hasn't been easy," Noah said.

"I'm sure it hasn't."

They shared a brief silence. Then Noah said, "Miriam and Aaron already know."

"I had assumed. Did you tell Ilana?"

"She was the first. I owed it to her."

Jonathan nodded. There were so many things he wanted to ask, but he restrained himself, knowing it wasn't appropriate then, or perhaps ever. He had to accept that Noah would share only so much, that the rest would simply have to be guesswork. And then there were the things he wanted to say, all of which he didn't yet know how to. "You're a good man, Noey. A really good man."

"So are you."

Jonathan felt himself getting choked up and struggled to maintain his composure. "I'll wake you for *shul* tomorrow?"

"Yes."

They shared what each experienced as the tightest hug ever. Jonathan stood up and started for the door.

"One more thing," Noah said.

Jonathan turned around to listen.

"Earthquakes have ripple effects."

Jonathan considered the point. "I know," he said, then added, "We'll just have to deal with that."

They looked at each other. "Good night, Dad."

"Good night, Noey."

From the den, situated just below the master bedroom, Sarah could hear Jonathan preparing for bed. She closed her medical journal, on which she wasn't really concentrating, and headed upstairs to join him. "How did it go?" she whispered as she entered the room.

"Okay… I suppose."

She could see he wasn't eager for conversation. "Tired?"

"Exhausted."

"You'll be all right tomorrow?" she asked, allowing herself just this last question. Saturday morning was the hardest time of the week—he had to be energetic, on his game, attentive, and wearing a smile.

"I'll be fine. What about you?"

"I'll be fine too."

They both knew there was much to discuss and that their future held some new, unforeseen challenges. At some point, they would need to talk it through. For now, they needed to digest things on their own. And get through tomorrow.

An uncharacteristic silence overcame them as they got into bed. A few minutes passed before Jonathan eased himself beside her and took her in his arms. It was no time for sex, he knew, but he just wanted to hold her. Sensing the same, she turned over, maneuvered him onto his back, and rested her head upon his chest.

"Good night," he said softly.

"Good night," she replied, closing her eyes and hoping, that sooner or later, they would both drift off to sleep.

16

BENJY MARCUS, AS USUAL, showed up right on time for *davening* the next morning, when only the most devoted and those needing to say the Mourner's *Kaddish* are present. *Kaddish* is a prayer offered following the death of an immediate family member and is said for eleven months for a parent. It also requires a quorum of ten men, a *minyan,* according to Orthodox tradition. In the morning service, it is one of the very first and very last prayers, prompting Jonathan to quip on more than one occasion that the rabbis had organized it that way to ensure that there were enough people who came on time and stayed till the end, "something Jews often don't like to do." For the afternoon and evening services, which were much shorter, the rabbis were far less concerned and thus left *Kaddish* till the end.

Noah also arrived on time, not because he was so dedicated, but because he was a Bauman. It was stressed by both Jonathan and

Sarah that the rabbi's sons were held to a higher standard than other boys in the community and needed to be in *shul* on Shabbos morning from start to finish. Unlike with Aaron, this had been a problem for Noah, especially as a teenager wanting to sleep late. That provoked many spats with his father who, when it came to this, always won. Truth be told, Noah never really put up too much resistance. He had always known the right thing to do.

Miriam, on the other hand, was completely left out of all this. Although obliged to pray at least once a day, according to many authorities, women weren't required to pray at specific times or with a quorum. Miriam and Sarah could actually get to *shul* when they wanted, but for appearance's sake, they were always among the first women to show.

Noah decided to say hello to Benjy before taking his seat beside his father. He noticed that Benjy's row was still empty except for Benjy, and that it was a good time to get a moment alone. They had always been close, and all three Bauman children regarded Benjy as a quasi-uncle.

"Noah!" Benjy said, his enthusiasm surprising considering his circumstances.

"How are you doing, Uncle Benjy?" Noah said while squeezing Benjy's shoulder.

"Oh, just peachy."

The two men looked at each other, each realizing there wasn't much to be said on that topic.

"Maybe by the time you finish Harvard Law, you'll help with my appeal?" Benjy gibed.

Noah offered a faint smile. "Let's hope it doesn't come to that."

"From your mouth to God's ears." Benjy said, his tone revealing his skepticism. "It's good to see you. I heard about you and Ilana. How are you holding up?"

"I'm okay." Tentative.

Benjy gave him a curious look but chose not to probe. "Everything works out for the best," he said, somewhat unconvincingly.

Noah simply nodded, also unconvincingly.

"We'll talk later?" Benjy said.

"For sure."

Noah moseyed over to his seat beside Jonathan. Engrossed in his prayers, Jonathan paused barely a second to lean over and plant a kiss on Noah's face. Nothing special or different, this was always the routine. And it was particularly crucial for Jonathan to stick to the routine, for he desperately wanted to communicate to his son that there would be no change in their relationship.

Noah opened his *siddur*, or prayer book, and started on his *davening*, but he couldn't really concentrate. He'd been up most of the night, tossing and turning, ruminating about this and that—his past, his future, how he wound up this way, and how he could possibly manage it all. And then there was his most pressing question, which he'd been struggling with since the moment he came to the realization of who and what he was: *If homosexuality is forbidden in the Torah, then why did God make me this way?*

He had asked this of Rabbi Kaminetsky, the student spiritual advisor at Yeshiva University. Kaminetsky was a young, easily approachable sort who was widely admired by the students as a keeper of secrets and dispenser of sound advice. But the answer he had given Noah—it's a test, we don't understand God's ways, control your impulses and stick with doing mitzvahs and studying Torah—ultimately proved vexing.

Presently, sitting here, *siddur* in hand, all Noah wanted was to pose this question to his father. He wouldn't. Not now, perhaps not ever. It was certainly a fair question to have, he thought, though not so fair to ask. Why put his father on the spot when he knew there wasn't a good answer?

Still, he wanted to, not for provocation or to even make a point. But for the most fundamental of all reasons: he yearned for his father to actually provide the answer, to say something that would finally solve the problem, to utter the magic response that would make him feel complete as both an Orthodox Jew and a gay man. Yet he knew that there was no such thing, that he would have to find a way to live with the question and create his own answer. And at this moment, sitting in this sanctuary beside the man he loved most in this world and praying to a God he also loved, it all seemed incredibly unjust.

Lunch was uneventful, facilitated to some degree by the guests at the table. Sarah and Jonathan usually preferred only family at meals when any of the children were visiting, but it wasn't always possible. They'd gotten away with it the night before, ironically, with the help of the Marcus affair, but today's guests—a young family of four who recently moved into the neighborhood—had been invited well before the news about Benjy broke. It was unavoidable, most definitely an imposition, but not enough to compromise the Baumans' usual graciousness.

For Noah, it was actually a welcome breather. He was glad for the distraction, a few hours of conversation having nothing to do with his issue. Not that Sarah and Jonathan would have pressed him had they been alone, but things certainly would have been strained. Even now, he sensed a slight uneasiness, albeit from his father more than his mother. An uneasiness born not from anger, he knew, but from sadness and helplessness, two feelings with which he was all too familiar.

Not surprisingly, no one brought up Benjy Marcus' situation either. Even in *shul*, after the service, the usual consorting and hobnobbing went on as if the entire Marcus matter hadn't existed. Noah had overheard some chatter about it from one or two congregants, but for the most part there seemed a prevailing and unspoken taboo on the subject. As for Benjy, Noah noticed that he had left immediately after the service and had avoided as much contact with others as possible. It was enough, Noah reasoned, that he had shown up for *davening* in the first place, and understandable that he would want to avoid the social scene.

As a mid-February Shabbos, the day was short, leaving barely any time for a nap between the guests leaving and the walk back to *shul* for *mincha,* the afternoon service. Usually, other congregants headed to *shul* would join Jonathan along the way, but on this particular freezing afternoon he and Noah wound up alone, each seemingly lost in his own thoughts, neither knowing quite how to start the conversation.

"I'm really sorry, Dad," Noah offered, ending the silence.

"Sorry for what, Noey? There's nothing to be sorry about!"

"I know, but I'm sorry for my timing. You and Mom have enough on your plate, with Uncle Benjy and all that."

"Our plate is always overflowing. And so, by the way, is our cup."

Noah smiled, admiring his father's knack for positive spin, a required skill for a good rabbi. "I appreciate that."

"It's not just words. Your mother and I really believe that the good in our lives far outweighs the challenges we face, and that, in ways we don't always understand, those challenges are good as well."

"*My* challenge is good?"

Jonathan took a breath. "Ultimately, I believe it will be. It may not feel that way now—not for you, not for Mom, and not for me. But I believe that in the end it will be so."

Notwithstanding the positive message, Noah noted diffidence in his father's tone. And he understood why. This had been a shock to Jonathan, and it was going to take a while for him to recover. It was obvious that he was dealing with this as best he could, even better than Noah had expected. Not that Noah had anticipated being disowned or anything of that sort, but he had expected a somewhat more severe reaction than this.

Noah also sensed his father's powerlessness and a myriad of other feelings lurking beneath the surface—frustration, anger, and disappointment undoubtedly among them. And while he appreciated Jonathan's uncanny ability to hold it all together, he just wasn't sure how long that would last.

Noah departed Saturday night, a disquieting undertone still discernible, with no further mention of the issue. Jonathan hugged and kissed him at the door, and Sarah drove him to the train station. Alone with his mother, he was more at ease. She was always the less austere one, often accepting departures from the norms his father held so sacred.

"Are you going to be okay?" she asked.

"I suppose." Noncommittal.

She thought a moment, wondering if there was anything she could say to make him feel a little better. "You do know that your father loves you, no matter what," she stated, though it came out sounding almost like a question.

Noah nodded.

"This just isn't... easy for him," she said.

"What about you?" he asked.

"Easier," she said. "But also not easy."

Noah considered her comment. "It isn't easy for me either."

"I know, honey. I can't even imagine what you've been through, or what you're going through now."

Noah's eyes began to tear.

"All I want is for you to be happy, to have a good life," she said, her voice a bit shaky. "That's the thing I'm really worried about—that it's just going to be harder for you."

Noah not only understood her point, he'd thought about it many times himself. As difficult as life was for gay people in society, it was far worse in the Orthodox Jewish world. Finding a partner and having a family that would be fully accepted in the community was virtually impossible. And a life outside of his community seemed equally grim, and sad.

Sarah pulled up to the curb outside the train station, turned toward him, and drew him into an embrace. "It's going to be okay," she said. "It's all going to work out."

He slowly withdrew from her, peered into her eyes, and said, "I better get going or I'll miss the train."

"Yeah," she said. "We don't want that to happen."

He exited the car, then opened the back door to grab his bag.

"Call me when you get home!"

"Maaaa!"

"Okay," she conceded. "Call me... whenever."

"I'll call you soon."

"Good. Soon is good."

They smiled at each other as he closed the door, then he turned and went on his way. The hardest part of all this was finally behind him. So he thought.

17

MIRIAM BAUMAN WAS PANICKED. She had thought it would be just another Saturday night get-together with friends, a couple of drinks, laughs, maybe a little weed, and then back to her place with Raj. They usually preferred her place. Her roommates were cool and quite discreet. His were rowdy and partied pretty much all night.

Such had been her plan, until she saw Zoe Gold, a ghost from her past who unexpectedly invaded what Miriam had believed was her private domain. She had never entertained the possibility that her old life might catch up to her new one. Yet here it was in the form of a high school "friend" from whom she had gradually drifted over the years.

It wasn't as if she and Zoe had ever been besties, for they hadn't really been that close. Zoe's family belonged to her father's synagogue and, as such, the dutiful rabbi's daughter was obligated to extend the hand of friendship. She had to do this so often and with so many of her peers that it grew to be almost meaningless. She could never really be authentic with any of them.

It wasn't Zoe's sudden appearance at the party, per se, that set Miriam out of sorts. It was the timing of her entrance: exactly at a moment when Raj had his arms around her. While that alone could have been interpreted as a friendly gesture, his tender kiss on Miriam's neck was unmistakably intimate. And Miriam was convinced that Zoe saw it all.

Oh my God, she told herself as she jumped from Raj's embrace. He looked at her inquisitively.

"It's someone I know from home," she whispered.

"Uh huh," he reacted, trying not to be offended. He was growing a bit weary of her conflict as of late, especially the rules on how they were to comport themselves in public. And while this particular crowd and venue had previously been considered safe, suddenly it wasn't. Not a good sign for their future, he mused.

Zoe was making her way through the room, headed in Miriam's direction, when Miriam figured out why she was there. The giveaway was Zoe's companion, David Felder, a classmate in Miriam's program. Miriam didn't know David very well, only that he was a southern Jewish kid, originally from Memphis, with no apparent connection to the Orthodox community. *So, what is he doing with Zoe?* she wondered, confident that she was soon to find out.

"Hiiiii," Zoe said gleefully as she embraced Miriam. "Oh my God, it's been so long!"

While Miriam unfailingly visited her parents at least once a month for Shabbos, many of the girls she'd grown up with, including Zoe, were on different schedules. It had been a while since they'd found themselves in the neighborhood at the same time. "I know," Miriam said, feigning the same enthusiasm. *Maybe she didn't actually catch that moment with Raj? Maybe I'm being ridiculously paranoid?*

"It's so good to see you," Zoe said, her hands clenching Miriam's as it slowly dawned on her why Miriam was at the party. "I'm a total ditz! David told me we were going to a party with his graduate school friends, and I just didn't make the connection—it never occurred to me that you and David go to school together! Holy shit! I'm so stupid!"

Miriam raised her eyebrows. She'd always known Zoe to be a scatterbrain, but still couldn't fathom how anyone could miss something like this. She decided to just let it go. "And you and David?" she asked as she looked from one to the other.

"Dating," David interjected, almost as if he didn't want to hear how Zoe might have described it.

Zoe acceded with a grin.

"Oh, I'm sorry," Miriam said. "I'm being rude." She turned towards Raj. "This is Raj."

Zoe wore a blank expression.

I guess she did see it. "So how and when did you guys meet?" Miriam said, hoping her efforts to direct the conversation weren't obvious. She glanced at David, wondering why he also hadn't made a connection between her and Zoe. Having only twenty students in their class, she was pretty sure she'd shared bits and pieces of her past with him at some point, and he must have known Zoe's back-story. Of course, it was possible that, despite his intelligence, he was as oblivious as Zoe. Or just a typical male who didn't pay much attention to such details.

Zoe and David looked at each other. "It's okay, we can tell her," she said to him as if the answer was some sort of secret. She then turned to Miriam and said, "JDate," with a slightly embarrassed mien.

Miriam's curiosity was heightened. The Jewish dating website lets people specify their level of "Jewishness." *So how did Zoe match up with David Felder?* Unless Zoe wasn't interested in an Orthodox guy at this point, which, Miriam had to admit, was entirely possible. She knew all too well how priorities can shift with time, sometimes slightly, sometimes dramatically. Orthodoxy aside, David had his appeal. Smart, a budding professional, handsome, humble, and not a jerk.

"Wow, that's so interesting," Miriam said, immediately realizing that "interesting" could sound a bit patronizing. "I mean, I think it's really cool that you guys met that way."

"It's as good a way as any," David said. Nonchalant. He clearly didn't share Zoe's embarrassment.

Miriam smiled and nodded. She took some comfort in thinking that Zoe's being with David made it more likely for Zoe to be discreet about her own situation. But she was far from certain. David was undoubtedly outside the box, considering where she and Zoe came from, but Raj was something else altogether. And at that moment, she was finding herself keenly aware that Zoe, too, appreciated the distinction.

"What about you?" Zoe said. "What's going on?"

Miriam figured this was Zoe's way of asking about Raj without actually asking about Raj. "I'm good," she said.

Zoe seemed to be waiting for more, then caught on that this was all she was going to get. "That's great," she said.

Raj, intently observing this interaction, couldn't help but imagine how the subtitles might read. He threw a glance at Miriam, which she didn't miss.

So that was it. Miriam was wondering about David, and Zoe was wondering about Raj. Miriam had no choice at this point but to cling to her hope that their common circumstances might serve to keep things under wraps, but in the end, she knew that secrets were always temporary. Sooner or later, one way or another, it was only a matter of time before the proverbial shit would hit the fan. The only thing left for her to dwell on was what to do about it.

Eager to close the conversation, Miriam said, "You know, we really should get together some time."

"Yes, absolutely! That's such a good idea," Zoe said, welcoming the opportunity to move on.

"I'll call you."

"Okay. I'll call you too."

The two women kissed, then Zoe and David slipped back into the crowd.

"Doesn't sound to me like anyone's calling anyone," Raj whispered.

"That's the least of it," Miriam said, wearing every bit of the angst that was consuming her.

The short walk to Miriam's building seemed to take an eternity. Usually, he would have his arm around her or hold her hand, but not tonight. He had sensed a distancing since the moment Zoe had appeared. It didn't take brilliant deductive powers to see that tonight's encounter had stirred something up.

They approached the entrance to her building. She took her keys from her bag. For an instant, it seemed almost as if everything was normal. Only, he knew it wasn't. "What?" he said. "What's wrong?"

Her eyes started to well up. "I can't do this anymore," she said as she reached out and placed her hand on his chest. "I'm sorry." She started weeping.

"What are you talking about?"

"We can't be together anymore. We just can't!"

"Miriam, what's this about?"

She took a deep breath, knowing she didn't have a good answer, at least not one he would understand. She'd tried hinting about her dilemma in the past, saying just enough to get him to comply with her rules about being touchy-feely outside their grad school circle. She knew her previous explanations had been cryptic and insufficient, and now she realized that she had no choice but to give him the full picture. "My parents are going through a really hard time with this Noah thing."

Raj looked at her curiously. He was aware that Noah had come out to her parents a few weeks ago, but he couldn't comprehend what that had to do with their relationship. He waited for her to clarify.

"My mother tells me my father's, like, depressed or something," she continued. "He's walking around in a fog or a daze and is hardly even talking. She doesn't know what to do." Her lips were quivering. "And if my mother doesn't know what to do, then it's really bad, because she usually knows just what to do."

"Miriam," he said. "I know this is really hard for you, and I don't want to sound insensitive, but I don't get what it has to do with us."

"Everything!" she said. "It has everything to do with us."

"How? Why?" Baffled.

"My father's an Orthodox rabbi," she said, more as an explanation than a fact.

He still looked perplexed.

She realized she had no choice but to elaborate, to say things she'd never wanted to say, things she knew would only hurt him and probably leave him feeling that she was a contemptible person from a contemptible family with a contemptible religion. And, she believed, he would have every right to feel that way. "My family, we're Orthodox, and being gay, it isn't okay." She paused to consider her words.

He waited.

"It's not okay," she continued, "because it's totally unacceptable in my father's world. It's against the religion, the Bible, everything. For my parents, especially my father, it's a *really* bad thing. It's probably destroying him inside. And now, on top of that, I just can't imagine what it will do to him when he finds out I'm dating a non-Jewish guy, because that's also against everything he believes. I don't even know which is worse in his eyes, but both of them together is just..." She couldn't find the words to finish her sentence.

"So, you're worried that Zoe's going to say something, and how your father's going to react? But what about you, Miriam? Do you feel the same way about me as your father does?"

"It's not about that. He doesn't have any bad feelings about you, he doesn't even know you. It's just that you aren't Jewish, that's all that matters."

"But if I were Jewish, and a dick, that would be okay?"

"You know that's not true."

He looked at her, unconvinced, wordless.

"The sad thing is that he's really a sweet and wonderful man, and he would feel that you are too, if he knew you."

"So, why isn't that enough?"

"Because it isn't."

"Even for you?'

She hesitantly nodded. "Look, it's not about what I feel or whether I agree with my parents. It's about what I have to do. I know this sounds terrible. I know I'm weak and I'm a really bad person, but I just can't…" Again, she couldn't get the words out.

"And how do you know Zoe will say something?"

"I don't. But it doesn't matter. Sooner or later, one way or another, it's going to come out."

"Maybe later, after your parents have adjusted to the news about Noah. Then it might not be as difficult for them."

"They're never going to adjust to that, and it's always going to be difficult."

Raj just stood there, once again speechless. For a moment, he imagined how his parents would have embraced and adored her. True, they were Hindus, but they weren't shackled to their tradition in the same way as her parents. All they wanted was for him to find pure love. And now, amid all this, he couldn't accept that there was anything more important than that.

Miriam lay in bed, staring at the ceiling after tossing and turning for almost two hours. She was all cried out, left only with ruminations about how awful a person she was. In her mind, the choice was simple—awful person or awful daughter—and somehow her own happiness didn't seem to matter. That's how she saw it. It was also becoming apparent to her that sleep wasn't in the cards.

She sat up on the side of the bed. In the darkness, she was still able to see the clothes she'd quickly tossed on a chair just a few feet away. She was usually more fastidious than that, never leaving things strewn about. Clothing was either rehung or put in the laundry basket. Everything was always tidy with her, except her present circumstances.

She stood up and walked to the bathroom. Not because she had to go, but because she didn't know what to do with herself. She splashed some water on her face, went back into the bedroom and sat down on the bed. Glancing again at her clothes, she decided to get dressed.

She finished dressing, grabbed her coat and her bag, and left the apartment. It was just after 4 a.m. Her roommates were asleep, and the street was empty. The Upper West Side was a pretty safe neighborhood, as far as city neighborhoods go, yet she knew it probably wasn't the best idea for a woman to be out alone this time of night. She didn't really care.

She started walking toward West End Avenue, then made a right and headed north. She was acting on pure instinct, lacking any forethought of the consequences for her behavior. She just felt that she had to go where she was going.

She came to Raj's building and pressed the front door buzzer. The voice on the intercom belonged to one of his roommates and sounded wide awake. She wasn't surprised. They were always up, especially on weekends.

He buzzed her in without a moment's pause. She assumed that he either had no clue about what had happened earlier with Raj and her, or he was stoned and had little idea of what he was doing. She also anticipated that Raj was likely already asleep, or at least hidden in his room.

When she entered the apartment, it was apparent to her that she'd been correct on both accounts. The roommate, Sonny, simply said hi and walked off. He was obviously out of it. She looked in the living room and saw three guys and three girls sitting around quietly, seemingly lost in their own worlds. One of the girls acknowledged her and lifted a hand, attempting a wave. Miriam responded in kind.

She made her way to Raj's bedroom, stopped at the door, took a breath and knocked lightly. No answer. She gently turned the knob, slowly opened the door and found him sound asleep, just as she'd expected. She couldn't help but admire his ability to do that. While the smallest of problems usually meant total insomnia for her, not even a nuclear attack could keep him awake. *Not even a broken heart,* she reflected.

She watched him sleep for a minute or so, not sure if she should turn on her heel and retreat or wake him and tell him she'd made a mistake. She stared at him, thinking what a beautiful man he was. *And what a confused woman I am.*

Suddenly, her hands started unbuttoning her blouse. Slow, hesitant, but determined, as if possessed by some external force. After undoing her belt buckle and unsnapping her pants, she froze again. Standing in her bra and undies, her pants gathered around her ankles, she took another breath, eased her feet from the pants, and walked slowly to the bed.

She lifted the blanket and managed to slip in beside him while he continued to sleep. She contemplated lying there till he eventually woke up. *And then what?*

She slid closer to him and started caressing him, at which point he opened his eyes and looked at her.

"Huh?" he uttered.

"Shh," she said softly. Talking wasn't on her mind.

No, he wasn't dreaming, he told himself. *She's here and I'm awake.* And, bewildered as he was, he kept silent as he rolled himself upon her and glided his tongue into her mouth.

Being beneath him in that way was more than she could bear. She could do nothing but surrender, which was exactly what she had done the moment she had left her own apartment. To what she was surrendering, she didn't yet fully grasp, and at that moment, she didn't want to think too much about it. All she knew was that she had lost any semblance of mastery over her fate, an acknowledgement that left her terrified.

He, on the other hand, was relieved to find that she couldn't just break away as she had attempted, that she was bound to him by a power far greater than the forces dividing them. But this, he feared, was only a reprieve and not a solution. Their future remained undefined and, notwithstanding their attachment to each other, was bound to be fraught with conflict and agony.

Could they survive all this intact? He, too, didn't want to think about it. For now, they belonged to each other, and that would have to be enough.

18

DAVID WEISBERG, IN HIS duty as treasurer, called to order Beth Israel's monthly board meeting. A managing partner at a downtown Manhattan accounting firm, and a respected Torah scholar in his own right, Weisberg, like Jonathan, was from rabbinic lineage. He owed his professional achievements to an unrelenting work ethic and a keen intellect. He too was reared in an elite Brooklyn yeshiva, similar to Jonathan's alma mater, and his accounting career was perfectly suited to his personality. He was a fairly rigid black-and-white sort, old-school, forever destined to view the world through the very same lens he had back in his yeshiva days.

Weisberg was a rather prodigious sort, large both vertically and horizontally. And always well put together: expensive Italian suits, freshly shined shoes, starched white dress shirt with a perfectly crafted Windsor. Conforming to his staunch religious leanings, his balding head was covered by a sizeable black velvet yarmulke. Less conforming was his clean-shaven, youthful face. He had once confided in Jonathan that his wife simply hated beards. "Everyone has his compromises," had been Jonathan's reaction, acutely aware that he was telling this to one of the least compromising people he knew.

Every synagogue had issues of dissension among some of its members. For Beth Israel, officially a Modern Orthodox synagogue, there was a split between its more and less observant families. At the start of Jonathan's tenure, the congregation had been fairly liberal by Orthodox standards, with some families barely keeping Shabbos while others were occasionally seen dining in non-Kosher restaurants. Over the years, things had changed. The arrival in the Five Towns of transplants from the fervently Orthodox enclaves of Brooklyn and Queens introduced a more devout demography, which initially filled the pews of some of the smaller and less established synagogues. Eventually, however, they found their way to Beth Israel. David Weisberg was among this crowd and a thorn in Jonathan's side from the moment he had set foot in the *shul.* Now he was the treasurer, the man who holds the purse strings and, after this meeting, likely the next president. Jonathan could certainly weather a president he didn't always seen eye to eye with—it had happened a couple of times over the years—but with the recent events in his family, he had a gnawing sense that things were destined to change.

"I have a letter here from Benjy Marcus," Weisberg said in his deep, hoarse voice. He then cleared his throat, which he did quite often as if it were a tic.

Everyone in the room looked at one another. They all knew what the letter said.

"He's resigning his position as president forthwith," Weisberg continued.

"And expresses his heartfelt apologies for any difficulties or embarrassment he has caused the community," Jonathan added. He made no secret of his continued fondness for Benjy.

Weisberg nodded. "The question is, what do we do now?"

"That's a good question," Meyer Strauss responded. Strauss, the synagogue's executive director, was an unassuming, gentle fellow with thick spectacles and a goatee. "I looked at the *shul's* bylaws earlier. There's a clause that says, if the president's term should be cut short for any reason, then the board is to elect a new president. It doesn't have to be the entire board, only a majority, which is what we seem to have here tonight. And there's no need for a congregational meeting."

"You mean there's no specific order of succession?" Weisberg said, surprised.

"It's been talked about, but we never actually got around to implementing it," Jonathan said.

The synagogue had been lucky that no past president had resigned or died while serving, at least not as far back as anyone in that room could recall. There had been one, Jake Friedman, who had taken ill with cancer and had wanted to resign, but the board had insisted he continue to hold the title while others actually did the work. There were a few vice presidents of this and that at any given time, and some talk, as Jonathan pointed out, of making one of them the next in order of succession. Somehow, other pressing matters always seemed to usurp the agenda.

"I guess we have to pick a new president," Strauss said.

Everyone seemed to nod in agreement.

"Who wants it?" Weisberg blurted out with a smirk.

Not a single response. It was a volunteer position requiring a great deal of time and work with absolutely no perks, aside from constant headaches. Jonathan was secretly hoping that someone other than Weisberg would step up. A mild irritant at any other time, Weisberg was beginning to look like a potential nightmare. Jonathan couldn't guess when Noah's situation would become public knowledge, but he could very well guess just how Weisberg and his ilk would react when it did.

"It probably should be you, David," Shmuel Ehrlich said. A medical doctor whose family had moved into the community just three years earlier, Ehrlich was one of the younger members of the board and, like Weisberg, a purist when it came to religious matters.

Jonathan felt some of the others looking to him for a response but remained impassive. Regardless of what he thought, it wasn't his place to weigh in on who became his "boss."

"Well, it looks like there aren't any other takers," Weisberg said. *Ahem.* He perused the room for a moment and waited for another suggestion. "Okay," he said haltingly, "I suppose someone should propose a nomination."

"Right," said Ehrlich. "I nominate David Weisberg for president of the *shul.*"

"Is there a second?" Weisberg asked.

The room was silent. Jonathan gazed over at Shelly Wolff, one of Sarah's closest friends, who was in charge of the youth committee, and nodded ever so slightly, hoping no one noticed. "Yes," Shelly said. "I second."

Shelly understood that Jonathan's signal to her was because he wanted to quash the tension in the room. This wasn't a time for debate or divisiveness. Their community was in crisis and needed to move on. He would do whatever it took to facilitate that.

"Okay," Weisberg said, followed this time with a major rumble. "All in favor, say aye!"

There were nine people present, all responding "aye," though some with more enthusiasm than others.

It will be fine, Jonathan told himself. He would make it work. He would figure it out. Just like everything else. *You always figure things out.*

Sarah was sitting up in bed, working on her laptop, when she heard the front door open. She looked at the clock: 9:36 p.m. Earlier than she'd thought he would get home. *There must have been little if any debate,* she told herself, correctly presuming the outcome.

She thought about whether she should go downstairs and join him. Usually at this time she would be on the den couch doing her thing while waiting for him. She'd taken to the bedroom about a week earlier, a reaction to his having become uncommunicative and withdrawn. She still wasn't sure whether this was a deliberate gesture on her part or just an instinctive response.

It wasn't that they were in a spat, it was that he had simply shut down and she noticed that it was only with her. She didn't personalize it, for she knew that he had no choice but to fake it with others, even their children. With her, however, it was different. His home was his refuge, the one place in which he was entitled to behave as he actually felt. And till now, she'd been thinking that this was probably what he needed.

But enough is enough, she told herself as she closed the laptop. She knew he was going through pretty much the hardest time of his life, and she was trying to be helpful. Leaving him alone, however, no longer seemed a viable option. It wasn't working for her and it wasn't working for him.

She got out of bed, put on her slippers, and came downstairs. He was already in the kitchen with his dinner. He looked up, almost expressionless, as she entered.

"How'd it go?" she asked.

"Oh, just great." Sarcasm.

"Is it Weisberg?"

"As we expected."

She could see that he was eager for his dinner and wondered if it was actually hunger or avoidance. "Want company?" she asked.

"It's okay, you can go back to what you were doing. I'll be fine."

"I think I'll join you." Resolute.

He looked at her, suspecting she was up to something. After two weeks of leaving him to stew in his despondency, she was shifting gears. He certainly wasn't in the mood for a "conversation," but accepted the fact that he didn't always get to decide. "Okay," he said, a bit more warily than he'd intended.

"Good," she said as she sat down.

"I think maybe I'll get myself a drink."

"Not a bad idea."

He cracked a smile, the first she'd seen in some time. "Want one?" he asked.

"No. I'm good."

He got up and sauntered over to the bar in the dining room. He perused his collection of single malts and bourbons, and reached for the Widow Jane 10-year-old, his favorite of the moment. He took a snifter from beneath the bar—he enjoyed his bourbon in a snifter—and poured himself what some might call a "double." Slightly over 2 ounces, twice his usual allotment, just enough to take the edge off. He surprised himself as he poured the glass. He had always been adamantly opposed to using alcohol for this purpose and had been quite outspoken about this publicly on several occasions. Another lesson in humility, he supposed, as he made his way back to the kitchen: be careful not to judge others.

"That's a nice drink," Sarah remarked as she saw how much was in the glass.

Jonathan sighed. "I know." He sat down, looked her in the eye, and took a healthy sip. He waited for the bourbon to go down. "Okay, I'm ready," he said.

"Ready?"

"You obviously want to talk."

She wore a curious expression. "Of course I want to talk. That's what we usually do, isn't it?"

Contemplation. "Yes, you're right. I guess I've been a bit of a grouch."

"That would be putting it mildly."

He took a breath. "I'm sorry."

"What's going on, Yoni?"

"*What's going on*? You know what's going on."

"I know what's going on with Noah. I just don't know what's going on with you."

He thought about that for a moment. "I can't help feeling that everything's been turned upside down."

She looked at him, waiting for more.

"This thing with Noah," he continued, "I honestly don't know how to process it, what to do about it." He stared at the snifter as he turned it in his hands. "The only thing I do know is that it's going to make life difficult for him. I worry about his being able to stay religious, how just about everything is going to be harder."

She nodded, indicating she shared the same concerns.

"And I don't mean to be selfish," he continued, "but I fear it's going to have other implications for us. I just can't help thinking that it's going to get out and it's going to cause some problems for us in the community."

"The community?" she said. "They love you!"

"They love me?" Reflective. "Maybe some, maybe even most." Hesitation. "But that love is conditional. They want their rabbi to be perfect, to live a perfect life, always say and do perfect things, and have a perfect family. They need for us to be exemplary in every way." He thought for a moment, then added, "Something like this could cause problems. I'm not saying they would be insurmountable problems, but there may be some rough times ahead."

"So, they'll just have to get used to us being human, just like they are," she responded.

"If they can," he uttered softly.

Finding herself at a loss regarding this part of their discussion, she decided instead to change the subject. "And what about the *halachic* issue?" she asked, referring to the Jewish legal position on homosexuality. She had been reticent to pose this question, knowing it touched upon what was probably his deepest inner conflict. But now that they were finally talking, they might as well get it all out.

"There's that," he responded sadly. "I can't deny it. It bothers me that my son will be living a life that is clearly prohibited by the Torah."

"But didn't God make him this way?"

Deep down, he felt her question was a good one, though on this he was truly torn. He believed that God created all types of people with varying inclinations, but that Jewish law still held every individual accountable for his or her behavior. And that was just it —the Torah didn't prohibit being a homosexual, it prohibited homosexual behavior. The proscription was simple: if one has homosexual inclinations, then one shouldn't act on them. The inclination itself is seen as yet another challenge from God among the multitude of challenges God often puts in our path. They are meant to be overcome, not indulged.

That was the lecture he could have given her but wasn't about to. It was the advice he could have offered Noah but had also chosen not to. Noah, like his mother, was well aware of the nuances of Jewish law, and any rabbi that Noah may have spoken to about this would certainly have stressed this principle. But he was a father in this, not a rabbi, and he could never ask his son to repress or deny his most basic instinct for love and intimacy. And while part of him vacillated over whether he should, he knew he never could.

"I know. I get that," he said. "I don't have the answer to any of this." His eyes welled up.

"You're not supposed to have the answer." She ran her hand through his hair. "Maybe there is no answer. We just have to live our lives the best way we can, take each day and obstacle as it comes and deal with it. Noah is hurting. Our priority is to be there for him and to love and support him no matter what. And the most important thing is that we do it together, not separately. You're not alone in this, and I want you to stop moping around as if you are!"

He looked at her, nodded, and wiped away his tears with his hand. She handed him a napkin and as he grabbed it, he relinquished any last semblance of control. And he wept.

She had never seen him this way, not even after his parents died. He had always been the one who held it together, and now their roles were reversed. She moved her seat beside him and wrapped her arms around him as he welcomed her embrace and buried his head on her shoulder. Exactly as Noah had on that Friday night that forever changed their lives.

19

AARON BAUMAN HAD SPENT the past month debating when and how to tell his wife about Noah. He was worried about how understanding she would be, yet realized he couldn't avoid it forever. She was the only family member aside from his children who didn't know, so he figured he no longer had a choice.

She had probed him about Noah and Ilana that night in New York when he and Noah had gone to the basketball game, and he had glossed over it at the time, telling her that Noah had simply attributed the breakup to "incompatibility." He had been feeling guilty that he'd misled her and wanted to set things straight. So now he was simply waiting for the right moment.

His reticence was rooted in what he truly believed was an accurate assumption: she would not take kindly to the news. Sheindy was a Borough Park girl, through and through, educated in right-wing, single-sex schools and a post high school women's seminary in lieu of college. Getting her out of Brooklyn had been arduous, to say nothing of moving her to LA. Most of it, he knew, had been about leaving her family. But there was also her desire to raise her children in an ultra-Orthodox milieu. She still hadn't given up on that and rarely squandered an opportunity to remind him how the heterogeneity of their current surroundings scared her.

On some level, he had to admit that this was one of the things that actually endeared her to him. She was truly zealous in her beliefs, outspoken and enthusiastic. It was part of what made her a great mother and a great wife, albeit not always the best *rebbetzin*. And while on the surface she appeared radically different from his own mother, in truth they were quite alike. Their philosophies may have been distinct, as they came from dissimilar backgrounds, but their strength of devotion to their respective families and ideals was identical.

Aaron looked up at the ceiling. They were lying in bed after just having put the kids down for the night. This was usually their together time, for chatting or, depending on the time of the month, sex. Sheindy wasn't due for the *mikvah*, the ritual bath, till tomorrow, which would then allow them about two weeks of physical intimacy. And, mindful of how a conversation such as this might get in the way of that, Aaron felt he didn't have any options. It had to be tonight, so it had to be now.

"I have some not such great news," he said, figuring that as good an opening as any.

She turned over to face him, looking at once both curious and concerned.

"It's about Noah," he said.

"What? What's wrong?"

Hesitation. "Well, when you asked about him and Ilana back in New York, I wasn't completely truthful."

She looked at him incredulously—she could never have imagined him being anything less than honest.

He realized that it would be best if he stopped dancing around the issue. Once he told her, he reasoned, she would understand why he hadn't. "Noah confided in me. It's a secret he's been hiding for a long time... He told me he's gay."

"Gay?" Astounded.

"Yes. Gay." He couldn't think of anything else to add.

"Oh my God!" she said, visibly shaken.

It was pretty close to what he'd expected, and he was fairly certain that there was little he could offer at the moment to mollify her. Yet he had to try. "Sheindy, I didn't say he has cancer. I said he is gay."

"I know what you said. It's still very upsetting."

He considered her point. "I agree."

"Do your parents know?"

He nodded.

"And how did they react?"

He took a breath. "Not well." He figured he didn't have to go into the details. She knew his parents and could easily imagine their reactions to such news.

"Your father must really be beyond upset."

He understood why she singled out his father. The differences between Sarah and Jonathan were apparent to all who knew them, and while Sarah was likely struggling with Noah's revelation, Jonathan was undoubtedly suffering. "That sounds about right," he said.

"And you?"

Her leaving Miriam out of the equation here was also understandable. They both knew that Miriam would be the last in the family to have a problem with anything of this sort. "I'm not happy about it. But he is my brother," he said.

She nodded. "This is horrible!" She wasn't one to mince her words. "For Noah, for you, for your parents." Hesitation. "And what about our children?"

He had anticipated this question. He too had been concerned about the same thing. "I don't know."

"What do we tell them?" she muttered under her breath.

They had a 4-month-old baby girl, a 2-year-old son, and a soon-to-be 4-year-old daughter, all obviously too young for any such conversation. But the future was another matter and certainly something to worry about. How, exactly, they would tell their children to accept or even embrace something so expressly forbidden in their world was an unnerving question indeed. "I don't think that's what we need to be thinking about right now," he said.

"I know. I'm sorry. It's just that..."

"I understand," he interjected. "But I really believe it's best if we take it one step at a time. Right now, I'm really worried about Noah. He sounds okay, but he can't be feeling good about any of this. He knows he's created turmoil in the family, and it's also probably going to cause some stress for my father regarding his position." He dropped his head. "It's a total mess."

"What about *your* position?" she asked.

He considered her question. "Honey, we're in California. Do you honestly think anybody in our community will care if their rabbi's brother is gay?"

She looked at him askance.

"I actually think it might have an opposite effect," he continued. "People out here want to be so enlightened, open, and modern that it might make them appreciate me more."

"Really." Sarcasm.

"Maybe."

It was apparent to her that he was just trying to brush the concern aside. *A weak attempt*, she thought.

"Well, if I'm wrong, it could work for you. They'll fire me, and then you can go back to Brooklyn," he said wryly.

She managed a smile. It was just like him to so easily turn a negative into a positive. It was one of the things she loved most about him. But still, she was far from convinced that any of this was going to turn out well—not for him, their children, his parents, or anyone.

20

ZACH ABRAMSON peered into Noah's eyes and was keen on what he saw. This was their third date since Noah had come out to his parents, and while there was still no real intimacy to speak of, something about this evening gave Zach a sense that it might very well end differently. He couldn't pinpoint exactly what it was, but it felt like Noah was turning a corner.

The setting was the Sony Atrium in Midtown, just outside *Pizza Da Solo,* a popular kosher Neapolitan pizza place. It was important to both of them to dine only at kosher establishments, despite the occasional risk of being noticed. It had been particularly challenging on their past two dates, with Noah frequently looking around to see who was there, appearing self-conscious. Tonight, however, he seemed less concerned.

They had just come from the latest blockbuster movie, Deadpool, and decided on a bite before heading back uptown. It was

Thursday night and many of the Atrium's aluminum tables were occupied by people who possibly could know either one of them, yet Noah was acting unfazed.

"You okay?" Zach asked.

"Yeah, why not?"

"Well, you don't look uncomfortable."

"Uncomfortable?'

"Yeah. You're usually uptight when we're together in places like this."

Noah considered his point. "I know," he said. He didn't feel the need to explain or defend himself. They were both more than aware of the issues. "Well, I'm not uptight tonight." A smile.

"That's good."

"Isn't it? See how that shrink's been helping?"

"Indeed. Maybe I should go see him."

"Find your own. He's mine!"

The two men looked at each other, sharing a moment of deep fondness, perhaps even more. "You think they know what we're about?" Zach asked, referring to the people surrounding them.

"Some probably do, or at least are guessing. But I think most of them just see us as two guys who can't get girls or something like that."

Zach contemplated. "Yeah, something like that."

Noah felt like he wanted to take Zach's hand, but their surroundings precluded such a move. He was definitely more at ease, but not recklessly adventurous. It wasn't about what anyone might think—he was definitely past that—but was very much about his parents and his brother. He didn't want to do anything publicly that might cause them difficulties. It wasn't necessary, and he could easily take Zach's hand when they were alone. Though, in his mind, he was imagining much more than that.

They finished eating fairly quickly, each sensing that the other was eager to get on to the next phase of the evening.

They arrived in front of Zach's building. Thus far, their routine had been for Noah to walk with Zach, who lived closer to the subway, and then proceed to his own place. Neither had actually been in the other's apartment. Along with their understanding of postponing sexual contact, they'd intentionally avoided situations that could make it difficult.

"So?" Zach said as they each stood shivering. He knew he didn't need to say more. It was clearly on both their minds.

"Is that an invitation?"

Zach nodded. "But decide quickly, please! It's freezing out here."

Having been the one who had originally put the kibosh on physical intimacy, the decision was clearly Noah's. Shivering from the cold made it easy to hide his nervousness, but he was still certain Zach could see it.

"Okay."

With that, the two men speedily entered the building. And with that, Noah Bauman took the next step toward what he had come to believe was his destiny.

21

JONATHAN BAUMAN BARELY STARTED to doze in his recliner when a knock on the front door jolted him awake. He removed the newspaper from his lap and was about to get up when he heard Sarah scuttling down the stairs from the bedroom. "That's for me," she exclaimed.

He took the paper from the table to resume his reading. Such was his routine every Shabbos afternoon: lunch, clean up, then the recliner. He always started with a religious book, until his concentration waned and he surrendered to either *The New York Times* or *The Wall Street Journal*. While most of his reading time—what little he had—was spent with Talmudic texts and the like, he was still fanatical about staying informed. Both papers were part of his daily routine, as was his fascination with their occasional discrepancies. But on Shabbos afternoon, the time of the week when he found himself most exhausted, they provided little more than a good nap.

He heard the familiar voices of Sarah's girlfriends. "I'm leaving. See you later," she called out as the front door closed behind her. Sarah had skipped the Shabbos walk for the past two weeks, explaining that she was feeling under the weather. He had been skeptical, assuming there was more to it, like not wanting to face her intimate circle so soon after the news from Noah. In any event, he was glad she went. He had been working hard to get back to his normal self, and seeing her do the same was most reinforcing.

He turned toward the window and watched the ladies stroll down the block. It was a sunny, pleasant day, the bitter cold of February having faded into an early March thaw. *A good day for a walk,* he considered, but he was way too glued to his recliner. He returned to his paper, hoping this time to get through a few more pages before drifting off once again.

The ladies were well into their walk, covering every topic from world politics to the latest price hikes at a local supermarket, and all but Sarah had updated the others on recent family happenings. "So, what's going on with your clan?" Aviva Mandel asked Sarah. Aviva was Sarah's oldest childhood friend and married to a pediatric oncologist with whom Sarah often shared referrals. In fulfillment of the girls' lifelong promise to always be close to each other, the Mandels had moved to Lawrence shortly after Jonathan had taken his position.

Sarah had anticipated this question with trepidation. Now she had to drum up an answer. She and Jonathan had decided that it wasn't their place to disclose Noah's situation. That was for Noah to do, as he saw fit, and they figured the news would spread from there. It always did.

She was tempted to go with a vague response but knew that would only arouse suspicion. These were her closest friends, it wasn't easy to conceal things from them. "Well, Aaron's doing great out there, but Sheindy still has her heart set on coming back."

"To live in Brooklyn?" asked Devorah Wasser. Devorah was Aviva Mandel's sister and the most religious of the group. She was married to an ultra-Orthodox rabbi of a small neighboring *shul*, but among her friends, she was known to occasionally say things uncharacteristic of her background and position. This seemed to be one of those occasions. "Who would want to live in Brooklyn when they could live in LA? Makes absolutely no sense to me."

"I agree," added Esther Marcus.

Esther, understandably, had also been AWOL for the past two weeks. The others were pleased to see her out and about once again and were impressed by her composure. She had been quite forthcoming just minutes earlier about her decision to stand by Benjy despite his dalliance with his assistant.

Sarah felt bad about being evasive while Esther was so open. But that was how it had to be. Esther's disclosure was about herself, whereas Sarah's secret was about Noah. And while she was confident that they would eventually find out, she was equally confident they would understand and forgive her for having kept them in the dark.

"She just wants to be close to her parents. I can understand that," Sarah said.

"So can I," said Giti Seif. Giti, a social worker who specialized in Orthodox Jewish teenagers at risk, had recently become a grandmother for the first time. "It's always better to be near family," she added with a touch of sadness, bemoaning the fact that her son, daughter-in-law, and newborn granddaughter lived across the world in Israel.

"And what's with Miriam and Noah?" asked Devorah Wasser.

The others looked uneasily at one another, realizing that Devorah didn't grasp that this was a sore spot for Sarah. Especially with regard to Miriam. Not that Sarah wasn't delighted with Miriam's accomplishments, for they all knew that she couldn't have been prouder. But Miriam's marital status weighed on her mother. It was flatly unusual in this community for a 24-year-old woman to be single without any prospects. And, as educated and enlightened as Sarah was, this was a hard pill for her to swallow.

As for Noah, there was—predictably—a slight double standard. Although he was approaching the upper end of acceptable age for a man to be single in their community, he was nevertheless granted more leeway. And while his series of failed relationships may have been cause for concern, his situation was still somewhat easier for Sarah to accept. Or so these women thought.

"They're both doing well. Miriam's really absorbed in school. She just finished interviewing for externships for next year and is waiting to see where she places. She seems stressed about it, and I can understand. I remember what I went through with residency."

"What's her first choice?" Giti Seif asked. Being in an allied field, she knew more than the others about the various possibilities.

"She's hoping for LIJ," Sarah said, using the acronym for Long Island Jewish, one of the area's more prestigious hospitals. "But it's very competitive."

"It certainly is!" Giti confirmed. "But she's brilliant, articulate, and beautiful. I'm sure she'll get it."

"From your mouth to God's ears," Sarah replied. She realized she'd said nothing about Noah and was hoping it would go unnoticed, that they could just continue on as if his name hadn't been mentioned.

"You know, I've been thinking about Noah," Devorah Wasser interjected. "If he's ready to date yet, I may have someone."

So much for that, Sarah mused.

Aviva looked at Sarah, her expression saying, *I know you'd rather be talking about anything other than this.* "Oh, I don't think he's ready to get fixed up yet," she said. "I mean, he just broke off a long relationship. The boy needs some time to recoup." She took a breath. "By the way, did you hear about Orit Harris?" she asked, referring to a young woman from the community who recently left her gap-year seminary in Israel to join the IDF, the Israel Defense Forces.

Sarah smiled at her old friend, acknowledging Aviva's artful way of changing the subject. *I owe you one.* And just like that, the discussion turned to Orit Harris, each of the women having a different take on how the young lady's parents were either oblivious, *plotzing*, or proud. It was occasionally a thing in their circles for a young man to join the IDF in lieu of, or after, his gap year in yeshiva. It was far less common for women, and even more unusual to drop out of seminary altogether.

"Orit has always been more independent-minded than many of her peers," Sarah said. "She's following her own path. It's a good thing." She thought a moment. "I'm sure her parents are conflicted about it, but I'm also sure they're proud."

"I couldn't agree more," said Esther Marcus. "Our kids usually do what we or their friends tell them to do. Orit is different. It's not every day an 18-year-old makes a major life choice based on values. I think she's very brave, and I think it's to be applauded."

"Well I don't," said Devorah Wasser. "The Israeli army is no place for a religious girl. Who knows what goes on there? I think it's a bad choice."

Sarah was a bit taken aback that Devorah, who didn't always stick to the ultra-Orthodox party line, was now doing so. She couldn't help but wonder how her friend would react to learning about Noah. She wanted to give Devorah the benefit of the doubt, but she just wasn't sure.

"I'm with Devorah on this," Giti Seif chimed in. "We send our children to Israel for a year or two believing it's good for them, and next thing you know they're not coming back. I don't know if they get brainwashed or what, but I'm not sure we're doing the right thing."

"I'm certain Orit's seminary didn't brainwash her into dropping out mid-year to go to the army," Sarah said.

Giti nodded, seemingly realizing she was focusing on her own situation and just using the opportunity to blow off some steam.

The group found itself standing in front of Sarah's house once again. The walk was over. Sarah was relieved. The Noah question had been forgotten and would have to wait till next week when, surely, it was bound to resurface. Who knew what would happen between now and then? They would either learn the truth from another source, or she'd have to figure out yet another way to dance around it.

Jonathan emerged from the house and headed down the front path toward them. He was on his way to the Synagogue, where he would wind down Shabbos with a late-day class, afternoon services, a small bite to mark the third required meal of the day, and the final evening service. These rituals attracted most of the men but only a handful of women.

"Anyone care to join me?" he said with a smirk as he approached the group. He knew there would be no interest from these ladies. It was the same scene that repeated itself on almost any given Shabbos afternoon when their paths crossed.

They all smiled back and said, "No, thank you," almost in unison.

"How was the walk?" he asked.

He heard the adjectives *good, great* and *fine*, while noticing Sarah simply nodding. He could tell from her expression that she had managed to get through the walk without any pitfalls.

"Well, you had good weather for it," he said to the group.

"It's about time," Aviva Mandel said.

"Indeed," Jonathan rejoined.

"You should get going," Sarah said to him.

He wasn't sure if she was eager to get rid of him or just to get herself back into the house so she could be alone. "Yes, it's not a good thing for the rabbi to be late," he said.

She nodded again, urging him to get moving. And as he turned and left, a vivid memory came to her of the very first time she watched him walk away like that, her thought then the same as now: he carries himself like a prince.

And for her, he was a prince—of God, among men—most importantly, her prince. Close to three decades together, and their biggest speed bump had been convincing her family and friends that he was the right one. It hadn't been easy, but not for a single moment since had she doubted her choice. And now, facing challenges far beyond either of their expectations, was no exception.

She understood why she was suddenly struck with such thoughts, and also understood the accompanying wave of heartache. She swallowed hard and told herself that whatever awaited on the horizon, she and he would face it together. And in the end, regardless of how things emerged, he would forever be her prince.

22

BENJY MARCUS SAT ACROSS from his attorney and friend, Avi Gerstein, silently processing the terrible news he'd just received. The latest offer from the state attorney general still required two years in prison. He had mentally prepared himself for six months, a year at most, but not this.

Far worse, he'd have to serve his sentence in a state prison. State prisons were dangerous hellholes and often quite a distance upstate. If they had kept the sentence to under a year, Benjy would have served it in Nassau County Jail, which was nearby, reputedly safer, and would have enabled Benjy's family to visit more often.

Avi was genuinely worried about how his client would fare being mixed in with hardened criminals and so far away from his family. Yet his clout as a lawyer and the sensibility of his arguments seemed useless against an AG determined to make an example of Benjy.

"I'm sorry, Benjy. My opinion is that the AG's political aspirations are getting in the way of his judgement. He wants to be governor or senator, and he sees your case as part of his ticket." Avi said.

It was the perfect case for such aspirations. The news had been replete with headlines like "Real Estate Magnate Charged with Bribing Highland Falls Mayor, City Council Members in Bid to Build Shopping Mall," and Avi believed that the AG was using the Marcus case to set an example for what was allegedly an industry-wide practice. And the fact that Marcus was an Orthodox Jew whose personal assistant and former lover had now turned state's evidence made it all the more titillating to the public.

Benjy remained speechless and seemed unable to find a relaxed position in his chair.

Avi felt awkward himself, watching one of the most confident men he had known crumble before his eyes. He also didn't know what to say next. "We can always push back, even threaten to go to trial. They might respond with a better deal," he offered, a bit less enthusiastically than Benjy would have preferred.

Benjy nodded. There was no one better at this than Avi Gerstein, he told himself. The lawyer was known for getting deals, sometimes even exonerations, for some very famous and infamous characters, many of whom had done far worse things than he. Avi would find a way. "It's okay," he said, also half-heartedly. "I'm sure you'll do all you can."

"And then some," Avi said, this time a bit more decisively.

Benjy lifted his head and leaned back into a more natural position, still trying to muster as much comfort as possible under the circumstances. "I guess that's it," he said.

"Well," Avi said, "there is another matter."

Benjy sat up.

"It's on something else altogether." Avi was hesitant, then added, "I know it's a bad time to bring this up, but it's about *Rav* Yoni."

Avi had Benjy's full attention.

"Actually," Avi continued, "it's really about David Weisberg."

"Weisberg?"

Now it was Avi shifting in his chair. Benjy just stared at him, wondering what was coming next.

"I've been hearing things," Avi said.

"What sort of things?" Edginess.

Avi breathed deeply. "I probably shouldn't say this to you, especially now, but I feel I have to. Despite everything, I want you to know that you're still widely respected in the community, and because of your closeness with *Rav* Yoni and Sarah, there are some conversations that are never held in your presence."

Benjy found the "widely respected" comment ironic. He was also fairly certain that he wasn't the only one in this room who was close with Jonathan. "What conversations?" he asked.

Avi pondered a moment before responding. "We both know that Weisberg isn't exactly a big fan of the rabbi."

Benjy nodded. He understood that Weisberg belonged to the *yeshivish* crowd—followers of the ultra-Orthodox way—as did many of the new young families in the congregation. And while Jonathan had originally come from that same background, he had evolved over the years toward a more compromising, modern approach. At least that was how it appeared in contrast.

"I'm concerned that he might try to make some changes."

"You mean replace *Rav* Yoni with someone younger and *frummer*?" he said, using the Yiddish term for more devout. "I've also had that thought, but I'm not so concerned. He really doesn't have the clout or the backing."

"I agree... But that could change."

Benjy raised his eyebrows.

"There's been some talk as of late," Avi continued. "I imagine in the end it's probably a lot of nonsense. But in the short run, it could be damaging."

"What's it about?"

Avi halted for a second. "Miriam."

"Miriam? What about her?"

Another pause. "There's a rumor floating around. Apparently one of the girls from the neighborhood ran into her at a party and says she was with a Muslim guy."

"*What*?"

"I know, it sounds ridiculous," Avi said. "But the way I heard it, they were holding hands and being *quite* friendly."

"Girl from the neighborhood! What girl from the neighborhood? And how does this girl know the guy was a Muslim?"

"All good questions, and I don't have any answers. I'm just repeating what I've heard."

"From whom?"

"From a few people. It's not important. I agree that it could very well be untrue, but you and I both know that it doesn't make any difference. It's all about perception."

Benjy nodded. He couldn't deny the point. "You really believe Weisberg's going to use this to undermine *Rav* Yoni?"

"I do. And there's more."

Benjy heaved a deep sigh. "More?"

"Again, just rumors and innuendos. This time about Noah."

Benjy's eyes widened.

"It seems," Avi continued, "some people... probably the very same group, are questioning his sexuality."

"I suppose that's not completely surprising."

"With his age, his history with women and all that, you can't tell me that you haven't considered the possibility," Avi said.

"I guess the thought had entered my mind once or twice. I've even joked with Noah about it. But Avi, you're a lawyer. His age and the number of women he's broken up with is hardly evidence of anything. I think he's just very choosy and hasn't found the right one yet."

"I hear you. But again, reality doesn't matter. When it comes to a position like *Rav* Yoni's, it's all about what people believe, not what they know."

Benjy was silent.

"Look, I'm sorry to saddle you with this. You already have enough to worry about. It's just that I suspect trouble's coming, and I frankly don't know who else to turn to."

Another deep breath. "I understand, but what can we do?"

"I don't know," Avi muttered.

"Neither do I." Contemplation. "Look, we both agree that *Rav* Yoni is as savvy as they come. I'm sure he's well aware of Weisberg's intentions, and he may have even heard the rumors about Miriam and Noah. My guess is, if he needs our help, he'll come to us. For now, I think we should just wait and see."

Avi nodded. "That's probably a good idea. Not much more we can do anyway."

"You know," Benjy said, "something like this could really split the congregation."

Avi nodded. "It could indeed." He considered his words. "Quite concerning."

"For you more than me," Benjy said with a smirk.

Avi looked at him curiously.

"I mean, I'll probably be sitting in a prison cell somewhere when it all comes down."

"Very funny."

The two men looked at each other, Benjy hoping Avi would say something reassuring like, "Don't worry, we'll figure out a way to get you less time," and Avi disquieted by the fact that he could offer no such guarantee. Two highly successful, powerful men. Two extraordinary problems, no solutions. A conundrum neither was accustomed to.

23

MIRIAM BAUMAN LOOKED AT her younger brother, observing an aura of equanimity that seemed somehow odd, distinctive from the subtle angst and unsettledness to which she had grown accustomed through the years. Sitting across from him and Zach, scrutinizing their every gesture, made her—she had to admit—uncomfortable. This would definitely take some getting used to.

It bothered her that it bothered her. After all, she was supposed to be the enlightened one. And it wasn't as if Raj, sitting beside her, fit neatly into their scheme either. But to her, he was somehow more suitable than Zach.

Perhaps she was convincing herself of this, she reasoned, to feel better about her own situation. But that couldn't be it, for she only felt worse. She just couldn't get her head around it, recalling simpler times, the days when she saw Noah as the dashing, charismatic lady's man for whom no woman would ever measure up. And now, here he was, finally finding fulfillment under the spell of another man.

She also wondered how much of her discomfort was due to the fact that Noah's situation made hers all the more impossible. It was easy to resent him for that, though she knew it was unreasonable. She couldn't blame him more than she blamed herself. After all, he really had no choice in this. She did.

Or did she?

They were at a table in the middle of O'Keefe's, an Amsterdam Avenue hot spot on most nights of the week, with a typical Irish pub motif: dimly lit bar, finished dark wood chairs and tables, and a rustic weathered oak floor. Being Tuesday, things were relatively quiet, exactly how they'd planned it.

The waitress arrived with a pitcher of Sam Adams' latest winter brew and four glasses, interrupting what was, in Miriam's mind, an exasperating conversation about the latest happenings in professional basketball. Despite her usual interest in the subject, her mind was as far away from this boyish, muscle-flexing, get to know one another ritual as possible.

"So, Zach," she interjected, "how did you guys meet?"

Noah threw her a curious look. "Didn't I tell you?" *I thought we weren't going to get into stuff like that.*

"I'm just trying to converse," she said. Slightly defensive.

"We are conversing," Noah responded.

"I'm bored," she said.

"It's okay," Zach said to both of them. "We met at a support group."

"Well, Raj, it's your turn," Noah said, leaning forward. "Where did you guys meet?"

"That's a good question," Raj said. He looked at Miriam. "Where *did* we meet?"

"In class," Miriam said. She looked at Noah and Zach, and said, "His head is sometimes in the clouds."

Ignoring her last remark, Raj said, "But we didn't *really* meet there."

"We saw each other. And we talked," she said.

"We talked?"

"Yes, we did." A little testy.

"If you say so," Raj uttered.

"So where do *you* think we met?" Miriam asked.

Raj paused to sip his beer. "I really haven't thought about it."

"And now that you are thinking about it?" she said.

Raj reflected for a moment. "I think it was actually the library."

"The library?"

Noah and Zach gazed on intently.

"Well, that's the first place I remember us speaking to each other."

"You're not supposed to talk in the library," Noah said glibly.

"That's why it stands out," Raj said. "Yes," he added emphatically, "that was our first meeting, if you want to call it that."

"How about encounter?" Zach asked.

"Well," Raj said, "it wasn't exactly our first 'encounter' either, but it was the first time we really talked. That's how I remember it. And, for me, that was when I started seeing her as more than just a classmate."

Miriam hit Raj on the arm. "Stop. You're being silly. And I want to hear more about my brother and Zach."

"Sounds like you had an agenda for this evening," Noah said to her.

"This evening was your idea, little brother," she responded. "*You* said you wanted me to meet Zach, and *you* were the one who suggested I bring Raj. So here we all are."

"Yes, here we all are," Zach said, trying to break the tension.

After a moment of silence, Miriam asked in a big-sisterly sort of way, "So, Zach, what are your plans?"

"My personal plans, or my plans with Noah?"

"I was actually asking about your plans with Noah, but you could tell me both."

"Unless you feel like you're being cross-examined," Noah said to him.

"No, I'm good," Zach said. He looked at Noah. "It's cool, really."

Miriam smiled. She was getting to like him.

"I'm going to law school next year also," Zach said. "But I'm sure Noah already told you that."

Miriam nodded. "He said you were going to Berkeley."

"I am," Zach said.

"That's complicated, you in California, Noah in Boston."

"It is that," Zach said, downing some beer.

"We haven't really thought about it," Noah said, also taking a sip. "We're kind of doing things day to day." He looked at Zach.

Zach nodded.

"What about you, Raj?" Noah asked. "What are your plans?"

Miriam threw Noah a look indicating her impatience with his not-so-subtle efforts to deflect the conversation.

Raj was hesitant. "To be a clinical psychologist," he said.

Noah peered at him inquisitively, awaiting more. Only, Raj wasn't taking the bait.

"I meant with my sister," Noah said.

"Noah!" Miriam said.

"If it's okay for you to ask Zach, it should be okay for me to ask Raj."

"It's different," Miriam said.

"Different?" Noah asked. "How so?"

"It just is," was all she could retort.

"What she wants to say," Raj interjected, "is that you guys are seriously involved, while we're..." He was having difficulty completing the sentence.

"What?" Noah asked. "What *are* you guys?"

Miriam and Raj looked at each other.

"We're," she said hesitantly, "undefined."

"Yes," Raj concurred. "We're undefined."

"How convenient," Noah muttered under his breath.

Miriam stared at him. "What? What does that mean?"

"I'm going to excuse myself," Zach said. "Nature's calling."

"Me too," Raj said eagerly as he stood up. He looked at Miriam and shrugged his shoulders. "Gotta go."

Left alone, Noah and Miriam looked at each other across the table.

"I have something I want to tell you, but I'm not sure if this is the time and place," Noah said.

"It's all right," Miriam said. "Say what's on your mind."

Noah thought for a moment. "Well, all I can say is, I've recently learned that it's very hard to live a lie." He waited a beat. "And even harder to stop living a lie."

"I'm not living a lie," she said insistently.

"If you say so."

She stared into space, contemplating the irony of the situation. She had always been the candid, upfront one, while he had been more mysterious and private. She had to admit, though, that he was wearing his newfound self rather well. Which was why she was finding it so difficult to respond. "I honestly think you're not being fair," she said.

He raised his eyebrows, waiting for her to continue.

"I've been with Raj for, like, three months and you've had your secret for how long? And I don't think I'm lying about anything. In fact, I don't believe I'd be telling Mom and Dad about Raj yet even if he was Jewish." She paused to drink as she saw that he was considering her points. "And there is one more thing."

"Which is?" he asked.

This was the very place she hadn't wanted to get to, yet here they were. *He wants the truth,* she told herself, *so give it to him.* "I don't know how to say this, so I'll..."

"Just say it."

"Well, I'm not claiming anything's your fault, and it really isn't. I mean, it's really great that you came out and that you're being who you are and all that..."

"But?"

"But." Hesitation. "I know it's not right of me, but I find myself blaming you for making my situation all the more difficult."

He looked away, took a deep breath, then turned back to her. "I know... I'm sorry for that."

"It's okay," she said, her voice slightly tremulous.

"Look, I know I didn't realize how my situation affects yours, but the important thing now is that we have each other's backs."

"And it's really good that we talked about it."

"Says the psychologist."

"Yeah. Says the psychologist."

Raj and Zach reappeared simultaneously, as if they'd deliberately waited till it seemed okay to return.

"Long bathroom break," Miriam said.

"Hopefully long enough," Raj replied as he took his seat. Miriam and Noah chuckled.

"Another pitcher?" Zach asked.

"We've barely touched the first one!" Miriam said.

"All the more reason for another," Raj said.

Noah attempted a sip. "I agree. This stuff is too warm."

"If you guys insist," Miriam said.

With that, they called the waitress, ordered another pitcher, and continued to talk as if everything was fine. Yet for her it wasn't. She could pretend for now, but a strain deep down in her psyche still gnawed at her. No longer a strain between sister and brother nor even the strain between boyfriend and girlfriend, which had also seemed to dissipate. But the strain within a young woman, caught between devotion to her parents and heritage, and her love for a man she wasn't supposed to be loving. And the frightening realization that she hadn't a clue of what to do about it.

24

SARAH BAUMAN SAT IN the driver's seat of her Nissan Rogue, double-parked on a narrow Queens street. Her ears were attuned to the classic soft rock of *The Bridge*, her favorite satellite radio station. Her eyes were affixed to the slightly unnerving surroundings. This part of Far Rockaway was but a stone's throw from the streets of Lawrence, yet twice the circumference of the earth vis-à-vis affluence and crime.

Of all her altruistic endeavors, the one she liked best was her Wednesday evening trips with Aviva Mandel delivering Shabbos food packages for the needy. Although it was safer to park the car and go into the apartment building together, there was seldom a spot to be had, so they usually switched between delivering and driving. Tonight was Aviva's turn to deliver.

Still, Sarah felt some guilt as she watched Aviva come and go. *The weather has taken a turn for the better,* she consoled herself. *At least the walk to and from the car is more bearable.*

Sarah was a little less worried about Aviva's safety walking around alone in the buildings than she'd been in the past. Their years of experience doing this had made them both a little tougher and bolder. She thought back to those first days, about a decade earlier, just before Miriam's Bat Mitzvah. During the months prior to the ceremony, all Bar and Bat Mitzvah candidates were required by the synagogue to take on a *chesed* project, a type of community service, for a few hours each week. This was how it all got started.

Aviva's daughter, Batya, was the same age as Miriam, so the four of them joined up with *Tomchei Shabbos,* an organization that provides the food and the routes. It was also an opportunity for these old friends to get their girls together, a relationship they had tried, albeit unsuccessfully, to cultivate over the years. The girls had gone through the same schools but always in separate social circles. It wasn't that they didn't like each other or were unfriendly, it was that they didn't have much in common. Batya was the quiet, reserved type, obedient and easy. Miriam was, well, Miriam.

The girls grew up and moved on but maintained a peripheral relationship with each other, occasionally exchanging Facebook messages. Now Batya was married with a newborn baby boy, and Miriam was doing her thing in graduate school. The mothers decided to continue the food deliveries without them. It was a good thing to do, and also a weekly opportunity to chat, just the two of them. It was time they cherished.

Sarah's meditation was interrupted by a knock on the window from Aviva. She unlocked the door. "All good?" Sarah asked, as Aviva got back into the car.

"Everything went well. Mrs. Stein, Marilyn, and the Nussbaums were all home and glad to see me," Aviva said. Mrs. Stein was an aging widow about whom little was known. They'd been delivering to her for at least five years, but the woman simply took the meals at the door and said little beyond "thank you" and "good Shabbos."

Marilyn was a talkative one. Somewhere in her late 40s, her mild cerebral palsy affected neither her intelligence nor her ability to communicate. She had no husband or children, so Sarah assumed that her proclivity to chew off one of their ears was probably the result of loneliness. She had once mentioned a sister in Florida, but it had sounded like there wasn't much of a relationship there.

The Nussbaums were an elderly couple, one of whom had an obvious hoarding problem. Aviva thought it was her; Sarah thought it was him. Either way, they did not relish the idea of being invited in. There was no place to sit, barely room to stand, and the place smelled awful. They'd made frequent offers to come another time, maybe help clean up the place, but the Nussbaums would have none of it. Sarah had even done a little research and found that the Nussbaums had a son in Brooklyn. A phone call from her, about a year ago, had produced nothing other than, "I'll look into it." There really wasn't anything else they could do.

These were their last deliveries for the evening. Their routine was to go to the local Starbucks and continue chatting over some decaf tea—hot in winter, iced in summer, whatever during fall and spring. Sarah put the car in drive and had barely pulled away when Aviva turned to her and said, "There's something I have to tell you."

"Sounds serious." Sarah could tell from Aviva's tone that this was going to be something she probably didn't want to hear.

"It is."

Sarah feared it was about Noah. It had been over a month since he'd come out to the family, so it was likely public knowledge at this point. It was also likely that her closest friend wouldn't be afraid to bring it up. That's how things were between them.

"It's about Miriam," Aviva said.

"Miriam?" Astonishment.

Aviva's momentary silence indicated to Sarah that she wasn't sure how to say what she wanted to say. And that it was bad news.

"Well?" Sarah said.

"I suppose I should just say it."

"Yes, you should!"

"I heard from Batya, who seemed to hear from some friends, that Miriam's seeing a guy who isn't Jewish."

"What?"

"There's more." Halting.

"What more?" *Is she now going to tell me about Noah?*

"What I heard is... he's a Muslim."

Sarah was tempted to tell Aviva that it really didn't matter to her if the guy was Muslim, Hindu, Christian, or whatever. A romantic involvement with any Gentile was clearly verboten in their world, the rest made no difference. To some, like Aviva, a Muslim might be considered worse. Many in their community were staunchly Zionistic, and as such tended to see Muslims as a threat, as enemies of the Jewish people and the State of Israel. But this wasn't the time to lecture her friend about the varying persuasions among Muslims and all the problems with generalizing and harboring stereotypes. She was way too caught up in her own shock for any of that.

"None of this means it's true, you know. It's all just a rumor, but I thought I should tell you," Aviva said.

"Yes," Sarah said contemplatively, her eyes welling up. "I understand."

"It's just a rumor," Aviva repeated.

"I get that," Sarah said, struggling to converse at all. "But where there's smoke, there's fire."

Aviva just listened and nodded.

"I think I'd rather skip Starbucks tonight, if that's all right," Sarah said.

"Of course it's okay."

They drove the few blocks to Aviva's house in silence.

"I'm so sorry," Aviva said as they approached her house.

"Really, you needn't be. You're a good friend, and you did the right thing."

They looked at each other, both with tears in their eyes. "I have something to tell you as well," Sarah said.

Aviva wondered what Sarah could possibly have to add at a moment like this.

"It's Noah," Sarah said.

Aviva waited for more.

Sarah stared into space. She had promised herself to tell no one, had convinced herself that this was Noah's story to share, and here she was about to violate that. But Aviva, her oldest and closest friend, had just delivered some very painful news. She felt like she owed it to Aviva to learn of this from her, and she was certain that what she was about to say would never be repeated. "He's gay," she said matter-of-factly, almost as if she were making a comment about the weather.

"What did you say?" Aviva asked. Disbelieving.

"You heard me right. Noah's gay."

Aviva sat there, absorbing what she'd heard. Questions flooded into her mind: *Is he sure? How long has this been going on? Is he actually dating men?* She decided to stifle her curiosity. If Sarah says Noah's gay then that was that. When and how it came to light was immaterial. "Oh my God!" Aviva said. "Not oh-my-God about Noah being gay, but oh-my-God about *all* this."

Sarah simply nodded in agreement.

"What are you going to do?"

"What's to do?"

"I mean, with Yoni being the rabbi and all that, this is going to be a real... shitstorm."

Sarah managed a smile. It was rare that she or her friends ever used expletives. "That's *exactly* what it is."

Sarah was relieved to enter an empty house. Even on a late night like this, she was home before Jonathan. Her mind was ablaze with questions: whether to call Miriam to poke around to see what comes up; whether to just ask outright; whether to pay a surprise visit and how, exactly, she would pull that off. And then there was Jonathan. Tell him now? Wait? And what if it is true? If so, he's going to find out. *So why does it have to be from me?* No answers.

She didn't know what to do with herself. Her life as she knew it was unraveling, and she felt completely incapacitated. She looked at the clock: 9:15. About 45 minutes or so before Jonathan's arrival. Quite uncharacteristically, she decided to pour herself a drink, and fixed her eyes on one of his bottles of bourbon. She didn't know one from another, and it didn't much matter. She took it neat, as he would, and managed to down it in one gulp, as he would never. Then she had another.

She sat down on the couch in the living room and stared into space, some of her tension admittedly eased from the alcohol. There was nothing she could do at this moment, at least nothing sensible. So she decided on just that—doing nothing for now, just waiting. She would somehow get through the rest of the night pretending everything was normal, and tomorrow she would figure out her next move. It was dishonest, she knew, but springing something like this on Jonathan without any confirmation was plainly out of the question. First learning the truth was her most prudent course. She could do this, she told herself. And she did.

25

SARAH BAUMAN PRESSED THE buzzer for apartment J-3, feeling a surge of anxiety as she waited for a voice on the intercom. She figured it would be either Miriam or one of her roommates, hoping for the latter, but no one seemed to answer. She had anticipated this possibility and planned to find a café, work on her laptop, and return in a couple of hours. She was prepared to do that again and again till they actually met up. But she decided to give this attempt a few more minutes.

She had debated whether to call Miriam the night before to say she was coming but had decided against it. She didn't want to be forced into having such a conversation over the phone or give Miriam the opportunity to push the matter off till some other, more "convenient" time. This had to be done face-to-face, and it had to be done today.

So here she was. She didn't feel like standing around by the door, so she stepped out onto the sidewalk. She had been imagining the possible outcomes in her head for about five minutes before spotting Miriam walking up the block. Miriam appeared to be meandering, lost in her own thoughts as Sarah waved to get her attention.

Miriam hurried toward her. "Mom! What are you doing here? Is everything okay?"

"I just thought I'd stop by to see my girl." Unconvincing.

"Mom, you *never* just stop by." She looked at her mother with concern. "What's going on?"

"Okay. Busted. There's something I need to talk to you about."

"Ever hear of a phone?"

"I wanted to talk in person."

Miriam stared at her. *OMG, she knows about Raj. Zoe Gold and her big mouth!* "Sure, Mom," Miriam said as she fumbled in her bag for her keys.

They sat on the couch in the living room after an unusually silent journey from the lobby to the apartment. For Sarah, it was fortuitous that Miriam's roommates weren't around. Though she wondered when they might return.

"So..." Miriam said. "What's going on?"

Sarah had spent the last fourteen hours anticipating this moment, replaying it in her head over and over, each time a little differently. Miriam's expression in the elevator suggested that the purpose of her visit was no longer a mystery, and that the news was true. Sarah was tempted to respond with, *I think you know*, but thought it better not to be presumptuous. There was still a distant hope she could be wrong. "I heard a rumor," were the words she found.

Miriam felt her heart pounding. What had been a wave of nervousness suddenly became an overwhelming, almost crippling torrent of dread. Over the years, there hadn't been much pretending between them, and she understood that now wasn't going to be any different. She just didn't know how to say it. "It's true," she managed, her eyes welling up.

Sarah's head dropped. "How could this happen?" she asked as if whispering to herself.

"I don't know. I've asked myself that same question more times than I can count."

The two women looked at each other, each teary, each not knowing what to say next. "Tell me about him," Sarah said, her tone obviously lacking the enthusiasm that might be attached to such a question under other circumstances.

"His name is Rajesh," Miriam responded. "But everyone calls him Raj."

"So he's..."

"Indian," Miriam interjected, aware that her mother would probably have guessed this from his name.

Sarah knew that her next question was delicate, but she figured this was more of a time for candor than tact. "I heard he's a Muslim."

Miriam appeared bemused. "Really? *That's* what you heard?"

"Not that it makes any difference, but that's what they're saying."

"That's what *who's* saying? Where did you hear this?"

Sarah took a moment. She had expected this question and was prepared to answer it, yet she found herself faltering. Aviva Mandel was her oldest friend, a quasi-aunt to her children, and known not to be a talebearer or gossiper. The last thing she wanted was to drive a wedge between Aviva and Miriam. But there had already been enough secrets between herself and Miriam. "Aviva," she said, tentatively.

"Aviva?" Miriam reacted, her surprise apparent. She thought about it, then added, "Who must have heard from Batya, who probably heard from Zoe or someone else that Zoe told."

"Zoe?"

"Yeah, Zoe Gold. She was at a party and saw me and Raj together."

"That sounds like a good possibility," Sarah said.

"More than a possibility, as far as I see it. And inaccurate."

Sarah raised her eyebrows. "Inaccurate? How so?"

"Raj isn't a Muslim. He's actually an atheist, and his parents are Hindus, though they don't really practice. I haven't actually met them, but we've talked about it."

Sarah contemplated. "I wish I could say I'm relieved."

"I know. It really doesn't matter."

They both took a few seconds to digest the conversation.

"I met Raj in school," Miriam said.

"He's in your program?"

"Yes."

"And how long have you been..."

"Seeing him? About three months."

"So, it's true," Sarah said, confirming that this was much more than a fling or flirtation.

Miriam seemed unable to respond. "I'm sorry," she said, visibly distraught. "I'm so sorry. I don't know what to do. I've tried to break it off, but... I can't."

Sarah instinctively reached for her and embraced her, wanting to say something like, *It'll be all right*, just as she always had when any of her children were hurting. But this was not that sort of thing. This was different. This was, for her, very much a tragedy, and any statement to the contrary would be dishonest. "I guess we'll just have to find a solution," was the best she could come up with.

Miriam sat upright. "Honestly, I've been trying to do exactly that. I haven't been very successful."

Sarah sighed, then shrugged her shoulders. "Maybe he can convert?"

"Mom, he's an atheist. We don't let atheists convert. And even if we did, I don't think I can ask him to. And even if I could..."

"I know," Sarah interjected, "it's very hard to ask someone to do something like that."

"Not just that. It's also a huge commitment from my end. It means I'm telling him that I want to be with him forever."

"Well, do you?"

Miriam thought about the question. "I don't know."

"Seems you have some things to sort out."

Miriam nodded, acknowledging her mother's point. "Seems you do, too," she said.

"Me?"

"Yes, you. Like, how are you going to tell Dad about this?"

Sarah was pensive for a few seconds. She wasn't bothered by Miriam's assumption that she was going to tell her husband. The Bauman children understood only too well that there weren't any secrets between mom and dad, and it was unlikely that Sarah could wait for Miriam find the "right" time to tell Jonathan herself. "That's a really good question. I do have to tell him before he hears it from someone else, and who knows when that's going to be."

"I know. I'm just so worried. With this, and Noah's thing, it's just not going to be good."

"That's quite an understatement," Sarah said, then paused as she considered whether to elaborate. On the one hand, Miriam was an adult making an adult choice, so why be coy? On the other hand, Miriam was her daughter and already suffering with guilt, so why add insult to injury? Again, she opted for candor. "I think it's going to be horrible, plain and simple. Just horrible."

Miriam knew her mother as someone who was neither dramatic nor apt to repeat an adjective in the same utterance. She nodded and said, "I know."

Sarah sat frozen, lost in her thoughts.

"Do you want me to tell him?" Miriam asked.

Sarah contemplated the question. "I wasn't going to suggest that, but since you did—yes, I think you should."

"I should."

They looked at each other.

"Just one thing," Sarah said.

Miriam raised her eyebrows.

"I don't want to pressure you," Sarah said. "But you can't take your time. It's just not right to keep him in the dark much longer."

Miriam took a deep breath. "I understand."

26

JONATHAN BAUMAN WASN'T ONE to feign emotions, a trait that often handicapped him in his position as a rabbi, and also drew occasional teasing from family members. But at this moment, Sarah was actually concerned. It was Purim, a holiday on which Jews are commanded to be joyous, even ecstatic, and Jonathan seemed anything but. This might have been okay with her, even understandable, if it weren't for the small matter of Miriam and Noah's scheduled arrival in a few short hours for the festive meal.

Like the rest of the day, the feast was to be filled with singing, frivolity, and even sanctioned imbibing to the point of drunkenness, all to celebrate the survival of the Jews from extermination at the hands of their Persian hosts of a prior millennium. For many, the day also symbolized survival from the malevolence of all the enemies of the Jewish people throughout history, a theme that usually resonated with Jonathan. But this year, his spirit was dampened by the expectation of a particular guest at their table, a new "friend" of Noah's.

Sarah could only imagine how much worse he would have been had he also known about Raj, though she suspected that this evening might answer that question for her. It had been more than two weeks since Sarah and Miriam had spoken, and Sarah was unnerved that Miriam had not yet talked to Jonathan. She knew that Miriam's plan was to stay the night, so it seemed a reasonable assumption that Miriam was going to talk to him once the others left. Sarah also assumed that Miriam wouldn't mind her being around the house, considering her many years' worth of expertise in mediating between father and daughter during tough times. And this was certainly shaping up to be one of those.

Sarah was torn over confronting Jonathan about his mood, but eventually decided she had no choice. She simply couldn't fathom the thought of her husband wearing his displeasure during their first encounter with Zach. Only, she was at a loss for a way to help him get past it. "Are you sure you're up to this?" she asked as he was setting the table.

He stepped back, examined his arrangement of china and cutlery, then responded, "Yeah, sure."

"I wasn't referring to the table."

He lifted his eyes to her and smirked. "I know."

"And?"

"I suppose."

"Yoni, I realize you're upset, but that's not a good enough answer."

He understood that they were both troubled by all this, and he admired her ability to deal with it. "I'll be okay," he said, somewhat unconvincingly.

She looked at him, hesitated, then said, "I need you to be more than okay."

A deep breath. "I'll try."

"It's Purim," she said, trying not to sound didactic.

"Yes, it's Purim, and our son is bringing his homosexual lover home to meet us. So, I guess we should all be joyful."

"Yoni!"

"I'm sorry." Reflection. "I'm just venting."

A sympathetic expression. "Are you all vented?"

A faint smile. "I suppose."

"Really?"

Hesitation. "Really."

She approached him and touched his face. "I love you. This isn't easy for either of us. But it's even harder for Noah, and we have to try to help him with that, not make it worse. We should welcome into our lives whoever he chooses." She suddenly thought about Miriam again, wondering what she would possibly say to him about that. She didn't want to think about it. *One crisis at a time*, she told herself, mindful that the next one was soon to follow.

Jonathan surveyed the people sitting around the table. Miriam, Noah, Sarah, and Zach—a small gathering compared to previous years. The absence of Aaron's clan, especially the grandchildren, rendered things somewhat quieter than he preferred. He loved the commotion from the little ones. On a day like this, it would have been just what he needed.

All considered, he had to admit that this particular Purim was going well. In contrast to previous years, in which there had been incidents in the community of public vomiting, passing out, and even alcohol poisoning, this one was relatively tame. He wondered if it had been due to the email he had sent to the congregation asking for moderation. In it he stressed how alcohol abuse was a growing problem in the community, and how the teens were undoubtedly emulating their parents. The adults needed to set an example, and what better time was there to start than with Purim.

He couldn't deny that he was pleased with the change and surprised at the possibility that his email could have had an influence. Still, he considered that there may have been another contributing factor: The Benjy Marcus matter had left the community embarrassed, especially his congregation, and it was entirely possible that this had engendered some sort of collective unconscious need to avoid any additional embarrassment. Either way, things had most definitely gone better than expected.

His attention returned to the meal. Sarah had outdone herself. The brisket was perfect—her usual recipe of mushrooms, onions, and God knows what else. It was soft as butter and just seemed to get better every time she made it. And the sides of kugels —both noodle and potato—sautéed broccoli, and roasted carrots were all delectable. The presence of beer and homemade sangria didn't hurt either. Intoxication was forbidden at the Bauman table, even on Purim, but there was nothing wrong with feeling a little good. It was, after all, a *mitzvah*.

Jonathan observed Zach. A nice-looking fellow, well mannered. And religious, a trait Noah made certain to include when he first told his parents of the relationship. Thus far, the conversation had revealed Zach as intelligent and possessing a good sense of humor. *Would have been a perfect evening, had he been Miriam's guest.*

It occurred to him that, aside from their introduction, he hadn't yet spoken directly with Zach. He decided it was a good idea to change that. He looked over at Zach, waited for eye contact, devilishly grinned, and asked, "Can I offer you something special?"

Zach appeared curious and not the least bit off guard.

"He's asking if you want to sample one of his better bottles," Noah explained. "He keeps them hidden for special occasions."

"Hidden?" Zach asked. "Who's going to drink them?"

"He will," Miriam said. "He thinks if he keeps them out of sight, he won't be tempted."

"An excellent psychological analysis," Jonathan quipped.

"Sure," Zach said, looking at Jonathan.

Jonathan stood up. "Be right back." He walked through the kitchen and took the stairs to the basement.

"I'm intrigued," Zach said to the others.

"You'll be impressed," Noah said.

Sarah was smiling. Her prince had somehow found it within himself to overcome his heartache. She wanted desperately to savor the moment, acutely aware of how fleeting it was to be.

The three young folks looked at one another as they heard Jonathan's footsteps climbing the stairs. He appeared in the kitchen as they turned to see the bottle in his hand. Noah's eyes especially lit up as he saw the Glenfiddich 25-Year-Old Rare Oak, not simply because he appreciated the bottle's exceptionality, but more for what his father's act portended.

Noah took the bottle from his father. "Pricey bottle."

Jonathan smirked as he pulled five scotch glasses from the bottom of the bar.

"I would never spend such money on alcohol," Jonathan said to Zach, assuming that Zach was wondering why he, a rabbi, would have a collection of this sort. "These extravagances are gifts from a special friend over the years, usually on my birthday." He circled the table, putting down the glasses.

The three other Baumans noted Jonathan's omission of Benjy Marcus' name, all concluding that he probably wanted to avoid the topic. Zach likely knew of Benjy Marcus and the whole ordeal—pretty much everyone did—and that would have necessitated some sort of explanation from Jonathan. This way, all was averted.

"Seems like a good friend to have," Zach said.

"Indeed," Jonathan responded as he began to pour each glass. Under normal circumstances he would have let everyone pour his or her own, but Zach's presence made him feel the need to play host.

Jonathan returned to his seat and lifted his glass. "*L'chaim*," he said with a smile as the others followed suit. He took a healthy sip and a moment to appreciate its excellence, then started humming a tune. He knew his melody would be familiar to the Baumans—it was a *nigun*, a song without words, composed by his great-grandfather for Shabbos and holidays, and known almost exclusively by members of the extended Bauman clan—but he was surprised to see Zach immediately sing along, an indication that Noah had apparently been sharing his heritage. Jonathan's voice grew louder as he swayed back and forth, his eyes closed, seeming as if he was getting lost in the melody, transporting himself to another dimension.

There was singing all around as Sarah, ever mindful of the other crisis on the horizon, managed a faint smile. Her prince was being true to form. He was figuring it out. *At least for now.*

27

ZACH ABRAMSON AND NOAH Bauman got to the platform just as the train to Manhattan was about to depart. Noah felt bad about having jumped out of his mother's car with one of the quickest goodbyes ever, but they were cutting it close and desperately wanted to avoid the hour's wait for the next train. There were hardly any other travelers at the Lawrence station, so the train itself was pretty empty. They managed to situate themselves in a private area, though it was likely that someone would eventually sit nearby.

"Well, that went well," Zach said.

"Yeah, good thing we got here when we did."

Zach looked at Noah sideways. *Dude, that wasn't what I was talking about!* "Right," he responded sarcastically.

"Oh, sorry. I thought you were talking about catching the train." On reflection, Noah realized he had actually understood what Zach was saying. But it was late, he was tired, and he simply hadn't wanted to get into a detailed rehashing of the evening. As to his knee-jerk response of avoiding and deflecting, he had to admit to himself that this came rather easily to him, far more so than he was comfortable with. And while he understood this as a byproduct of living in the closet for so many years, it was becoming increasingly unacceptable to him. He made a mental note to work on it. "Yes, it did go well," he said.

"Better than I'd thought it would."

"Me too." Noah had never imagined his father capable of being rude or unpleasant, but he had still been fearful of some kind of awkwardness or tension. That the evening had gone so smoothly was something to be glad about.

"I know this is challenging for your folks. I mean, it was difficult for mine too, and my father isn't a famous Orthodox rabbi," Zach said.

Noah nodded. "And it's only going to get worse. I suspect Miriam stayed there tonight to drop the Raj bomb."

After Miriam's encounter with her mother, she had immediately phoned Noah in a panic to tell him all about it. Noah had updated Zach, and they both had wondered when Miriam was going to tell her father.

"I feel bad for your father. In some ways, his world is kind of crumbling."

"You think?" Noah said sardonically.

"Well, he seems to be trying," Zach responded. "At least as far as we're concerned."

"I agree. But Raj is a whole other thing."

The train stopped at the next station. Five people entered and scattered themselves throughout the car. Two teenage boys, both with headphones, took seats directly across the aisle. "We can talk about something else," Zach suggested.

"No, it's okay," Noah responded, realizing that the newcomers were absorbed in their music. For his part, he would just as soon have changed the subject, but Zach had been anticipating this evening with trepidation, and now needed to talk about it. "I'm sure they can't hear us."

Zach nodded. "Raj is a *really* good guy."

"I agree." Pensive. "But that only makes it worse."

Zach nodded, acknowledging that Raj's positives were the very source of the problem. "Yeah, I guess it does."

"She's not going to give him up," Noah whispered, as if contemplating out loud.

"That should be a good thing."

"Yeah, it should be... But it isn't."

28

JONATHAN BAUMAN WAS JUST finishing up his last phone call when Miriam appeared at the doorway to his study. He gestured for her to enter and sit. "Okay," he said to the person on the phone. "So, tomorrow at 5 p.m. I'll see you then."

Noah and Zach had left for the city about an hour earlier. Miriam's plan was to spend the night and leave in the morning. Sarah was upstairs mulling about, trying to make herself sparse.

Jonathan hung up the phone. "Not even an hour since Purim ended, and this woman, who isn't even a congregant, calls and says she needs to see me. Marriage problems. Says she has no one else to turn to."

"You could refer her to a therapist," Miriam said.

"I tried. She won't go. She says she will only speak to a rabbi."

"So, why you?"

"Good question. She sounds very *frum*, believes her rabbi will side with her husband, and she wants someone objective."

"Okay. I think you can do objective."

"I suppose."

They looked at each other.

"You were really great tonight," she said.

"You mean with Zach?"

"Yes, with Zach."

"Hardly."

She smirked. "Just like my father to downplay his accomplishments."

"I barely spoke to the guy."

"Dad, no one was expecting you guys to become best buddies right away. You broke the ice, and you did it with style."

"Style?"

"Yeah. The drink thing was brilliant."

"Funny you see it that way. I thought it was a little desperate."

"Well, you may have felt desperate, but you acted... classy."

Jonathan smiled widely; he certainly wasn't accustomed to receiving a compliment like that from her. "Thanks," he said. It occurred to him it had been some time since they'd really spoken one-on-one. "So, how have you been?"

She considered her response. "Good, I guess."

He paused, also considering her response. "Doesn't sound too convincing."

"No, I'm really okay. Just stressed with school and stuff."

He wondered what "stuff" meant, yet asking about her social life was off limits. She never took well to that line of inquiry from him, and at this stage of the game, that wasn't likely to change. In truth, he was really worried about her religious observance. For a single female on a university campus, he knew there were many challenges to maintaining one's Orthodoxy. He knew it was unwise to broach that either. "Yes, graduate school can be quite demanding," he said.

She nodded.

"But you are the smartest person I know," he added.

"Dad!"

"You are." Resolute.

"If you say so."

"I've *always* said so."

"I know."

He smiled. "You sure you're okay?" he asked, sensing that something was up with her.

"I'm sure." Slightly more convincing.

He looked at her intently and decided to change his line of inquiry. "So, what else?" he asked, betraying that he was enjoying this time with her and wanted it to continue.

"Nothing really." Hesitation. "I was just thinking that you'll probably be gone by the time I wake up in the morning, so I wanted to come down and say hi and bye."

"I'm glad you did."

"Me too."

He stood up. "I'm quite exhausted," he said.

"Same here."

He walked around his desk, drew her into a hug, and planted his lips on her forehead. "You know I love you," he said.

"I love you too," she replied as she squeezed him tightly, fighting back tears.

Sarah heard their footsteps ascending the staircase and, completely to her surprise, laughter. *She didn't tell him.*

She closed her laptop, got up from the bed, and came out to the hallway as they bid each other good night. *Definitely didn't tell him.*

"I'm going to bed," Jonathan said to her as he slipped past her into the bedroom.

"Right," she said impassively. "I'll be a minute." She then looked at Miriam bewildered.

Miriam walked into her own bedroom as Sarah followed her and closed the door. The two women looked at each other. "What?" Miriam said.

"What!" Sarah struggled to keep her voice down. Jonathan probably figured mother and daughter were spending a few minutes chatting before bed, and she wanted it to stay that way. "You promised me two weeks ago that you were going to tell your father about..."

"I know," Miriam interjected, also concerned about the decibel level.

"Then, what?"

Miriam stood frozen.

"Why didn't you tell him?

Still frozen.

"I've never kept a secret from your father." Still attempting a whisper. "And now, for two weeks, I've kept a secret—*your secret*—and only because you promised me you were going to tell him."

Miriam's eyes started welling up. "I couldn't."

Sarah just looked at her.

"I couldn't," Miriam repeated.

"I don't understand."

"I couldn't tell him."

"And I can't keep it a secret from him anymore," Sarah said.

"I get that... But things are different than they were two weeks ago."

"Different? What's different?" Sarah asked, her exasperation growing.

Miriam stared into space, her cheeks wet with tears. She wiped her eyes and said, "I'm pregnant."

Sarah covered her mouth. "Oh my God!" she muttered as her own tears began to flow.

"I'm sorry," Miriam said.

Sarah stared at her. "How did this happen?" she asked as hushfully as possible.

"What do you mean, how did it happen? It happened!" Miriam responded, also trying to keep her tone down. "We were reckless, drunk, a moment of passion, unprepared, and voilà. That's how it happened. Do you want more details?"

"Don't be snide with me!" Sarah said. "I think that's the last thing you want to do right now."

"You're right." Miriam took a breath. "I'm sorry."

Sarah sat down on the bed. "How far along are you?"

"I'm not sure. I just took the test last week." Miriam sat down in her old desk chair, the same chair in which she had once drawn pictures, written poems, and done homework. Now here she was talking about this.

"Did you repeat it?" Sarah asked, hoping for the remote possibility of a false positive.

Miriam nodded. "Yes."

Hesitation. "What do you plan to do?"

"I don't know." More tears.

Sarah's mind was swirling. She couldn't help but think about the possibility of an abortion. It was a complicated issue in their world, but she had to admit she was tempted to mention it. They could seek a *heter,* a rabbinic dispensation, though permission for early abortions was granted only for significant medical complications or psychological duress, and she wasn't sure there was a strong argument for either in Miriam's case. And even if she could put aside her own religious concerns and quietly arrange for an abortion, that would mean yet another secret from Jonathan, one she would have to take to the grave.

Then there was the possibility that Miriam would want to keep the baby, which, at the moment, seemed a rather scary scenario. But if Miriam were to make that decision, Sarah could never, in all good conscience, dissuade her from it. "What about Raj?" Sarah asked.

"He wants me to keep it."

Sarah looked surprised. She'd assumed a young man in his position wouldn't want to be saddled with such a responsibility.

"He wants to marry me," Miriam added.

"He does?" Sarah reflected. "And you?"

Miriam was silent.

29

RAJESH BHATT GAVE UP on the hope of drifting off to sleep. After ruminating, tossing, and turning for the past three hours, he didn't know what to do with himself. He stared at the ceiling, considering his options. He could go into the living room and turn on the TV, and at least get some distraction from these thoughts. But what he really wanted to do was wake up Miriam and tell her what was brewing in his head. He just couldn't bring himself to do it. She had spent her last hours of wakefulness crying, bemoaning their situation, so he knew she must have been exhausted. It was quite the role reversal—he usually slept while she bounced around.

He, on the other hand, had mostly listened, primarily because he hadn't known what more to say. He had already voiced his desire to keep the baby and get married, and without her explicitly saying so, it seemed clear to him that the latter was out of the question. As for the baby's fate, he wasn't sure what she was thinking.

Frustrated from his musings, he put his hand on her shoulder. Lacking any response from her, he applied a bit more pressure.

She awoke startled. "What? What?" She looked at him. "Is everything okay?"

"I'm sorry, I just couldn't sleep."

"*You* couldn't sleep?" She was truly surprised at this, then added, "So I have to be awake too?"

He paused. He wasn't used to such a harsh tone from her but understood it as symptomatic of the circumstances. "Sorry, but... I needed company."

She shifted over to face him. "Okay, I'm awake."

"I've been thinking." Hesitation.

"Thinking what?"

He took a deep breath. "What if I convert?"

"Convert?"

"Yeah, convert. Like, become Jewish."

"You can't convert," she said rather matter-of-factly.

He looked at her curiously.

"You don't believe in God," she said. "And that means you *can't* convert."

"Well, maybe I believe... a little bit."

Now she looked at *him* curiously. "You said you were an atheist!"

"I know, but I've been thinking."

She smiled. "Thinking that you want to be with me and raise our child together, so now you suddenly believe?"

"Sort of."

She thought a moment. "Sorry, but that's not good enough."

"Why not?" he asked.

"It's complicated. But the long and short of it is that if your conversion—so to speak—is going to mean anything to my parents, it would have to be Orthodox. That involves a whole lot of things, including believing in God. Are you ready to keep kosher? Not drive or use electricity on Shabbos? There's so much involved in being Orthodox."

"I've been with you for a while now, so I'm well aware of the Shabbos and kosher restrictions. They don't bother me at all. I also know about a lot of other things. I've done some research."

She sighed. "I'm sure you have." *Such a geek! Always researching.*

"I'm being serious," he said sternly.

"So am I. You're also being ridiculous."

"Ridiculous! Why do you say that?"

"Because the idea of you converting is just that—ridiculous. First, I would never ask you to convert. Second, regardless of what you know from me or your research, you really have no idea what you would be getting into. And third, what about your parents? What would they say?"

"My parents?" he said reflectively. "I honestly don't think they would be upset at all. They don't practice Hinduism, they don't even believe in it. They eat meat, they drink alcohol, they're totally secular. And they're both doctors, and most of their friends are Jewish."

"And that means they would be perfectly fine with it." Sarcasm.

"You can believe what you want, but I know them. All they care about is my happiness. If they knew that I loved you and wanted to marry you, they would be all in."

"Don't be so sure," she replied.

He considered her point, then said, "Actually, I think you're projecting."

"*Projecting*? Are you playing shrink with me?"

"I guess you could put it that way. But as I see it, since you can't imagine your parents accepting me even if I do convert, then you certainly can't imagine my parents accepting us either. Sounds like a pretty solid analysis to me."

She thought about that, admitting to herself it had merit, but still saw the entire conversation as ludicrous.

"I promise you," he said. "My parents will be fine."

"I'm sure they will be, because it's not going to happen."

"You don't have to be so mean."

"Sorry." Conciliatory.

"It's okay," he said gently. "I know it's all very stressful."

"I'll agree with you on that."

He smiled.

As did she.

"You know," he said, "maybe this is all part of God's plan to keep us together."

"You don't believe in God."

"Like I said, maybe I'm starting to."

"Right." Sardonic. "Can we go to sleep now?"

"Just one more thing," he said.

"And what might that be?"

"I know I told you already, but I'd really like you to keep the baby. It's your decision, and I respect whatever you want in the end. I'm just stating, or restating, my preference for the record. And whether I convert or not, whether we marry or not, I'll always be there. I just want you to know."

She took a moment to process what she was hearing, then said, "I do know. And *for the record*, you needn't worry." She began to tear. "I'm keeping it. I couldn't live with myself any other way."

30

JONATHAN BAUMAN SCANNED HIS audience as he was about to start his daily 6 a.m. Talmud class, noting that the usual group of about twenty had progressively dwindled to fewer than ten over the past two weeks. The Talmud class, held in the *beis midrash*, or study hall, immediately preceded the daily 6:45 morning service held in the same room. Many of those missing from the class had been regulars for years and all of them—to a man—were still attending the 6:45 service. That not one had even bothered to approach him with an excuse or apology for skipping the class had left him wondering.

He couldn't help but connect this to the vibe he had gotten just a few days earlier on Shabbos morning. A cold shoulder from David Weisberg, the new president, was nothing new, but this one had seemed a tad colder. The disinterest he sometimes sensed during his sermon felt more widespread, and the lack of well-wishing or even eye contact from some when the congregation gathered after services was most unusual.

They must know about Noah, he told himself. He had been expecting this in one form or another for a few weeks, and at this point there was simply no other explanation for what was happening. He wasn't surprised that some of his congregants would have difficulty with their rabbi's son being gay, he just hadn't expected it to be so blatant. From the moment Noah came out, he had imagined that his tenure in this position might be compromised. Now he had no doubt.

He had spoken to Sarah about this on Shabbos, and she had agreed, saying she had the same perception. He had decided not to dwell on it, for her sake more than his. He knew that, despite her outward equanimity, she too was feeling quite vulnerable, and he didn't want to make things worse. But it was there, and they both knew it.

Presently, he needed to confirm that all this wasn't just in his head. He had a pretty good idea of how he would go about that, though it wasn't going to be so easy.

He opened the book in front of him, smiled at the few faces eagerly awaiting the lesson, and said, "So, where did we leave off yesterday?"

Benjy Marcus had been making it a habit to scoot out early from the daily morning prayer service to avoid having to talk with anyone. It was hard enough for him to show his face in public these days. He certainly wasn't up for inquiries about his predicament, genuine or otherwise.

Jonathan respected that, and admired Benjy for not buckling under the pressure and totally hiding. Benjy had done some pretty bad things and would soon pay dearly for them, but he was still determined to remain part of the community as best he could, continuing both his philanthropic commitments and his attendance at *davening*. He was also just about the only one in the room, at least at that moment, who Jonathan fully trusted as a friend and ally.

As in many Orthodox synagogues, the décor of the *beis midrash*, the second-largest room in the building, was utilitarian. Institutional carpet with checkered shades of brown, library-esque walls lined floor to ceiling with jam-packed bookshelves, and twenty or so walnut tables with matching chairs. The usual crowd on a weekday morning was about forty men, and occasionally two or three women in a small separate section on the side. Jonathan's seat was in the front, and Benjy, who used to sit beside him, had recently taken to the back of the room to facilitate a speedy and inconspicuous departure.

The service was drawing to a close when Jonathan turned around, hoping to catch Benjy's eye. Seeing that Benjy was occupied with folding up his *tallis*, or prayer shawl, Jonathan sauntered toward the back, trying not to attract attention. He approached Benjy, put his hand on Benjy's shoulder, and whispered, "Do you have a few minutes?"

Benjy looked at him curiously. It was unusual for the rabbi to initiate any discussion until the prayers had completely concluded.

"Just something I need to talk about," Jonathan explained, again whispering.

"Sure," Benjy responded, hiding any compunction over having to stay longer than he'd planned.

Wanting to express his awareness that he was asking Benjy to do something uncomfortable, Jonathan said, "I appreciate it... It's important."

"Of course," Benjy said.

Benjy still managed to sneak out of the sanctuary early, made his way into Jonathan's study, took a seat, and waited. The office was a handsome space, refurbished about five years earlier when the board decided that the dark paneled walls, thick red carpet, and worn furniture were rather dated and unbefitting their then beloved rabbi. In fact, it was Benjy's wife, Esther, a celebrated interior designer, who had taken the task upon herself. She had the paneling ripped out, the built-in redwood bookshelves refinished, the walls painted a soft white, and upgraded the lighting, art and furniture. Sarah had distanced herself from the project for obvious reasons—the rabbi's wife really shouldn't be involved with such matters—but ultimately thought it quite tasteful, though perhaps a bit too ostentatious for its purpose. Esther had reassured her that everything had fallen well within the budget, and that nobody would have any basis for comment. Sarah accepted her friend's explanation about the cost, but was skeptical about the latter part of Esther's claim. She knew there would always be someone to comment.

Benjy took in his surroundings, appreciating how his wife's furnishings melded with Jonathan's books, plaques, and pictures, and realizing that this very room personified the intertwining lives of the Marcus and Bauman families. Lives that had been filled mostly with joy and achievement over the years, but which were now burdened with difficult obstacles.

It was only another month or so before his court date, when he would announce his plea. That would be his last day of freedom for quite a while. He would be fine, or so he kept telling himself. His wife and kids would be okay as well. Finances were ample and in place, everyone would be taken care of. He needed to stay positive. It was either that or go insane, and the latter simply wasn't an option.

He found himself staring at three particular framed photos on a bookshelf facing Jonathan's desk, each featuring Jonathan and Sarah with one of the three children at the Western Wall in Jerusalem. It was a Bauman family custom for Mom and Dad to take each child to Israel before the celebration of his or her Bar or Bat Mitzvah, and these photos were from those trips. Benjy had seen these a hundred times before yet somehow never noticed the intensity of the smiles of the children and Sarah and the extraordinary twinkle in Jonathan's eyes. He had to admit he'd been seeing things a lot differently these days.

A few years back, Jonathan had confided in Benjy that he strategically placed those photos so he could glimpse them over the shoulders of whomever he was meeting with. In this room, people came with all sorts of vicissitudes, sometimes challenging even for Jonathan to process. It helped that he could simply shift his eyes a bit to gain some perspective.

Benjy found himself drawn to the photo of Noah and felt a twinge of heartache, then he scanned to the photo of Miriam as the heartache deepened. He had learned about Noah and Miriam recently, as had most everyone, and hadn't had been ready yet to approach Jonathan about any of it. These days, with social media, privacy was a relic of the past. He assumed that no one else in the congregation would have the temerity to approach the rabbi about this stuff either and wondered just what, if anything, Jonathan actually knew. He had a strong suspicion that the conversation he was about to have was going to answer that.

Benjy's reflections were interrupted when the door opened. Jonathan entered wearing the same somber expression he'd had a few minutes earlier and took a seat on the couch underneath the family pictures. He didn't need to be behind his desk, this was a conversation with a friend. "Thanks for taking the time," Jonathan said.

"For you? Never a problem."

Jonathan nodded. "So..." Reluctance.

Benjy nodded, waiting for more.

"We haven't really spoken in a while," Jonathan continued.

"I know."

"I figured you just want to be left alone."

"That's true."

Jonathan leaned forward. "How are you doing?"

"I'm hanging in there," Benjy said. "Seems Avi managed to convince the attorney general that eighteen months is enough for what I did. They originally wanted twenty-four, so who am I to complain?"

"Eighteen months," Jonathan said, his tone somber.

"Probably out in thirteen or so, if I behave."

Jonathan just looked at him, unsure how to react.

"Anyway," Benjy said. "I'm sure you didn't ask to talk to me about this."

Jonathan nodded. "Right. I didn't. But I want you to know that Sarah and I will be there for you, Esther and the kids throughout everything. Whatever's needed."

Benjy just looked at him wordlessly, obviously discomfited. It was clear that he preferred Jonathan move on to the real purpose of their meeting.

"I don't know quite how to put this without sounding paranoid, but I've been sensing something that's bothering me, like people are somehow unhappy with me. The morning class is down to maybe ten, when it used to be more than double that. And on Shabbos, it felt like people were snubbing me." He paused, then, "Wow, that does sound paranoid, doesn't it?"

"Actually, it sounds rather accurate," Benjy said. "You're not being paranoid at all."

"What's going on?" Jonathan asked, showing more concern than alarm.

Benjy found himself tongue-tied. Sure, he'd anticipated this moment, but that didn't make it any easier.

"Is it about Noah?" Jonathan asked, realizing he was violating his and Sarah's rule about bringing this up with others. But Benjy wasn't just anyone, and he likely already knew about Noah, their sons being close friends and Noah being out of the closet for some time. And beyond that, Jonathan felt his question was unavoidable. To him, there was no other possibility.

Benjy nodded, then said, "And Miriam."

"Miriam?"

Benjy realized that Jonathan knew only half of what everyone else knew about his children, and that this really was going to be even more difficult than he'd imagined.

"What's going on with Miriam?" Jonathan pressed, as if Noah's situation was suddenly inconsequential.

Benjy took a deep breath. His friend was waiting for an answer, and he had no choice but to oblige. There was no delicate way to put it. "The word is—I'm not saying this is true—but the word is... she's dating a non-Jewish guy."

"What? Whose word?"

"Rumors, that's all. Maybe none of it is even true, but it's out there and people are talking, both about that and Noah."

Jonathan dropped his head in his hands, suddenly besieged by an unbearable, overwhelming sense of dread that made it almost impossible for him to breathe. After several moments, he lifted his head and asked, "How is it that everyone knows this, and I don't?"

"Because no one would dare say anything to you."

"Not even you?"

"Yes, not even me."

Jonathan looked away a moment, as if ashamed, then dropped his head once more into his hands.

Benjy just sat there, again wordless.

Realizing he had to somehow hold it together, Jonathan lifted his head again and sat up straight. "What they're saying about Noah, it's true," he said.

"I know," Benjy said.

"But this thing about Miriam... I just can't imagine."

"Neither can I. I've been telling people not to talk, but you know how it is."

"What else are they saying?"

Benjy had naively hoped this question wasn't coming, but here it was. He understood at this point that he could no longer hold back. "Again, these are just rumors..."

"I know," Jonathan interjected. "What are they saying?" Edgy.

"Some are saying he's a Muslim, but I've also heard he isn't. No one seems to know for sure."

No one but Miriam, Jonathan thought. *And maybe Sarah.* The possibility that Sarah knew about this somehow didn't seem to amplify his distress. He could imagine her struggling to find a way to share such a thing with him.

And then there was the possibility that it was all false, that maybe Miriam had been seen with a man who didn't look particularly Jewish—whatever that meant—and the rumors started from there. *A possibility indeed, but not very likely.* "If it's true," Jonathan said, "then it doesn't really matter what he is. It matters only what he isn't."

Knowing Jonathan as he did, Benjy was unsurprised by his friend's words. "I agree," he said.

Both men sat silently for a moment before Jonathan said, "I hope you won't take any offense if I'd like to be alone for a little while."

"Of course not." Benjy stood, leaned over, put his hands on his friend's shoulders, and added, "If you still need to talk, you know where to find me."

Jonathan looked up. "I know."

With that, Benjy turned and left, and as the door closed behind him, Jonathan remained on the couch, listless, staring into space. He had just begun to get a handle on the situation with Noah, adjusting to the fact that his family was turning out differently than he'd ever imagined, coming to grips with the possibility that his future in his position was tenuous, and now this. He so wanted to believe that this news about Miriam wasn't true, that it was just nasty gossip, but he couldn't help but think otherwise. Some of it had to be true, maybe all of it was. And that being the case, what was he to do?

Strangely, he found himself beyond tears or anger, not knowing quite what he was feeling, barely grasping what he was thinking. It struck him that he and Benjy had barely spoken about Noah. Perhaps there hadn't been anything more to say about that. It was what it was. He couldn't blame Noah for his situation nor could he blame himself and Sarah. Noah hadn't chosen this, and it didn't take much insight to understand how he must have suffered all these years, trying to fight and deny something so fundamental, so inescapable.

Let them judge, he told himself, recognizing his powerlessness over the perceptions and opinions of others, and over most of the things that were happening around him. A rude awakening for a rabbi, whose job it was to teach and influence. *Let them judge.*

But this thing with Miriam, this was different. Perhaps he and Sarah had played a role. After all, Miriam had been the rebellious child who won just about every argument they ever had. He had wanted to be stricter, while Sarah had constantly urged for leniency.

"You'll lose her," Sarah had often warned, and he had always acquiesced. Thus, it wound up being one year of seminary in Israel after high school instead of the two years he had wanted. "She didn't even want to go at all," Sarah had told him, "but I helped her realize how much it would break your heart if she didn't.

"But two years will really give her the foundation she needs, especially her," had been his response.

"A second year will make her miserable, not religious, I assure you."

Who could argue with that? Well, he could have, but it would have fallen on deaf ears. He was always outnumbered, and sometimes outsmarted, at least when it came to the women in his life.

Then there was the co-ed Cornell University versus Yeshiva University's Stern College for Women. "She needs to be in a structured, religious institution where she won't be exposed to all the nonsense the kids are involved with at other colleges," he had argued.

Again, the claim about her being miserable, and: "Who are you kidding? You think the girls at Stern don't know from drugs and sex?"

"Not nearly as much!"

"Maybe so, but Miriam is the last person on earth to be influenced by her environment. She marches to her own drumbeat and will do so wherever she is. Don't you see that the happier she is, the more likely she'll stay away from those things?"

And at some point, these discussions just ceased. He wondered: Had he seen the light, or had he just given up? And were they now paying the price?

As for Sarah, he was confident she already knew about Miriam. He was also certain that she must feel awful, both about the situation and also for having kept it from him. But what could she have done? he pondered. How was she to have approached him about something like this? Soon enough, he would relieve her from that quandary, and the two of them would have to face yet another upheaval in their lives. As for exactly how they would manage these things, he hadn't a clue.

His mind turned to the fact that he and Benjy hadn't mentioned how all this would bear upon his position as rabbi. Perhaps that discussion was yet to be had, but in any event, he was fairly certain that Benjy would have dismissed any notion of him leaving. "Anyone who wants you to leave can just leave themselves," was probably how Benjy would have put it before declaring that most of the congregation would want him to stay put.

Not so simple, he contemplated, knowing all too well the complexities of serving as a religious leader of an Orthodox community. People looked to their rabbi as an example. And at this point, he wasn't feeling like much of one, not in the way they needed.

Jonathan stood up from the couch but was still feeling lost, clueless as to what to do next. He considered calling Sarah, but she was busy with patients. As much as he needed to talk to her, it would have to wait. He also thought of calling Miriam, but that he deemed a very bad idea. He hadn't an inkling as to what he would say to her or how he could even start the conversation—a rather rare predicament for him—so he thought it best he speak with Sarah first.

He looked at his chair behind his desk, wondering if he should sit in it and start to work. He had classes and a sermon to prepare, and an article he'd been working on for a law journal contrasting Talmudic and American tort law on a specific form of liability. He didn't have the head for any of it. He also had a few appointments scheduled, mostly for counseling, and he wasn't up for that either. Truth be told, he couldn't do anything.

He sat himself back down on the couch, contemplating how he needed to stay composed, yet realizing that he presently had about as much control over his own state as he had over the actions of anyone else. Still no sadness. Still no anger. Only a crippling sense of despair.

Ironic, he mused, considering he was usually the one who dispensed advice and guidance. Regardless of the matter, he was always propped up as the one who would *figure it out*—an expectation that, to his mind, had never been anything more than utter foolishness. And this was especially true now, when the only thing he knew for certain was that he had no answers whatsoever.

31

SARAH BAUMAN LOOKED AT the couple sitting across the desk from her. This was what she loved most about her work, though the young lady's pregnancy, about 30 weeks along, had her thinking a bit too much about Miriam. It was the end of her workday, the time she preferred to have such meetings. With her appointments finished and her staff busily wrapping up any administrative matters, she could patiently address whatever questions and concerns the expecting parents might have.

Getting together with the pediatrician before the birth of the first baby was fairly common, and some couples used the process to shop around for the doctor of their choice. With Sarah, however, these meetings were seen more as an opportunity to get to know each other. Her position in her community, as well as her reputation among her medical colleagues, placed her at the top of the list for many prospective parents.

The personal touch was an important component of the way she practiced, so much so that she'd long resisted the trends of joining group practices or selling to one of the large hospital corporations. A group practice would mean that patients would see different doctors, depending on when their appointments were, and selling to a corporation would render her an employee with time limits and quotas for patient visits. She wanted every patient to see only her and would take as long as needed for every visit. That was the way she did it.

She had explained much of this to the couple, not to sell herself but rather to set their minds at ease. She had also explained her position on the benefits of breastfeeding, vaccines, her general medical approach, and, since the sex of their baby was already known, proper post-circumcision wound care. She was confident she had managed the discussion fairly well despite having been terribly preoccupied with everything that was happening with her own family.

The meeting ended and they all stood up. The young lady reached out, took Sarah's hand, and said, "Thank you so much, Dr. Bauman. We really appreciate your taking the time." The young man nodded and also offered his gratitude but, being an ultra-Orthodox Jew, didn't extend his hand. Sarah, of course, understood and smiled. As a rabbi's wife, she too would never offer her hand to another man, though if one were offered to her she would most certainly shake it. She believed that any man who held a hand out to her was probably unaware of the prohibition, and that it was a worse transgression to embarrass someone than to shake his hand. It was also easier not to have to explain such things to people.

She saw them out, closed the door, and sauntered over to the window. Her office was on the ground floor of a two-story building on Central Avenue, a major thoroughfare running through three of the Five Towns: Woodmere, Cedarhurst, and Lawrence. She didn't see much aside from traffic and a few pedestrians. It was shortly after 4 p.m. on a sunny, mild late-March day. Some of the trees were starting to bloom. Spring was her favorite season. Though not so much this year, she pondered.

It had been just over a week since she'd learned of Miriam's pregnancy—a long, trying week, and somehow she'd managed to keep it from Jonathan. It was the only secret she'd kept from him since the day they'd met, sort of, aside from that "little white lie" he had caught her in six months after Aaron was born. A faint smile came to her as she remembered.

Jonathan had been starting out as assistant rabbi, and she had just started medical school, so money was tight. With a new baby and a new house, however, some expenses were unavoidable, and the credit card bills seemed to be causing some tension. As newlyweds, inexperienced with the tests that marriage can occasionally bring, they managed to negotiate their disagreements on what was essential and what was frivolous. She had tried hard to stick to the plan, but then there were those occasions when she just saw something nice and couldn't help herself. Between the stresses of medical school during the day and taking care of the baby at night while also studying—and with Jonathan working so many hours in his new position—sometimes she just needed a bit of retail therapy.

The actual incident occurred on a Saturday night in February. They had been on their way out for their first annual synagogue dinner, putting on their coats. The babysitter, Sarah's college roommate, Jennifer, had been in the bedroom, cooing over little Aaron.

"That coat doesn't look familiar," Jonathan remarks, trying to downplay his anxiety over yet another purchase.

"Oh, this?" Sarah says. "I had it before we were married. I just never wore it with you."

Jonathan, about to say something like "oh" or "I see," loses his chance as Jennifer emerges from Aaron's bedroom with an enthusiastic, "Wow, Sarah, nice new coat!"

Sarah does her hand-covering-her-mouth thing and turns red.

"Did I say something wrong?" Jennifer asks.

"No, of course not," Jonathan says somewhat humorously, looking at Jennifer. "It's only that Sarah was just telling me how she had that coat before we were married, so it's kind of strange that you don't recognize it."

They all look at one another.

"Oops," Jennifer mutters.

"Busted," Sarah says sheepishly.

Jonathan smiles widely, seeming more amused by the uncovering of Sarah's ruse than distressed about the coat. His reaction also breaks the tension, as he hoped it would.

Sarah returned to the present. She had once tainted the truth to avoid conflict on what was such an important evening, and Jonathan had made light of it for the very same reason. It had been what each of them had needed to do at the moment, and it had worked. And even when he had teased her about it once or twice during that dinner and more than a few times over the years, it had always been with the very same smile. He had a little something on her, and to him, that was all right, for it was yet another discovery about the woman he loved.

Her smile faded as she thought about her current dilemma. This time, her deception was far more serious, and she expected Jonathan's reaction to be much less forgiving. She couldn't recall ever feeling so helpless. Much of her life seemed beyond her control.

Sarah, too, had sensed something in the synagogue this past Shabbos, a kind of coolness or distance from some of their usual enthusiasts. That, along with her recent conversation with Aviva Mandel, had her concluding that the news about Miriam and Noah must have spread. When later, at lunch on Shabbos, Jonathan had mentioned his feelings, along with his suspicion that it might have been related to people finding out about Noah, she confirmed having had the same experience and simply responded, "I wouldn't be surprised if some of them know." She realized at that very moment that she had reached the height of her deceitfulness, and she was ashamed for all of it.

She turned her thoughts to a phone conversation she'd had with Miriam the night before, during which she chastised Miriam for continuing to delay the inevitable confrontation with her father. As if her guilt over Jonathan wasn't enough, she was also reproaching herself for pressuring her daughter, understanding all too well that Miriam had more than enough troubles besides this. It wasn't an unfamiliar experience—guilt over simply telling one's child to do the right thing—but she knew she had no choice. It had to happen.

Okay, okay! I'll come tomorrow night, were the words resonating in Sarah's mind as she tried to visualize what the evening ahead portended. And all the images that came to her filled her with trepidation.

She pulled her car into the driveway and was surprised to see Jonathan's car already there. She was always home several hours before him, so she wondered what was going on. Her worried mind already started imagining the worst of things, like maybe he wasn't feeling well. But if that were the case, he would have texted or called her. *It must be something else.*

All she could come up with at that moment was: *He knows.*

She entered the house and, while removing her coat, called out, "Yoni."

No answer.

Her first instinct was to check the bedroom. Perhaps he really wasn't feeling well but hadn't wanted to alarm her at work. She moved toward the staircase when suddenly the silence was broken.

"I'm in the den," he said, his tone low and frail.

She entered the den and found him sitting on the couch, staring into space, his face fallen, his body still. *He knows.* "Is everything okay?" she asked, anticipating the answer.

He fixed his eyes on her.

She sat down on the other end of the couch, wondering if he was acting this way because he had just found out that other people knew about Noah. But they had both expected that news to spread, she told herself, and they'd been preparing for it mentally. What she was seeing now, she realized, was something else. Something new. Something she'd never seen before, not even after Noah came out to them. "I guess you've heard," she said.

"I guess it's true," he responded.

She nodded.

"And you knew," he said, his tone surprisingly unaffected.

"Yes."

"You know, Benjy knows, everybody seems to know except me."

That he'd found out from Benjy didn't surprise her. "I wanted to tell you, but I thought it best that Miriam tell you herself and she agreed."

He took a deep breath. "And when was this supposed to happen?"

"Last week, but..."

"So why didn't she?" he interrupted.

"I was about to say—something came up."

"Something came up," he reflected, looking at her curiously. "What could have come up that would interfere with this?"

Not too many things, she said to herself, realizing that at this point there was no turning back. Once he knew part of the story, he should know the whole story. At least that's how she saw it. And though Miriam's arrival was but a few hours away, she felt she couldn't keep him in the dark any longer. "It's complicated," she said.

"What's complicated?" he asked reluctantly, as if afraid to know the answer.

Sarah looked away a moment, contemplating what would happen next. Sitting before her was the man she had come to know as a pillar of fortitude. Aside from skillfully helping myriads of people with the most challenging of life's tribulations over the years, she had watched him deal with the loss of his own beloved parents and his turmoil over Noah being gay, and she had truly come to believe that he would somehow find a way to deal with his daughter being with a Gentile. But now there was this other situation. And everyone, no matter how strong, has limits.

She turned back to Jonathan and said, "She's pregnant."

32

RAJESH BHATT STOOD, SEEMINGLY helpless, as Miriam gathered her things together. "Are you sure I can't come with you?" he asked.

"For the tenth time, I'm completely sure," she snapped, realizing he'd actually only asked her twice. Her exaggeration had been born of intense agitation, having received a rather upsetting text from her mother just a few minutes earlier:

"I don't know how to tell you this, but Dad knows everything. It's been very tense in *shul* this past week. People have been talking, and he found out about you and Raj this morning. I'm sorry, but I had no choice other than to tell him the whole story. I can't get into details right now, but I don't think it's a good idea to come tonight."

Her heart dropped the moment she'd read those words, but she concluded that this didn't change anything. And as upsetting as it was to have her father hear such a thing from others, it wasn't exactly shocking. On the contrary, she should have seen it coming. It had been naïve of her to wait this long.

She wanted to ask her mother why it was a bad idea for her to show up, but the answer seemed obvious: her father was in no state of mind to handle seeing her right now. She wanted to ask how long it would be before she could come home, but that was too uncomfortable a question to ask, and probably even more difficult for her mother to answer. She wanted to know if her father was okay, at least physically, but she was confident her mother would have mentioned something if there'd been a problem in that regard. So, not really knowing what to say or do, she simply responded: "I'm coming anyway."

It had been about ten minutes since she'd sent her response, and there had been no reply. She wasn't sure what to make of that, thinking perhaps that her mother just wasn't up to getting into a back and forth with her about it. She assumed that this was probably the same reason her mother had chosen texting rather than calling her on the phone, reminding herself of that old family trope of how nobody ever wins with Miriam.

In any event, her mother's text sounded to her more a suggestion than an insistence, so she decided to stick with the plan.

"You don't have to be so angry," Raj said.

"I'm not angry," she said as she scurried about, throwing things into an overnight bag. "Just frustrated and edgy."

"You're really going to spend the night?"

She looked at him, sighed, and said, "That's a good question." She thought a moment. "I would like to. Just not sure he even wants me there at all."

"At all?"

"Yes, at all, as in *ever again.*"

"That sounds very harsh."

He really doesn't get it. "It's actually quite realistic."

"I don't believe it."

She walked over to him and put her hand on his face. "I know you don't. It's because you don't understand."

He looked at her exasperated. They'd been through this conversation before, and now when it was all coming to a head, she was locking him out, not letting him be a part of it. "Well, I hope you tell them that I'm converting."

"Why would I tell them that?"

"Because it's the truth."

Fearing he was becoming more serious about this idea, she responded, "No, it isn't."

"Yes, it is." Unflinching.

"Listen, Raj. I've already told you: you need to get that ridiculous idea out of your head. You hate religion, you don't believe in God, you're not converting!"

"But I love you."

"I know you do, but that's not a good enough reason to convert."

It bothered him that she didn't say that she loved him back, but he understood there were more pressing things on her mind at that moment. "I'm aware that it's not a good reason to convert. The rabbi said the same thing."

She looked at him incredulously. *He's been talking to a rabbi?* "Rabbi! What rabbi?"

"Rabbi Samuels from Habad," he said, referring to the Chabad rabbi on campus, who he knew she respected.

"It's *Ch*abad," she said, emphasizing the *kh* pronunciation that many have difficulty with, and doing so a bit more snidely than she'd intended.

"When I become Jewish, I promise I'll pronounce everything properly."

"I'm sure you will." Her turn for exasperation. "What else did the rabbi say?"

Raj appreciated her curiosity, thinking maybe he was getting somewhere. "He also reminded me how people are often motivated by many factors in the choices we make. Since we're getting our PhDs in psychology, that shouldn't be news to us."

"It isn't," she said under her breath, "but that doesn't matter."

He stared at her inquisitively. *Why not?*

"Look," she said. "I agree that a person could start the conversion process because he or she loves someone who is Jewish, and that's probably the most common reason people do so. I get that such a person might eventually come to love Judaism from studying and becoming more familiar with it. But you're not that person. You don't believe in God, you've never missed an opportunity to tell me how you hate religion, and you don't want to be a Jew any more than you want to be a Hindu. So, it's out of the question."

"Sounds to me like *you* really don't want me to."

"There you go playing shrink with me again, and you've made this silly point before."

"Yes, I have, because I don't think it's silly, and I'm not playing anything. I think my point is quite valid."

She finished packing her bag, closed the zipper, and turned to him again. "Look, Raj," she said, her voice tremulous. "This whole thing is a big mess. I'm pregnant, I'm keeping the baby, and, even if we did get married, an Orthodox conversion takes time. I'm not walking down the aisle pregnant, so our baby will have to be born—God willing—before we're married. Not exactly what I ever envisioned for myself, and certainly not what my parents imagined. So, whatever scenario I come up with, it really sucks. Get my point?"

He nodded and said, "I do... No pun intended."

She smiled. "Funny, but not the best timing."

"Yes, not the best."

They looked at each other, some of the tension having dissipated.

"There are a lot of problems here," she said.

"But we can face them." Resolute.

She took a deep breath. "Maybe *we* can. I'm just not sure that my father can."

33

NOAH BAUMAN HUNG UP the phone with a sense of despair. Not even on the night he had come out to his parents had he felt so bleak. The news his mother had just given him shocked him as much as it had her. Not the part of the community knowing all about him—he'd been expecting that—but the part about his sister. *Miriam pregnant! How could she not have told me?* And now, with Miriam on her way to face their father, who his mother described as "practically catatonic," Noah feared that the situation could get even worse.

His mother had called him because she had no one else she could turn to at a time like this. That in itself scared him. Like his father, she had always been a problem solver, always in control and always confident. Never did any of the Bauman children sense a chink in their parents' armor. Not until recently. Not until his revelation. And now this. Everything was changing.

Miriam's predicament aside, Noah couldn't escape his own guilt for having started what now seemed to be the potential unravelling of his family. He realized he was being irrational and unrealistic, for there was really nothing he could have done to prevent this, but that didn't change the way he felt, the way he would probably feel for the rest of his life.

He needed to do something. Miriam was on her way home to deal with what was certainly her issue, but the entire family was affected. Even Aaron, the only one still in the dark about all this, would soon be involved.

And his mother *had* called him. Perhaps, without her having asked, she was hoping he might show up. Perhaps she and his father needed him to be there, either as a buffer or just for support. He wasn't sure.

He realized he was in a bad place emotionally and didn't want to make a rash decision. He looked at the clock: 5:10 p.m. Zach's classes ended at 5:00, and he would either be headed home or to the library. Noah dialed.

Zach picked up on the third ring. "Hey."

"Hey."

Zach sensed something. "Everything okay?"

"Not really."

"What's going on?"

Noah proceeded to update him, uninterrupted, concluding with the present dilemma of whether to go home or stay put.

"Wow! Oh my God!" Zach responded. "I think you should go."

"I'm just not certain if my presence is the first or the last thing they all need right now. I'm also feeling kind of responsible for at least some of this, and I don't want to do something foolish just to alleviate my own guilt."

Zach thought a moment. "I think you should go."

The next question Noah could have asked was "Why?" but it wasn't necessary. He understood Zach's thought process, and while Zach's reaction seemed impulsive, he knew it wasn't. Zach was usually quick on his feet, and his intuition was consistently spot on. The Bauman family was in crisis and Noah should be there, it was that simple. It didn't matter whether he'd be a help or a hindrance, he was a part of this.

Noah also took note of Zach not addressing his guilt, which to Noah's mind was consistent with Zach's tendency to focus on solutions. There had been times in the past when this had upset Noah, but at this moment, he actually appreciated it.

"Okay, I hear that," he said. "But maybe I should wait a couple of hours and then go? My guess is my mother's going to give them time together and stay just close enough in case it goes really bad. I'm thinking I should come later for the same reason."

Zach considered Noah's point. Noah's mother would somehow find a way to get her head around all of this, but the rabbi was clearly the wild card. "Sounds about right to me. Just don't wait long enough to talk yourself out of going altogether."

"I won't. I know what I have to do."

A brief silence.

"Will I see you later?" Zach asked.

"Probably not. I'm taking a bag, may have to spend the night. Possibly a few nights. Who knows?"

"Yeah, I understand... Call me later?"

"Definitely. Love you."

"Love you, too."

They hung up, and Noah started gathering his stuff together. While doing so, he felt himself getting choked up. In the past months, he'd gradually come to see Zach as a lifelong partner, and at this point he had no doubt about it. What their lives together would look like, he couldn't predict. But he was confident—especially now—that whatever came, they would face it as a team. He used to have the same conviction about his family These days, he wasn't so sure.

It occurred to him that his first instinct had been to call Zach rather than Dr. Rosen, and in that he found some much-needed comfort. He had come quite far from who he had been just a few months earlier. Mindful of this, he found himself feeling less despondent and more determined. With all he had been through, the years of self-loathing, torment, and struggle, he was finally seeing himself differently. What confronted him at this moment was no doubt a tall order—probably the tallest he would ever encounter. But maybe he could do some good, maybe he could help his family through this, maybe even his father.

34

MIRIAM BAUMAN LET HERSELF in and was immediately struck by the pervading silence. Not quite what she'd expected. She put her bag down, removed her coat and walked from the foyer to the den, wondering if anyone was even in the house. She hoped to see her mother first, to get an update on what was going on with her father before actually having to face him. She walked to the staircase, presuming the likely scenario of Sarah being in the bedroom and Jonathan being in his study. As she climbed the stairs and heard movement from the bedroom, a semblance of relief came upon her. At least this part she had gotten right.

The door was slightly ajar but still she knocked gently, as if afraid to disturb the quiet. A still voice, her mother's, said, "You can come in."

Miriam opened the door and entered. The two women stared at each other. "You okay?" Miriam asked.

"Not really," Sarah answered, surprised by her own honesty, by the ease with which she was able to flout the instinct to shield her child.

Miriam's face fell. She'd expected this, but actually experiencing it was a whole other matter. "Where's Dad?" she asked.

"Last I saw him, he was in the den."

Miriam figured that, whether from the den or his study, Jonathan most likely had heard the front door, her footsteps and, for all she knew, even some echoes of this conversation. "I'll go look for him," she said.

Sarah simply nodded, her face markedly undemonstrative.

Finding the den empty, Miriam made her way to Jonathan's study. The door was closed. She listened for sound but heard nothing. She couldn't recall a time when she hadn't heard him through that door, either humming over a page of Talmud or conversing on the phone. But never such silence.

She had a fleeting thought that maybe he wasn't there, maybe he'd left the house. She doubted he would have gone to the synagogue, not in the state she imagined him in. A walk outside, however, wasn't inconceivable; after all, it was a mild night. It then struck her that her mother would most likely have heard him leave.

No, he's on the other side of that door, she told herself, also realizing that he probably knew that she was standing there.

She took a deep breath and, with some hesitation, lifted her hand and knocked on the door.

No answer.

She knocked again, this time with a bit more determination.

Still, no response.

Suddenly, in her mind's eye, an image of herself as a child, 4 years old, bursting in on him with no warning while he met with a congregant.

Startled, he looks at her and says, as gently as possible under the circumstances, "Miriam, honey. How many times have Mommy and I told you that you're supposed to knock?"

"But, Daddy, I have to go to sleep," she says, as if that explains it all.

He smiles, as does the congregant, and says, "Yes, sweetie, you do," as he approaches her and picks her up. Hoisting her high, toward the ceiling, she shrieks with joy. He then kisses her, puts her down, and adds, "Now off to bed you go!"

With hesitation but compelled to proceed, she reached for the doorknob, slowly opened the door, and found him sitting in darkness, his eyes open but looking at nothing. He was expressionless, as her mother had been, seemingly unresponsive to her presence. "Daddy," she said softly.

He turned to her, still impassive.

"Can I sit?"

A reluctant nod.

She took a seat as she felt her eyes welling up. All the crying she'd been doing these past few weeks was really getting to her—just another thing in her life over which she held no sway. She had left the door slightly ajar for some light.

She had spent her train ride from Manhattan rehearsing various scripts in her head for this moment. But now, sitting in his presence, her mind drew a blank. "I'm so sorry about everything," was the best she could do.

He stared at her as if looking through her, somewhat at a loss himself. "I am too," he uttered.

A fleeting moment of curiosity, then she realized that he wasn't apologizing—he was expressing grief. "I don't know what to say."

"That's a first," he said, his voice slightly more animated.

She managed a faint smile. He couldn't pass up the opportunity for a tease, even at a time like this. It was his way of breaking the tension and, for a brief moment, it worked. "I know I've ruined everything," she said.

He considered her comment. "Well, your situation certainly does create a few problems."

While she appreciated his attempt to qualify things less severely than she had, his doing so only made her feel worse. Outrage, invective, recrimination—*those* she could have dealt with, but *this* only heightened her guilt. He simply loved her too much, and she knew it. And even with what she'd done, she could see that he was unable to countenance her anguish. Yet she had hurt him so, and the very thought of that was more than she could bear.

"I'm really sorry you had to hear about this the way you did," she said. "I was planning to tell you, and then I got..."

"I understand," he quickly interjected, as if he didn't want to actually hear her say the word.

She thought it best not to finish her statement. "I didn't know what to do," she said, tears covering her cheeks. "I still don't."

Prior to her entrance, he had been consumed by his own agony over what she had done, and now all he could feel was concern for her. "Are you asking me for advice?" he said.

She gazed at him, wondering what advice he could possibly offer. She couldn't imagine him recommending an abortion, and she simply didn't see him telling her to get rid of Raj under these circumstances. She also couldn't imagine him suggesting a conversion and marriage without knowing anything about Raj or the nature of their relationship. "I don't know that there's anything you can tell me," she said, cautious not to sound disrespectful.

"Neither do I," he reflected, admitting his question had been rhetorical, likely because he hadn't known what else to say. There were, however, real questions that he did have, but he wasn't sure exactly how to pose them. The last thing he wanted was for her to feel defensive or interrogated. "Can I ask you something?" he said.

She considered his request, fully aware that things were going to get even more uncomfortable, yet equally aware that this conversation was long overdue. "Yes," she said.

A slight hesitation, then, "How did this happen?"

"I really don't know," she answered. "He's a guy in my program. His name is Raj. There are only about twenty of us, and most of us are sort of friendly. So, Raj and I became friendly. Then, friendly turned into friends, which eventually turned into good friends, and one thing led to another." She considered what she was saying. "Honestly, I didn't even realize what was happening, and by the time I did, I guess it was too late."

"The heart is a funny thing."

"True," she said with a sigh. "Sometimes it can be brutal."

Jonathan nodded. "Your mother tells me he's a Hindu."

"Well, his family is, sort of... they don't really practice. He identifies himself as a 'none,' doesn't believe in any religion or God, but he says he's rethinking all that—it's complicated."

Jonathan was aware of the new term that some atheists were using these days, particularly popular among Millennials. "What's complicated?" he asked.

She figured, at this point, that she might as well tell him everything. "He says that's all changing now, that he wants to convert." She searched Jonathan for a reaction, but his expression was unrevealing. "Don't worry, I set him straight."

Jonathan raised his eyebrows. "Set him straight," he repeated, pondering her words. "And how did you do that?"

"I told him it was out of the question."

"Ah, out of the question," he uttered, again echoing her statement. "And why did you say that?"

"For the most obvious reason: he doesn't really want to be Jewish. He just loves me and wants to solve our..." She gestured, raising her hands, palms up.

"Problem," Jonathan added.

"Yeah," Miriam said. "Problem."

An exchange of meditative glances.

"Do you love him?"

Miriam nodded, surprising herself at how quickly she was able to respond affirmatively to that question. She wiped her cheeks. Jonathan slid over a tissue box. "Thanks," she said as she took a few.

"I have another question?" Jonathan said.

"I know." She paused, looked him in the eye, and added, "I'm keeping it."

Jonathan considered her response. "So Raj wants to convert, but you say he can't. You love him, and you're having his child." He paused for a second. "How, exactly, do you imagine this all turning out?"

"Not well."

"You're going to be a single mother of a Jewish child whose father is a *none*?"

"I guess so." Tentative. "I really don't see any other choice. Do you?"

He reflected on her question. "Perhaps I do."

She knew where he was going with this and threw him an incredulous look. "You can't be thinking that he'll convert? I told you, he's..."

"Yes, I heard everything you said." His eyes opened widely. "I'm the rabbi in this house." He pointed to his *smicha*, or rabbinic degree, on the wall. "I believe I'm qualified to decide who can and cannot convert." *Though I may not be the rabbi in this community for much longer.*

"*Really*, you think he can?"

"If he wants to as much as you say he does, then yes, I believe he can."

"But I thought that he has to really want to be a Jew, that he has to commit to observe all the commandments, and he has to really mean it."

"That's true."

"But that's exactly the problem. There's no way he's going to commit to be an Orthodox Jew!"

"Says who?"

"Says me, Daddy!" Indignant.

He looked at her askance, the same way he always did when they got into arguments. "How about this, Miriam? Instead of us getting into our usual back-and-forth about this, why don't you let *me*—you know, the rabbi in the house—worry about those details."

"I just don't understand how you think this could happen."

"How does *his* family feel about it?" he asked, seemingly ignoring her last comment.

"He claims that his parents don't care about religion, that they're very secular. They're doctors, lots of Jewish friends, that sort of thing. He says that all they want is for him to be happy."

He paused, considered what he was hearing. "Why don't we start with me talking to Raj?"

"You want to talk to him?"

"Actually, I want to meet with him. And I can't speak for your mother, but I suspect she does too."

She looked at him, astounded.

"At the very least, we *should* meet him," Jonathan said. "After all, he is going to be the father of our grandchild."

Miriam took a moment to digest all this. "So now *I* have a question."

His expression said *go ahead, ask away.*

"Well," she began, "let's say, for argument's sake, that you pull off Raj's supposed conversion and I do marry him, which sounds to me what you want—" *And that completely blows my mind, though it probably shouldn't.* "You and Mom are gonna throw me a wedding as a pregnant bride? That'll be a first in the annals of Orthodox Judaism!"

Jonathan actually managed a smile. "Yes, it would, and it would also be rather awkward. But that's not the plan, because a proper conversion can take about a year, and by my calculation that's longer than nine months."

She gazed at him wide-eyed. *Humor? At a time like this?* "And what about me giving birth out of wedlock?" she asked. "That's not going to look so good either."

"No, it won't," he said, his face turning serious again. "What can I say? God created a less than perfect world."

She considered his point and offered a faint smile of her own. "He did indeed."

35

NOAH BAUMAN CAME UP the front walk to the house when he heard the familiar sound of a bouncing basketball coming from the backyard. First asphalt, then backboard, then the unmistakable reverberation of the rim. He looked at his watch: 10:20 p.m. It was a mild enough late-March evening, but who could possibly be shooting hoops in the yard, especially at this hour? He returned his key to his pocket and decided to walk around to see.

"Dad!" he proclaimed upon observing Jonathan draped in a hoodie, throwing the ball at the net.

Jonathan stopped and turned to him. "Yeah?"

"What're you doing?"

Jonathan regarded the ball in his hands. "Looks like I'm shooting baskets."

Noah looked at him wide-eyed. "When was the last time you did this?"

"Can't really remember. Probably when you or Aaron were in high school."

Noah nodded. To his recollection, Jonathan used to shoot hoops with the boys regularly until Aaron, the phenom, was about 15, and the old man couldn't keep up anymore. There were a couple of times after that when Noah and Jonathan threw the ball around, but mostly it was Noah and Aaron, with Noah always striving to keep up with his brother's superior abilities.

"That's a long time ago," Noah said. "You suddenly felt an urge?"

Jonathan took a breath. "Needed to blow off some steam. Couldn't think of anything else." He turned to the basket, shot and missed, and clumsily went for the rebound.

Noah smiled. He had to admit, this was about the last thing he'd expected to find upon his arrival, but considering all the possible scenarios he'd been dreading, *this* seemed pretty good. "You need some work," he remarked.

"I suppose I'm a bit rusty," Jonathan responded. He looked down and saw that Noah was actually wearing sneakers, and said, "You came prepared," as he tossed him the ball.

Noah regarded his footwear, New Balance running shoes, not exactly the wisest choice for the pivots and twists of a serious game of one-on-one. He lifted the ball just above his forehead and took a shot. Thirteen feet, more or less. Swish.

"Not too shabby," Jonathan exclaimed, grabbing the ball. "You still have it."

Noah chuckled. "It was just one shot."

Jonathan passed him the ball again. "Okay, try another."

Noah looked at the ball, then at his father.

"Come on, Noey. I'm waiting."

Noah bounced the ball twice, set up his free-throw stance and went for it. Off the backboard and down through the net.

"Like I said," Jonathan said.

"I play now and then."

"It does seem that way. Now let's see what you can do with me guarding."

"Dad, you're being ridiculous."

"Why, because you think I'm old? I'm only 59. I run almost every day. I can handle this. Compared to what I've been handling lately, this is nothing!"

Noah raised his eyebrows. "This is a little different than a relaxed, slow-paced run."

"Don't worry. I got this," Jonathan said, offering his best imitation of a cocky adolescent.

Noah started dribbling. "Okay, if you insist."

Sarah stood at the bedroom window observing the commotion below. Ten minutes or so earlier, when she'd first heard Jonathan shooting baskets, she was a tad bewildered, as it had been years since she'd seen him use their backyard court. Knowing him as she did, however, she realized that he needed to do something physical to vent his frustration. They had often talked about getting rid of that old rickety basket, but the boys did use it from time to time when they visited, and most recently Aaron had been using it with his son. Good thing they left it intact, she thought, smiling as she saw Noah outmaneuver his father with a smoothly executed layup.

She had contacted Noah out of desperation but hadn't expected him to drop everything and show up. When he quickly texted her back to say that he was coming, she'd responded: Good. She hadn't been sure why she wanted him there or what his presence would accomplish, but now, watching the two men together, she knew it had been a wise idea.

She watched them finish up and head into the house. Supposing they would talk some, she thought it best to stay upstairs and leave them be. She turned from the window, walked into the hall and approached Miriam's bedroom door. She could see the light was on through the bottom of the door, but beyond that, she had no idea what Miriam was doing inside. She listened for a clue. Nothing. No typing on a keyboard. No movement whatsoever. Eager to learn what had occurred between Miriam and Jonathan, she knocked.

"Come in," Miriam said.

Sarah opened the door, the hinges of which seemed to squeak louder than usual amid the quiet. She looked at Miriam, lying in bed, phone in hand, and guessed that she had probably interrupted a texting conversation, most likely with Raj. "How'd it go?" she asked.

Miriam bobbled her head a bit. "Okay… I think."

"Anything you want to share?"

Miriam considered the request. "Raj and Dad think Raj is converting and we're getting married."

Sarah wasn't completely surprised about Jonathan's idea, especially since Raj, apparently, was thinking the very same thing. "Sounds like you're not in agreement with that plan," she said.

"I don't know what I'm in agreement with."

Sarah nodded. “I understand. It’s a lot to process.” She thought a moment. “What about Raj’s parents, do you know how they feel about this?”

“Funny, you and Dad always ask the same questions.”

“It happens when you’re married close to thirty years.”

Miriam smirked. “I told Dad the same thing I already told you: Raj says they don’t care about religion.”

Sarah nodded, acknowledging the conversation they’d had a few weeks ago. “They may not care about religion, but that doesn’t mean that they won’t care about him converting. They may not be so comfortable with him going from being a secular Hindu or atheist to becoming an observant Jew.”

“What can I tell you? He says they’ll be good with it.” Miriam stared at her mother a moment. “I’m not prepared for any of this,” her eyes welling up once again.

Sarah sat down on the bed. “I know, neither are we.” She put her hand on Miriam’s back and started rubbing. “We’re just going to have to get through all this together.”

Miriam wiped her tears and managed a smile. “I don’t think I’ve ever cried so much.”

“That’s only because you don’t remember when you were little.”

Noah and Jonathan sat in the den, each with a snifter in hand, sharing a glance of approval over Jonathan’s latest discovery, Blanton’s Single Barrel bourbon. “This is really good!” Noah remarked.

“Told you so.” Jonathan had tasted it at a wedding a few weeks earlier, had gone to three different liquor stores before finally getting lucky: he was informed it was the only bottle left of the seven allotted to the store, and no one knew when the next shipment might arrive. With all that was going on, Jonathan still appreciated that he could share this with his son.

"It's good to see you," Jonathan continued. "To what do we owe the pleasure?"

Noah understood that his father really knew why he was there but figured this was probably as good a way as any to start the conversation. "I heard Miriam was coming to talk to you. Thought it might be a good idea for me to be here as well."

Jonathan nodded, taking it in.

"So," Noah said cautiously. "You and Miriam talked?"

"We did."

"And?"

Jonathan took a breath and reflected on the question. "We have some things to work out."

Noah nodded and took another sip. "I'm sorry that my situation makes things even harder."

"You being gay has nothing to do with this," Jonathan said.

It didn't escape Noah that this was the first time he'd actually heard his father refer to him as gay, rather than talking around it. He knew that Jonathan was coming to grips with the fact, but actually hearing the term articulated to him in that way made him realize that his father was much further along on this process than he'd thought. "But it does," he responded.

Jonathan knew what Noah was getting at, that despite Noah not having had a choice in what or who he was, there was a cumulative effect in the eyes of the community of the rabbi having two children who have gone so far "astray."

"For some, it does," Jonathan said, "but for me, it doesn't. I understand what you've been through. I understand the challenges you face. And I understand that this wasn't your choice."

"I know you do," Noah said. "And I know that this may not make sense to you. But I've been thinking a lot about it, and I'm not convinced that Miriam's circumstances were completely by choice either."

Jonathan considered Noah's statement. "That, my son, is part of a much larger philosophical and psychological debate, and I think, right now, it's beside the point."

"Yeah, I suppose it is," Noah said, appreciating how his father was grappling with the practical issue of what to do going forward. "Are you and Miriam okay?" he asked.

"We're fine." Definitive. "The situation, however, *that's* a different story."

Noah took another sip, which prompted Jonathan to do so as well. "So, what's the plan?" he asked.

Jonathan thought for a second. "Miriam says Raj wants to convert."

Noah raised his eyebrows. "Really?"

Jonathan nodded. Another sip. "Really."

"And she wants to marry him?" Slightly bemused.

"She says she loves him."

Noah nodded. "Well, he is a really good guy. Super smart, good looking. And very much a *mensch*," he said, using the Jewish term for a "fine person."

"You've met him?" Jonathan asked, realizing that it was a sort of silly question, considering how close Miriam and Noah were.

"Yeah," Noah said haltingly, aware of his father's hurt from having been left out of the loop. "A few times," he added, only for the purpose of lending credence to his opinion of Raj.

"Seems I'm the last to know," Jonathan said, reflecting.

"Not quite," Noah said. "You're forgetting about Aaron."

"Aaron's in LA. Around here, I'm the last."

"With something like this, does that surprise you?"

Jonathan reflected again. "No, I suppose it shouldn't."

A moment of silence.

"Well," Noah said. "If Raj actually does convert, that certainly seems to solve some problems."

"Some, but not all."

"That's true... but it's a start."

"Yes," Jonathan said, "it's a start."

36

AARON BAUMAN STARED AT the phone in his hand not knowing what else to do. He had just received the troubling tidings of his family's latest dilemma. Having heard it from his father made it all the more palpable. Miriam with a Gentile, and pregnant, on top of Noah being gay. He couldn't imagine how his parents were surviving; he couldn't imagine how he would either.

He found Sheindy in the kitchen, cooking up a storm for an abundance of guests they were expecting for Shabbos.

"You look like you just saw a ghost," Sheindy observed as she was moving about, her attention mostly on her preparations.

Aaron just stood there, unresponsive.

"Aaron," she pressed, her focus now solely on him.

"Yeah. I'm sorry," he said. "Just got a call from my father and heard some really bad news."

Concerned, she waited for more.

"My sister's dating a Gentile," he said, his tone deliberately robotic, trying to hold it together.

"*Miriam?*"

He nodded, finding himself unable to tell her the other part of the story.

"Dating, as in *seriously* dating?" Sheindy asked, immediately realizing the answer to her own question. A phone call from Aaron's father meant it had to be serious.

All he could do was nod.

"Oh my God!" Her face rapidly turned crimson.

"That's not all of it," he said cautiously.

She peered at him, her eyes asking, *What more could there possibly be?*

He stared back at her, hesitated, then said, "She's also pregnant."

Sheindy reached for the countertop to steady herself. Tears formed in her eyes, and she was mute.

Aaron stepped forward and took hold of her as she buried her head in his shoulder. "It isn't all completely bad," he said, his tone warming.

"What? What's not completely bad?" she asked, withdrawing from him.

"Miriam says the guy wants to convert."

Sheindy took a breath. "Convert? What is he now?"

"Hindu. Sort of."

"Sort of?"

"Supposedly, he doesn't really believe in it. Neither does his family."

"But he believes in Judaism?"

"It's complicated."

"I'll bet it is!"

"I think they'll work it out." He tried to sound reassuring, but realized he wasn't doing the best job of it.

"It's a lot to figure out, especially considering your father's position in the community."

"That's going to be a big problem."

Sheindy hesitated, then asked, "And what about your position here?"

Aaron contemplated her question. "You think it could have an effect? All the way out here in LA?"

"News travels. And Jewish news travels even faster."

"I guess it's possible," Aaron reflected.

"I think it's more than possible."

"Okay. Maybe. But why would it really matter?"

"I'm not saying it would be as bad as what your father has to deal with, but it's *your* brother, *your* sister. Some people are bound to say things, look at you funny. For a rabbi, that can be a problem."

"Let them talk! Who cares?"

"I'm just saying that it could get... difficult."

"Only if we let it." He thought a moment. "Look, I can't be held responsible for what my brother and my sister do."

"I know. And most of the community adores you, but there are a few who always have something to say."

"You're right, there are probably a few who will have something to say. But if it isn't about this, it'll be about something else. I honestly don't think it matters."

"Okay," she uttered, somewhat unconvinced. "I hope you're right."

"And if I'm wrong, then we'll leave. We'll go back to New York," he said, his tone unexpectedly stolid.

"And do what?"

"Well, you'd be closer to your parents and happier about that. And I... I guess it would be hard to get another pulpit." Pause. "I suppose I'd have to find a teaching job or something."

"I don't think you'd be happy with that."

"I'm not so sure." He looked away for a brief moment, wondering. "To be honest, a part of me feels that maybe I should be there, especially now."

She approached him again and took his hands. "You don't need to worry about me. I've adjusted to being here, and I can be happy here or there. I understand that this is probably going to get even harder for your parents, so you need to decide what you want to do to help. Whatever that is, I'll be okay with it."

"Thanks," he said, feeling himself getting choked up.

She pushed herself against him, and as his lips settled upon her forehead, their moment was interrupted by the sound of a crying baby. "It's your turn," she said.

37

DAVID WEISBERG CALLED TO order an emergency session of the Beth Israel Synagogue Board of Trustees. The topic: what to do about the looming community "crisis." All fifteen current board members were present, plus Benjy Marcus, who enjoyed lifetime board membership, and Avi Gerstein, the synagogue's legal counsel.

Though pleased with the attendance—it was rare for more than ten people to show for any meeting, much less an impromptu one—Weisberg was concerned about Marcus and Gerstein. Not as much with Marcus, who had lost some credibility and influence and was soon to be sentenced to prison. But Gerstein was unquestionably a highly respected member of the community. He knew both men would adamantly oppose what he was seeking to accomplish yet was confident he had enough other votes to override them.

He also knew that one could never be certain of anything before the actual votes were in.

When the chatter faded, all eyes were on Weisberg. He observed his surroundings. He had decided to hold the meeting in the basement of his bayside home, a nice-sized colonial in what was known as Old Lawrence or Back Lawrence, across the street from the 11th hole of the Lawrence Country Club golf course. Weisberg was worried that it might get loud and felt that any room in the synagogue would be too public, as there were always people mulling around the building for one purpose or another.

Marcus and Gerstein had objected on the grounds that the synagogue's policy of transparency allowed all members of the congregation to observe all board meetings. They were also annoyed that the rabbi wasn't invited. They claimed the meeting was inappropriately clandestine, labelled it illegitimate, and threatened to boycott. But upon learning that only one other board member, Shelly Wolf, a close personal friend of Sarah's, agreed with them, they decided it was better to attend. Weisberg had scored first blood.

"I won't beat around the bush," Weisberg opened. "We're here to talk about what's going on. Everyone knows what that is. It's causing a rift in the community and we have to deal with it!"

"Everybody knows what's going on?" Benjy Marcus remarked, his tone skeptical.

"I believe so," Weisberg rejoined.

"Then tell me," Benjy said. "What exactly *is* going on?"

Weisberg leaned forward in his seat, projecting confidence. "Come on, Benjy, you know why we're here!"

"Because our rabbi is having some family problems?" Benjy asked.

"Not just family problems," interjected Shmuel Ehrlich, the young MD, and a staunch ally of Weisberg. "These are issues that are embarrassing the entire community."

"Are you referring to the rumor that one of the rabbi's sons is gay?" Avi Gerstein inquired in a lawyerly manner.

"That's only one part of it," Weisberg responded. "And if that were the sole issue, we wouldn't be having this meeting."

"I'm somehow not convinced of that," Benjy remarked.

"Think what you want, Benjy," Weisberg said. "In my opinion, the real problem here is the rabbi's daughter."

"And what about the rabbi's daughter?" Benjy asked.

"That she's dating a Muslim, for God's sake!" Shmuel Ehrlich blurted out.

"Actually, that's not true," Shelly Wolf chimed in.

"That's right!" Benjy said. He looked around the room. "It seems some people don't know what they're talking about."

"Okay, Benjy," Weisberg said defensively. "Why don't you tell us what *is* going on with the rabbi's daughter?"

"I think *you* should be the one to tell us! *You* convened this meeting." Benjy knew that, at the end of the day, it wouldn't make much of a difference whether Miriam was with a Muslim, Buddhist, Mormon, or whatever. The Muslim thing may have made a difference for some, but for most, a non-Jew of any kind was problematic enough. All Benjy wanted at that moment was to challenge and discredit Weisberg's entourage as much as possible, and by the look on some of their faces, it appeared he was making some headway.

It seemed for a moment that nobody had anything to say until Weisberg declared, "Look. Whatever. We may not have all the facts exactly right, but something is going on with the rabbi's daughter, and we all know it. We also know the situation with the rabbi's son. The community's in an uproar. We're the board, and we have to do something about this!"

"What do you suggest?" Shelly Wolf asked. "It is true that there are rumors of Miriam Bauman dating a non-Jewish guy and Noah Bauman being gay. But should we fire our rabbi, who's been here for almost thirty years, because two of his children may fall short of our view of perfection? As if none of us have children who have strayed from the path in one way or another? Who are we kidding?"

"We're not kidding anyone," Weisberg shot back. "Sure, many of us have had difficulties with children or other family members. We all understand that there's no escaping that. But this is our rabbi, our community leader, and he and his family should set an example."

"Exactly!" Avi Gerstein interrupted. "That's exactly what *Rav* Yoni is—exemplary! A role model *par excellence*. The type of person we should all emulate. He is a towering intellect and scholar, a spiritual and compassionate personality, and the fact that his children may not be completely perfect in our eyes makes him all the more human. And, actually, a better leader."

"And let's not forget Sarah," Benjy Marcus added. "Let's not forget all those midnight phone calls and house calls when our children were sick, or the endless other sacrifices she's made over the years and continues to make. Is all that rendered meaningless because of this 'crisis' you talk about?"

Again, the room turned silent. Avi Gerstein scrutinized the faces of those who hadn't yet spoken up, surmising that most were probably conflicted and taking it in. "I suggest we adjourn this meeting to give ourselves more time to think all this through," he said.

"We can't just let this be!" snapped Shmuel Ehrlich. "Already people are leaving the *shul* and joining other congregations. It may sound harsh, I understand, and I don't know how else to put it, but a lot of people don't want a rabbi with so many stains."

"You don't know how else to put it?" Shelly Wolf challenged. "There are a thousand better ways to put it than that. For God's sake, family problems *aren't* stains!"

"But they can be when it comes to the rabbi of a community," Weisberg said. "Whether that's right or wrong, it's how people see it. The viability of our *shul* is at stake here. We simply can't financially afford to lose more members."

"Has anyone considered how many members we might lose if we *do* fire the rabbi?" asked Rafi Aranov. A Sephardic Jew, Aranov was originally from Afghanistan and part of a large family in the diamond and rare-jewels business. It had become more common in the past few years for Orthodox Sephardic Jews, who were generally staunch traditionalists, to join Ashkenazic synagogues. Such a comment from Aranov, regarded by all as the perfect gentleman—reserved, thoughtful, and genteel—was taken as a good sign by the rabbi's advocates.

"Yeah," Benjy Marcus responded, "I wonder how *that* would impact upon the *shul's* viability."

"You're right," Weisberg conceded. "We're in trouble either way. But if we find a young, dynamic, energetic replacement, I believe we will grow again in time. If we do nothing, I'm afraid we're doomed."

Marcus and Gerstein looked at each other. They understood that "young, dynamic, and energetic," was Weisberg's way of disguising his true agenda of finding a rabbi with ultra-Orthodox leanings, something he'd wanted long before the scuttlebutt about Miriam and Noah. They also understood that Weisberg was right that ultra-Orthodoxy was growing rapidly around them, and that Beth Israel was one of the last hold-outs in the Five Towns for Modern Orthodoxy.

"Am I to take it that you want a vote here and now on whether to fire the rabbi?" Marcus asked.

Weisberg nodded.

"Well, I hate to tell you this," Avi Gerstein said contemptuously, his eyes on Weisberg, "but you can't do that."

"Why not?" Shmuel Ehrlich inquired.

Weisberg was silent because he already knew the answer to Ehrlich's question. In fact, he suspected this was coming the moment Gerstein showed for the meeting. A minor hurdle, he told himself, though he was certainly aware that it could turn into much more than that.

"There's a small matter standing in the way," Avi said, his tone mildly derisive. "It's called the New York State Religious Corporations Law 200." He turned again to Weisberg and said, "David, I'll let *you* explain to everyone what that is."

The others in the room looked to Weisberg.

Weisberg halted for a second, examining some of the faces. "The law that states that the board of trustees of a synagogue cannot fire a rabbi. It can only be done by a vote of the entire membership."

"If you already knew this, then why did you call this meeting?" Shmuel Ehrlich asked.

"Because I thought it was important first to get some kind of consensus from the board before we took it to the entire congregation," Weisberg replied.

"Doesn't seem to me that you have such a large consensus," Benjy Marcus said, realizing that he was voicing more a hope than a reality. It was still anyone's guess what some of the others were thinking.

"Well," Weisberg countered, "we won't know till we actually vote."

38

My Dearest Friends,

As you all know, our synagogue executive board has called for a meeting of the entire congregation next week to discuss issues concerning my position as Rabbi. As you also know, my family has recently been beset with considerable challenges that have, in turn, engendered questions among some regarding my fitness to continue serving as rav of our community. After lengthy and soul-searching deliberations, I have decided to compose this email to all of you, as members of the synagogue, to share my thoughts and feelings about this matter.

Let me start by saying that there are very few, if any, among us who haven't faced difficulties with some of our children. As your rabbi, I have seen firsthand how such situations can often be quite vexing for any family, and tear at the fabric of the relationships we hold most precious. For those who have sought my advice throughout the years, I must admit that I have never felt quite prepared for that role and have frequently found myself praying to Hashem for guidance. This inadequacy has more recently encountered its greatest test in my own life. For both Sarah and me, it has been a time of profound introspection, struggle, and, I hope, growth.

In the past few weeks, as the news of our family's situation has spread, it has become apparent to us that the community has approached a crossroad. We had surmised that this might happen well before any meeting had been scheduled, but we had hoped, perhaps unrealistically so, that you, the members of our dear and beloved congregation, would have taken such tidings in stride. I understand now that it had been naïve of me to have imagined such a situation not causing a schism among you, and I want all of you to know that Sarah and I cannot find it within ourselves to either blame or judge you for this. We wish it could be otherwise, but we understand that it isn't. I can go on ad nauseum about the reasons for this—how Orthodoxy feels assailed on all fronts by the threats of the modern world, how it sometimes chooses insularity and dare I say intolerance as its defenses—but I am confident that nothing I could offer at this point would change anything.

To be clear, my intention is not to cast aspersions on our community. On the contrary, intolerance can be a positive force, an unadulterated expression of one's values and positions. And I freely admit that, in this regard, there are many things of which I am intolerant. The problem is that it too often becomes a negative force, and as we all know, there is much calamity that follows in its wake. Ours is at once a strong and vulnerable community, and what has happened here is just the latest incarnation of a very old story. I know that there are those who argue that the only way forward for us is through rejectionism rather than accommodation. In all honesty, and perhaps because of my own personal predicament, I'm just not convinced.

As I compose this email, it occurs to me that I cannot do justice to describing the anguish that Sarah and I are experiencing over having become a source of dissension and divisiveness among those we hold so dear. It is this very same anguish that has led me to the decision to resign my position as rabbi forthwith, as I am unable to go even one more day knowing that I am the source of disunity in a community that I have served and loved for almost thirty years. There is simply no way I could continue to be effective in my role if even a small minority of the congregation has lost confidence in me.

Notwithstanding my resignation, I do recognize that the Passover holiday is approaching, and while there are plenty of rabbis in the area to field your questions about the detailed and arduous preparations, I will also make myself available in this regard. If any of you need assistance, just call.

I would also like to inform you that Sarah and I aren't going anywhere, certainly not in the near future. Although many rabbis tend to relocate when they leave their positions, usually to another pulpit, that will not be the case with us. We love our home, our friends, and our community. Sarah's practice is here, and we have no plans to change that. We are staying put.

As for how I will be spending my "retirement," I do have an idea or two, though now is neither the time nor place to discuss this. What I do want to stress, however, is the need to stay together and unified, to continue to build and grow as we move beyond what I hope will turn out to have been only a brief disruption.

Toward that end, I would encourage you not to cancel next week's meeting, but rather to set its agenda to exactly the opposite of what had been intended. It is my deepest hope that all of you attend, explore your disagreements in a civil and constructive way —something quite unusual in the greater world in which we live— and proceed as one community with common goals and aspirations.

With that in mind, Sarah and I offer you our sincerest thanks for all the good and wonderful times we have shared over the years.

Warmly,

Yonasan

39

JONATHAN BAUMAN LOOKED OUT at his audience. Six months standing behind this lectern, and still not completely accustomed to the crowd, the room, the venue. Each day it still felt novel, yet he had to admit he was enjoying himself.

He perused the eager, bright, captivated faces before him and savored the contentment that had enabled him to move beyond the lingering sadness over what he'd left behind. He was okay with the choices he'd made, as painful as they had been, and was excited for what the future held, whatever that might be.

It had been close to a year since he last stood at the pulpit of Beth Israel. No regrets. It had been time for the next chapter, for him and his family.

Despite Jonathan's resignation, his supporters tried to encourage him to fight, as they firmly believed the vote would be solidly in his favor. Their thinking was that Weisberg hadn't really cared if he lost the vote. His ambition, they believed, was to publicly exploit the issues, strengthen his faction, and walk away with a consolation prize: a separate Shabbos *minyan* for the so-called *yeshivish* crowd, otherwise known as the "black hat" crowd.

Jonathan had also understood Weisberg's intention from the start: create a "second congregation" within the same building to re-engage those who had already left, and attract new, young, and more strictly observant families. A breakaway *minyan* instead of a breakaway *shul*. Not a novel idea, and as usually happens in these situations, the breakaway would probably grow and eventually usurp the entire congregation.

So, that had been Jonathan's conundrum: fight and hold on while presiding over a split congregation and await the inevitable, or walk away. For him, it had been a no-brainer. He had meant every word of his resignation letter.

And here he was in his new post: law professor at Fordham University, his alma mater. He didn't mind the daily commute to the city. It was just a few blocks' walk from the house to the Long Island Rail Road station, and it hadn't even taken a week before a small group, some of whom had been congregants, had approached him and asked him to give a daily Talmud class on the train. He had been flattered by the request and happy to oblige. Before he knew it, he was surrounded by attentive participants both to and from Manhattan. And now, seven months into this new routine, he couldn't really think of anything to complain about. And that, in and of itself, took some getting used to.

As for his newfound happiness, he could thank his law school mentor and former professor, Arthur Carmichael. All those years of incessantly prodding Jonathan to teach at Fordham had finally paid off. The last of their annual lunches was fortuitously held about a month after Noah had come out, and it had taken a different turn. Jonathan sensed even then that changes were looming on his horizon, and Carmichael noticed that he had a more receptive audience than usual.

"I must say I'm surprised, Mr. Bauman," Carmichael says, using the same formal title for Jonathan that he used for all his students, even after many years of friendship.

"Surprised at what?" Jonathan asks.

"That you're not dismissing me so handily with that usual stuff about how you're happy where you are and with what you're doing." Carmichael pauses. "Tell me, what's going on?"

Observing the sizeable lunch crowd around them, Jonathan grows concerned about privacy. He is fairly well known and certain that there are people in the room who would recognize him. Normally, that wouldn't bother him at all, but today, this meeting, requires some additional discretion.

Being the one with dietary restrictions, he always chose the restaurant and, considering the cost of kosher food, he always picked up the tab. Not that the professor didn't protest about paying at least his own portion, and not that they didn't do the same dance every time the bill came. But Jonathan could be both insistent and persuasive, and this was one of those situations in which he made sure to draw upon those skills.

Jonathan had come to know Carmichael as one who was particular about food, so he routinely went out of his way to find impressive places. This time it was Les Marais, an upscale French eatery in Midtown. The motif was typical steak house, greeting its customers with a butcher-shop-style glassed display of choice meats, followed by an ornate and impressively stocked bar, and eventually leading to a dimly lit dining area with tawny wooden floors and dark wood tables and chairs.

Mindful of the crowd, Jonathan leans in and delicately responds, "There have been some changes this past year."

"Changes?"

"Some family issues." Jonathan looks around, gathering his thoughts. "I can't go into the details right now. But suffice it to say that your offer is sounding more appealing."

Carmichael notices Jonathan looking to and fro and recognizes his student's reticence to go any further. He knows he will learn everything in time. "Must be some pretty serious issues."

Jonathan nods, his face solemn.

"I'll make a few calls," Carmichael says.

Jonathan smiles. He knows Carmichael resigned as dean several years earlier and is teaching only part time at this point. He also knows that Carmichael is chairman of the academic search committee and still enjoys boundless influence. A few calls, so to speak, is as good as a done deal. "I appreciate that."

The waiter, a short, heavyset, balding fellow with a French accent, sets down their plates. "Enjoy," he says. "Let me know if there's anything else."

"Thank you," Jonathan and Carmichael say in unison.

Carmichael observes his burger, which Jonathan and the waiter assured him would be one of the best he'd ever had. "Well, it's certainly a big one."

"That it is," Jonathan says as he stands to go wash his hands. There is no need to formally excuse himself, as Carmichael is accustomed to his ritually washing his hands before breaking bread.

"I'll wait," Carmichael says.

"No need," Jonathan replies, watching the professor practically salivate. "Go ahead, dig in. I'll be right back."

Carmichael is already about four bites in by the time Jonathan returns. "This is spectacular!" he utters amid his chomping.

Jonathan sits, tears off a small piece of the bun, and whispers the Hamotzi, *the traditional blessing over bread. "I'll bet it is," he says as he lifts the burger to his mouth.*

Jonathan returned to the present. And here he was, in the very same room in which he had sat as a student so many years earlier, facing about eighty 1Ls. The subject: torts, his area of expertise. He especially loved comparing American and Talmudic discussions on such matters, but since this was a first-year class with an abundance of material to cover, he kept that to a minimum. Once in a while he managed to sneak it in, but only to whet their appetites for his elective on that subject, which they could take in their second or third year. All in all, he had to admit, he was having great fun.

He was also spending a good amount of time these days writing, and he appreciated having much more leisure to do so than in the past. When he had been in the rabbinate, most of his publications appeared in secular legal journals, which had positioned him well for this job, though that had never been his intention. And now that he was teaching law full time, his writing focused almost exclusively on Judaic topics. An irony indeed.

He took in the room yet again, as if to perform a reality check on where he was. Perhaps one day, maybe even soon, he would get used to this. For now, it all continued to seem surreal.

"Shall we begin?" he announced to the class.

40

THE BAUMAN FAMILY, FIRST night of Passover. Present: the entire clan, including the former LA contingent now residing in NY, and newcomers Zach Abramson, Rajesh Bhatt, and three-month-old Maya Bauman-Bhatt. The family table was now twelve strong.

Amid the many weeks of preparations—shopping for *Pesach* provisions; sterilizing sinks, countertops, and ovens; changing dishes, silverware, and glasses; turning the house upside down to ensure every last breadcrumb had been exiled—Sarah Bauman finally allowed herself to take a breather and enjoy her family.

Jonathan Bauman, too, was in better spirits than he'd been in quite a while. He was, of course, surrounded by those he loved most. And he also took solace from the knowledge that his close friend Benjy Marcus had been granted an early release from prison—courtesy of a plethora of pleas from politicians and community leaders. He imagined Benjy enjoying his own family Seder at that very moment. And he was heartened that Esther Marcus had found it within herself to forgive her husband's transgressions. It had to have been unbearable for her, and Jonathan would have understood had she chosen otherwise. But presently, it seemed to be working out for the best. At least for now. And that was all one could hope for.

Jonathan thought about this as he was about to recite the *Kiddush* prayer over the wine, sanctifying the holiday and fulfilling the first of the famed four cups of wine required during this sacred meal. He wasn't sure why these were the thoughts creeping into his head at this moment when he should be focused on fulfilling the commandments of the Seder. Perhaps it was because he was reflecting not just about his friend, but about himself and the others sitting around the table with him. Their tribulations, fealty, endurance, and triumphs. And all this, in a way, was what this celebration was really about for him: freedom, God having granted us the ability to make choices, the inherent difficulties often accompanying such choices, and the inevitable consequences and responsibilities that follow. This was what occupied his mind as he raised his cup to begin his recitation.

He glanced around the table one more time, his eyes settling on Raj. The two of them had grown quite close this past year, as Jonathan had assisted indirectly with Raj's conversion. Having been his future father-in-law, and no longer officially in the rabbinate, Jonathan couldn't play a formal role, but he still made sure they met for weekly study sessions. He had come to admire Raj's intellect and honesty, and he had grown to understand exactly what Miriam saw in him, why she had fallen in love.

His mind turned back to what had been one of their most memorable interactions, six months earlier, when they were supposed to have been studying the laws of Shabbos.

"I'm sorry to change the subject, but I have a question that's really been bothering me," Raj says.

Jonathan looks at him admiringly. It isn't the first time Raj suddenly veers off subject, and Jonathan has come to appreciate these diversions as always interesting and challenging. "Okay," he reacts.

" Well," Raj begins hesitantly. "I know I'm supposed to believe that God has a special relationship with the Jewish people."

Jonathan nods, waiting for the question.

" How, then, do you explain the Holocaust?"

Jonathan had anticipated that this issue would come up sooner or later. It was a most common perplexity for would-be converts, skeptics and agnostics, and even some thoughtful devotees. " I'm glad you didn't ask me anything difficult," he says with a smirk.

"I'm sorry. It's just something that's been on my mind...for a while."

Jonathan nods. "I suppose that's a good thing."

" That I've been thinking about that?"

" Yes."

" How so?"

" Well," Jonathan says in his thinking-aloud voice, "I assume you're not asking this to challenge me, but because it's actually bothering you."

" That's fair."

" Which means, at least to me, that you're starting to grapple with issues of faith rather than merely dismissing them."

Raj looks down, contemplating. "Could be."

Regarding Raj's non-committal response as a sign of both progress and candor, Jonathan reacts with a tender smile.

"So back to my question," Raj says.

"Right." Jonathan strokes his beard. "Back to the most difficult question ever asked."

Raj considers Jonathan's framing. "One of the most difficult questions," he rejoins.

"Of course," Jonathan says. "Pardon my hyperbole. There are definitely other equally perplexing questions."

Raj smiles, seeming to appreciate the clarification.

"As for an answer," Jonathan continues, "to be honest, I really don't have one. But there are several good books on the topic..."

"I know. I've read a few," Raj says. "I just haven't found any of them convincing."

"Me neither," Jonathan reluctantly confesses.

Raj, stirred by Jonathan's admission, widens his eyes.

"When I was younger and thought I knew everything, I suppose I had an answer to this question. And it probably sounded good to me at the time."

"What was it?" Raj asks.

"I don't recall exactly because I no longer think that way, but it was probably something like God abandoning his protection over the Jewish people because they weren't..."

"Behaving?"

"Something like that."

"Are you saying you no longer believe in reward and punishment?"

"No. I do. It's just... not simple." Jonathan pauses to gather his thoughts. "As time goes on, it seems harder and harder for me to identify what's a reward and what's a punishment. And hardest of

all, I think, is determining what's a sin. In some ways, these have all become nebulous terms to me, so I no longer use them very much."

"But doesn't the Torah teach about reward and punishment, good and evil, right and wrong and all that?"

"Yes, but it's not as clear-cut as one might think." He hesitates again, trying to best formulate what he wants to say. "You see, in life, it all gets very complicated. On the surface, the Torah tells us that if we follow God's commandments, it will go well for us, and if not, it will go poorly. Great rabbis throughout the ages, on the other hand, recognized that things don't often work out that way, so they offer a more obscure and nuanced perspective. The Talmud at times suggests there isn't any actual reward and punishment in this world, and that true justice only exists in the world to come."

He wavers a moment, realizing the potential weaknesses in his explanation, seeing Raj sitting there in silence, fully engaged, as if inviting him to do better. "For me, it's all a complete mystery. I don't understand the Holocaust or any form of suffering. That's not to say that I don't believe God always has a plan. I believe He does, but I also believe His presence is hidden, and nothing is obvious or even explicable in ways that we can understand." Jonathan pauses once again, obviously measuring every word, then adds, "There are those who claim that the Holocaust was a punishment. Personally, I see that as a very cruel portrayal of God, and way too simplistic. I also think it's arrogant to believe that one can truly know God's mind, no less arrogant than it is to be certain there is no God."

Raj takes a moment to consider the point, then says, "Well put. Not completely different from some of the things I've read, but to hear you say it that way makes it a little more compelling."

"Only a little?" Feigned disappointment.

"It's a very deep level of faith that you express." Defensive. "If I'm going to be truthful, I'm not quite there yet."

"That's okay. 'Yet' works for me," Jonathan says, his smile fully revealing how much he values this journey they've been sharing.

Jonathan reflected on the itinerary of that journey beyond the actual conversion: the birth of Maya, and finally the wedding. He also reflected on the journey of Noah and Zach, staunchly bonded together while struggling to maintain challenging identities in contradicting worlds. And he reflected on Aaron and Sheindy and their family. Aaron had grown uncomfortable in his position, knowing that some of his congregants—albeit a small minority—were disgruntled over the rumors they had heard. Like his father, he hadn't wanted to be a source of contention for those he served. But mostly, it had become increasingly difficult for him and Sheindy to be living so far away from loved ones. So here they were, back in New York.

He turned his attention once again to the cup in hand and began his recitation of the blessings. His first blessing was on the wine itself, the second on the sanctity of the day, and the third, the *Shehecheyanu*—his favorite of all—thanked God for sustaining our existence and bringing us time and again to this place of celebration.

As the words flowed from him, his eyes moved to Sarah, who appeared to be full of joy. Almost thirty years since she first reached out her hand to lead him along the way, and still his rock, his confidant, the love of his life. She had always insisted they allow room for modernity in their religious lives, and he had complied as best he could. Meanwhile, his brother and sister had eleven children combined, all very much entrenched and cloistered in the ultra-Orthodox culture of his youth, with the next generation likely to continue in kind. What the future held for his own grandchildren, however, he truly couldn't predict.

He concluded the blessing, and everyone leaned to the left to drink in the manner of royalty, the traditional expression of freedom. As he drank, the shrill sound of a baby's cry pierced his ears. He finished his wine, sat upright, fixated on Miriam attempting to soothe her child and smiled as widely as ever.

"May I?" asked Noah, reaching out for Maya.

"Sure," Miriam responded, perhaps a tad overeager to rid herself of the task as she handed Maya to her brother.

Noah began to rock the child on his knee, and Zach quickly got in on the action, trying to distract and soothe little Maya with funny faces and sounds.

Jonathan, intently watching this, experienced a huge lump in his throat, holding his smile while fighting back tears. This was his life, his universe, and he was still finding his way along its many paths and detours. On the one hand, he couldn't deny that a part of him would have preferred things to have turned out otherwise, more "according to plan." On the other hand, sitting at that table, surrounded by his cherished clan, listening to the sounds of his granddaughter, he couldn't help but realize that he wouldn't have it any other way.

And he also understood, after all was said and done, that he was finally figuring it out.

Acknowledgments

I am fortunate to have close friends who see the world quite differently than I do. Ira Wolff and Leeber Cohen have taught me much, though I have never admitted this to either of them until now. They gave of their precious time to painstakingly review the manuscript, and each offered comments and critiques that proved invaluable. Thanks, guys.

As for seeing things differently than I do, my wife, Debbie, undoubtedly takes first place. Her influence permeates this story, and her editorial contribution was, as usual, superb. Without her, I would not have become the person I am, and this book would not have been written.

I suppose it could be said that nobody ever really listens to me, save you, my audience. At least some of you. Even my precious children, Jessica and Max, have clearly followed their mother's lead in challenging me at every turn. Their thoughts, feelings, and voices have had a profound influence on all my stories. Max, this one's for you. And please try not to be too embarrassed by the dedication page. I know I use that description of you frequently, and that you don't love it. But in truth, it's simply what always comes to mind.

Berwick Court Publishing has been wonderful to me. This is our fourth book together: two from inception and two republished. Matt Balson, you are a gem of a publisher and a good friend. I don't quite know what I've done to deserve all the attention and devotion I get, but keep it coming. Yes, you can be nit-picky, and as you know it often drives me nuts. But I am always beyond appreciative of what emerges. And finally, my undying gratitude to Dave

Balson, editor extraordinaire. Every single page of this book attests to his gifts. Thanks, Dave, for being there when I needed you.

Book Club Questions

1. In the beginning, Sarah saw Jonathan as too *frum*, but eventually came to understand that his relationship with religion was complex and malleable. Some of his congregants see him as too lax. He is in some kind of middle space, trying to find balance on the head of a pin. Sarah is always gently tugging him toward "modernity." How much of his resistance is about appeasing his detractors versus being true to his own beliefs? As to the latter, do you ascribe it more to a desire to follow God's word or a duty to follow cultural traditions?

2. Throughout her childhood Miriam had fantasies of growing up and enjoying the religious lifestyle of her family, but her teenage and young-adult years steered her toward more liberal, secular and modern choices. This is not an uncommon path for children who grow up in religious households: a more rebellious youth, followed by a move to stricter adherence to religion as they get older. This story eludes to a transition that sometimes occurs in which individuals will be more secular in their youth and then become more religious as they get older. Is this just a natural consequence of the fact that the prefrontal cortex is still developing until your mid-twenties? Or is it just a youthful desire to test the waters, and push boundaries? If the goal is to keep your children in the orthodoxy of your ways, is it better to allow teens to test these boundaries, as the Amish do with their Rumspringa, so they don't wonder what they are missing? Or are they better off protected from such temptations?

3. Did Miriam have more of a choice than Noah when it came to finding a mate that would have been considered acceptable to her community? On a larger scale, he couldn't find a partner that would fit in the community, but theoretically she could have. But on a micro-scale is her attraction to Raj any more under her control than Noah's attraction to Zach?

4. When the board is discussing Jonathan's ouster, there is a discussion of a New York law that says the trustees cannot fire the Rabbi, only the entire congregation can. This would seem to conflict with the "ministerial exception" doctrine in US law, which says that, under the First Amendment, the government cannot interfere with a religious institution's decision to hire and fire clergy. Should the state be allowed to regulate the synagogue's process of hiring and firing a Rabbi? Likewise, should employees of religious institutions be protected from discrimination based on gender? What about race or sexuality? How far should this protection extend? Or should it exist at all?

5. When disclosing his legal troubles to Jonathan, Benjy said, "You know how it is–if they look, they find." And Jonathan nodded. Is Benjy right? Jonathan, for instance, was not concealing crimes, but his family was concealing secrets. Does Benjy's statement reflect a morally compromised view of the world or does everyone have something to hide? At this point in the book, Jonathan didn't yet know about Noah or Miriam. Do you think his nod was because he agreed with Benjy's statement? If he didn't agree at this point, do you think he does later in the book?

6. Benjy Marcus was being shunned by some of the congregation because of his corrupt business dealings. Does Benjy bear any less blame for being a cog in a corrupt system he didn't create? Is there a place for shunning in society? Author Brené Brown distinguishes shame from guilt, saying guilt ("I did something bad") can

be productive but shame ("I am bad") is always destructive. Is she right, or does shame have a place in social groups to discourage bad behavior?

7. Noah and Miriam spend so much time worrying about the impact of their decisions on their parents lives. Is that fair to them? Once children are grown, do they have as much of a duty to protect their parents, or do parents always have a greater obligation to protect their children? Is there an age or stage of life at which that changes?

8. In society, we generally treat religion as if it were heritable (people almost always follow their parents' religion). But we also treat it as if it is a choice ("faith" implies a conscious effort). Is it a choice? Can people force themselves into a belief system? Participation in a religion is both internal and external. If Noah truly believes and follows the tenets, but is shunned, where does that leave him? Can one truly be a practicing Orthodox Jew without the acceptance of the community?

CPSIA information can be obtained
at www.ICGtesting.com
Printed in the USA
FSHW011034300819
61547FS

9 781944 376086